ALL THE RIGHT REASONS

"Perhaps you should call someone else in on this case," Clay said, looking into her brown eyes. "I'm getting too personally involved."

Georgie stared up at him. Her pulse sounded like a drum in her ears. Was it adrenaline from her latest brush with death, or was his nearness the cause? It was a chemical reaction—a strong one.

"Oh, why not," she said aloud suddenly. "Who knows if I'm even going to be alive tomorrow."

She tiptoed and kissed him squarely on the mouth. Caught by surprise, Clay stumbled backward under the assault, but quickly recovered. His strong arms enveloped her and the kiss deepened.

"Sorry, Boston," Georgie said when she came up for air. "You just looked so kissable. Forgive me?"

"Only if you forgive this," Clay said as he bent his head and kissed her again.

SENSUAL AND HEARTWARMING ARABESQUE ROMANCES FEATURE AFRICAN-AMERICAN CHARACTERS!

BEGUILED   (0046, $4.99)
by Eboni Snoe
After Raquel agrees to impersonate a missing heiress for just one night, a daring abduction makes her the captive of seductive Nate Bowman. Across the exotic Caribbean seas to the perilous wilds of Central America . . . and into the savage heart of desire, Nate and Raquel play a dangerous game. But soon the masquerade will be over. And will they then lose the one thing that matters most . . . their love?

WHISPERS OF LOVE   (0055, $4.99)
by Shirley Hailstock
Robyn Richards had to fake her own death, change her identity, and forever forsake her husband, Grant, after testifying against a crime syndicate. But, five years later, the daughter born after her disappearance is in need of help only Grant can give. Can Robyn maintain her disguise from the ever present threat of the syndicate—and can she keep herself from falling in love all over again?

HAPPILY EVER AFTER   (0064, $4.99)
by Rochelle Alers
In a week's time, Lauren Taylor fell madly in love with famed author Cal Samuels and impulsively agreed to be his wife. But when she abruptly left him, it was for reasons she dared not express. Five years later, Cal is back, and the flames of desire are as hot as ever, but, can they start over again and make it work this time?

ALL THE RIGHT REASONS

Janice Sims

Pinnacle Books
Kensington Publishing Corp.
http://www.pinnaclebooks.com

PINNACLE BOOKS are published by

Kensington Publishing Corp.
850 Third Avenue
New York, NY 10022

First Printing: June, 1997
10 9 8 7 6 5 4 3 2 1

Printed in the United States of America

This one's for my mother, Lillie Jean Hammond. She's my most faithful cheerleader. Mom, as Cassie, one of the characters in this story, says, "You can't pick your parents." If I could have, I would have still chosen you because you're simply the best!

A book is always a collaborative effort. Therefore, I'd like to offer my sincere thanks to the following people: My editor, Monica Harris, for challenging me; and all the ladies at The Cooper Memorial Library for always finding the reference material I need, no matter how obscure, especially you, Ginger.

Also, a big thanks goes to my husband, Curt, and our daughter for putting up with the long hours and eating take-out.

Finally, I have to thank all the readers who wrote me letters expressing their appreciation of *Affair of the Heart*. Your letters were so uplifting to me, guys. I hope this story does the same thing for you.

Love, like an uninvited guest,
marches in displaying boisterousness
Shoves aside your common sense
then takes up permanent residence.

—*The Book of Counted Joys*

Prologue

As the fog rolled in across San Francisco Bay, the night seemed to take on a preternatural silence. Hurrying along the darkened streets of Haight-Ashbury at 2 a.m., Margery Devlin, nineteen, attempted to convince the elderly midwife, Mrs. Brooks, to quicken her pace. Margery could hear her own labored exhalations in the still air around them. Panicking, she was steadily becoming irritated with Mrs. Brooks because of her nonchalant attitude.

"It's just a little further," she encouraged the woman. "Please. She's in such pain. I'm afraid something is terribly wrong."

"Unwed mothers," Mrs. Brooks grumbled. "What is this world coming to?" Margery had taken her from a warm, cozy bed and she wasn't at all pleased about it.

Margery stopped at a run-down apartment house. Three stories up, a light shone in the only illuminated apartment in the building.

Heading for the stairs, she glanced back at Mrs. Brooks who was just entering the building.

"What, no elevator?" the woman complained. Having already given Margery a heavy duffle bag to carry, she handed her the remaining bundle in her arms. "You're young and strong."

Margery readily accepted the bundle which looked like a thick, white sheet rolled into a ball. It was heavier than she assumed it would be. No matter, her best friend was lying upstairs, possibly dying, and she'd do anything within her power to see that her friend got the help she needed.

Mrs. Brooks was out of breath by the time she reached the third level. She leaned against the door of the apartment, looking at Margery with an exasperated expression on her brown face.

"Why didn't you take her to a hospital?" she asked. "I told her that if she goes into labor in the middle of the night to go to a hospital. She could have gone to San Francisco General, they take indigents over there."

Dropping the bag onto the floor, Margery knocked on the door.

"She's stubborn," she said of her friend. "We tried to talk her into going to the hospital, but she said she didn't want her baby born in a cold, unwelcoming environment. She was born at home and she wanted the same for her child."

Shaking her head with disdain, the midwife followed the girl into the small but clean apartment. She sniffed at the decor: bean bags placed around the room, a battered couch that looked like they'd rescued it off a street corner. Multi-colored beads hung in lieu of the door that led to the hallway.

The girl who'd let them in was around five-six, slender, pretty and had an air of serenity about her. She smiled at the old woman.

"Thank you so much for coming," she said, placing a friendly hand beneath the woman's elbow. "I put her to bed as you suggested."

They pushed past the beads into the lighted hallway and walked to the second door on the right. Margery followed with Mrs. Brooks' belongings.

The air in the bedroom smelled of jasmine. A couple of incense sticks burned in a glass holder on the nightstand.

A young girl sat on the side of the bed. She was tall and full of vitality, even in the throes of labor. Her golden-brown complexion was covered with a layer of perspiration, yet she seemed to glow.

"I felt the urge to push so I sat up," she told the midwife.

Showing an alacrity that surprised the two young women behind her, Mrs. Brooks crossed the room. She firmly pushed the girl back onto the bed. "Lie back, child. Let me examine you," she said with irritation.

Looking into the face of the midwife, Antoinette Shaw thought of her mother, Marie. How she wished she was there now. But she'd decided from the moment she learned she was pregnant that she wouldn't shame her parents. It was her responsibility alone.

Connie Moore hastened to fluff up Toni's pillows, propping up her friend to a sitting position.

Margery looked on from the doorway, still holding on to the duffle bag and bundle of sheets.

"Come here," the midwife spoke to her. "I'll need that bag."

Margery hesitantly moved forward. Unlike Connie, she was very uncomfortable being present during her friend's travail. She had pressed Toni to go to a hospital instead of engaging the services of Mrs. Brooks. What if something went wrong, like a breech birth? Toni could require surgery. Then what? Mrs. Brooks didn't look as though she could handle those complications. It wasn't unusual for a mother to die during childbirth even in the enlightened age of Aquarius: 1968.

Toni suddenly moaned loudly and Mrs. Brooks, peering at the obvious crowning of the infant, snapped an order to Connie. "I want you in bed, behind her. You'll need to brace her back."

"And you," the midwife said sharply to Margery. "Unroll those sheets and place them beneath her. Hurry!"

The two girls did as they'd been told. Connie gently kissed Toni's cheek, speaking consolingly to her. "Find your center, Toni. Remember how we practiced. Focus, darling. Focus on something wonderful."

Margery felt faint when she spied the infant's head, bloody and covered with a thick, white mucous, slowly exiting Toni. Soon, the shoulders slipped out and the midwife grasped the child and adeptly pulled its body all the way out. The umbilical cord was promptly snipped as the child lay crying on the clean sheets the midwife had provided. With practiced precision, the woman suctioned the child's nose and mouth. The baby wailed.

"It's a girl," Mrs. Brooks announced. She smiled for the first time that morning. Looking at Connie, she said: "Did you prepare the water as I taught you to in childbirth class?"

"Yes," Connie replied, her face mirroring the wonder she felt at witnessing a new life coming into the world. "Margery, it's in the kitchen. You'll have to get it."

Margery was happy to have something to do outside of the bedroom. She disappeared into the hallway and was back in a couple of minutes carrying the basin of lukewarm water.

The midwife immersed the child in the water, carefully removing the blood and mucous. She then dried the child, diapered it and wrapped it with its arms at its sides in a thick, white cotton blanket. Finished, she placed the girl-child in her mother's arms.

Toni, looking spent but happy, cradled her child in her arms.

"Welcome, Georgette Danise. I'm your mother," she said as tears rolled down her cheeks.

"She's beautiful," Connie said, still sitting behind Toni. "She looks just like you."

"Mmm . . ." Toni groaned. She worriedly glanced up at the midwife for some explanation.

"It's only the afterbirth," Mrs. Brooks assured her. First-time mothers were always a little frightened when, after giving birth, they experienced further labor pains. "Believe me, it won't be as painful as the birthing."

The afterbirth did pass from Toni's body. However, a few seconds later, the midwife saw something which made even *her* slow heartbeat accelerate. Toni was crowning again.

The midwife shoved the basin into Margery's hands. "More water."

When Margery didn't immediately go to do her bidding, the midwife turned and shrieked at her: "Now!"

Looking into Toni's terrified face, Mrs. Brooks forced a smile. "Sugar, there's no need to get upset. You're just having another child, that's all."

"Connie," Toni cried. "Oh Connie, what am I going to do?"

"Bear down," the midwife replied in answer to her query. "Connie, take the first child and place her in her crib, then you get back behind Toni and help her push this child out."

By the time Margery returned with the clean water, Briane Marie had made her way into the world. Drenched in perspiration, exhausted from the labor and doubly so by the shock of becoming the mother of two within the space of twenty minutes, Toni fell gratefully back onto the bed.

Margery calmly placed the basin of lukewarm water atop the bureau and stood staring first at Georgette Danise, crying in the crib next to her mother's bed and then Briane Marie, wailing at the top of her lungs as the midwife held her upside down removing the excess mucous from her nose and throat.

Her eyes rolled back in her head and she fainted dead away.

Going to her and placing her head in her lap, Connie smiled down at her. "Margery, you should save your theatrics for the stage."

Margery's eyes fluttered open. "How are we going to take care of two babies?"

"You're such a worrywart, Margery," Connie told her. "Toni is a mother now and we'll be 'aunts' to two beautiful girls. Can't you be thankful that mother and children survived the ordeal and let the future take care of itself?"

"You've been listening to too many Joan Baez records," Margery told her spiritually-centered friend. "Girl, we're up the creek without a paddle."

Connie simply smiled and smoothed an unruly lock of hair out of Margery's face as they sat there. "Years from now, you'll think back on this and laugh."

One

Clayton Knight's footfalls made crisp, decisive taps on the hardwood floor of the Waters mansion as he followed the man-servant, Carson, down a long, portrait-lined hallway.

This wasn't the first time he'd been in a home like this. He'd had wealthy clients before, however none as reclusive as Charles Edward Waters. Always a man who zealously guarded his privacy, Waters became even more secretive five years ago when he lost his wife and only child, son Charles Edward the third, in an automobile accident.

Waters no longer bothered going into the office, preferring instead to run his frozen foods processing empire from his home. Only key people ever saw him. There were rumors that he, like his family, had died and the company chose to propagate the ruse of his continued leadership in order not to precipitate a panic among stockholders. Waters Foods supplied retail supermarkets and fast food chains with foodstuffs ranging from frozen orange juice to gourmet dinners. They were currently number one in their field with no competitor close enough to nip at their heels.

Clay perused the oak-lined splendor of the study while Carson took his leave.

"Mr. Waters will join you in a few minutes," the old fellow said in a cultured Boston accent. He disappeared like an apparition, leaving silently through the double oak doors and closing them behind him.

Clay sat down on a mauve wing chair near the French doors that led out to the most magnificent rose garden he'd ever glimpsed. Actually, upon closer inspection, he noticed that the roses were thriving in a clear glass enclosure, a very large green-house. Waters apparently spared no expense on his gardening staff. Roses in winter . . . seeing them made him think of Josie. Turning away, he wished he could insulate his heart from the pain, the way those flowers were protected from the cold by the greenhouse. He forced himself to consider why Waters himself was seeing him this afternoon and not one of his underlings. Usually, when he was hired by a company like Waters Foods, he worked to acquire information on a rival company, something unavailable to the general public. Instinctively, he felt that Waters didn't operate in that manner. No. There was something extremely personal weighing heavily upon Waters' mind to cause him to hire a detective.

His hazel eyes narrowed, Clay sat back on the chair and looked around him. Rich cherry wood furnishings surrounded him. The air was redolent with its slightly sweet smell and that of furniture polish. Old money. No doubt that Waters could trace his ancestors back to one of the original freedmen who had helped settle Boston in the seventeenth century.

His strong fingers fiddled with his watch, a nervous habit he practiced whenever he was kept waiting. Waiting was a big part of his job, but it was something he'd never gotten used to. He was basically a physical animal. Sitting, even for short periods, made him antsy.

Within five minutes, a side door that obviously led to Waters' inner office opened, and a trim man of average height strode into the room.

He paused in front of Clay and extended his right hand in greeting.

"Mr. Knight. So good of you to come. I'm Charles Waters."

Clay rose, towering over him. He shook Waters' hand. "Clayton Knight. How can I be of service to you, Mr. Waters?"

Charles Waters took a seat on the matching wing chair directly across from Clay. Clay wondered, fleetingly, if the creases in his immaculate trousers would actually bend when he sat down. They did.

Waters undid the buttons on his suit jacket as he got comfortable.

"You're a direct man. I like that, Mr. Knight."

He frowned, the lines around his light-brown eyes becoming more evident.

For a man who likes directness, Clay thought, he seems to be having some difficulty getting started.

Clearing his throat, Charles began. "Nearly thirty years ago, I fell in love with a young woman. We subsequently ended our relationship, and I wed a marvelous woman who gave me a son. Two years after our break-up, this first particular woman phoned me with the unbelievable news that we had a child together. The possibility that I had an illegitimate child and the kind of scandal it would cause if the news got out scared me. I was rude to her and accused her of wanting money, which I knew wasn't true. At any rate, she never called back. I had a wife and a child to think of, so I didn't try to pursue the matter."

"And now?" Clay prompted him.

"Now I really don't care about the consequences, Mr. Knight. My family is gone—killed in a freak accident. I will be retiring in a little under a year and my nephew, Benjamin, will be taking over the company. Finding the child I abandoned all those years ago is uppermost in my mind. I must find her."

"Her?"

"Oh yes. I have a daughter, I'm certain of that much. About five years ago I hired another firm and they got photos of Toni with two young women. She had two daughters; one of them has to be mine."

"Toni? Is that short for Antoinette?" Clay asked.

"Yes. Antoinette Shaw. Perhaps you've heard of her."

"Toni Shaw? The sixties activist?" Clay said excitedly.

"The one and only," Charles confirmed, smiling at the detective's enthusiasm.

"Pardon me, sir, but how could you allow a woman like that to get away? Toni Shaw was every man's dream. She's intelligent, talented, and she was the bravest woman I ever heard of," Clay said with passion. "I was nothing but a boy when I used to watch her on television protesting the Vietnam War. I often wondered what happened to make her drop out of sight. I assumed she was being hounded by the FBI."

Charles was smiling as he regarded the younger man. "I can see you've given this some thought. Yes, Toni was a marvel. She was always larger than life, even at eighteen, when I knew her. I adored her."

"Then what happened?" Clay wanted to know.

Charles sighed. "My parents were what happened. They were mortified when I brought Toni home to meet them. Imagine a couple of conservative, Republican Bostonians and Toni in the same room. When we left that weekend to return to Berkeley, my parents had made it clear to me that unless I distanced myself from Toni, I could forget about any inheritance. And don't think Toni was any less adamant. She told me I must have been adopted—there was no way I could come from such stodgy, judgmental parents. We argued and that, my friend, was that."

"What a shame," Clay said, meeting Charles' eyes. "You know, she never married."

"Who would marry an icon?"

I would have in a split second, Clay thought. Unfortunately, he and Toni were from different generations. He fell in love with her as a young boy, seeing in her an ideal. To a lonely boy, she became someone to look up to during a troubled childhood. He'd been drawn to her sweet image and thought that if someone as wonderful as Toni could exist in a chaotic world, then there was hope for the future.

"Why don't you simply pick up the phone and call her?" Clay asked.

"I've tried that," Charles replied sadly. "She won't talk to me. She won't talk to my lawyers. She returns my letters unopened. She refuses to tell me which of her daughters is mine."

"You must admit, she has no reason to be cooperative at this late date," Clay said as he rose from his chair. He was six feet, two inches and a man to whom the gym was like a second home. Inertia wasn't his friend.

Charles got to his feet, also, feeling inept under the big man's scrutiny.

"Don't you think I know that?" he said, voice rising. "I've apologized over and over again. She'll never forgive me. If I am ever to see my daughter, I must take drastic measures."

"Hold on now," Clay said calmly. "We don't need to go there just yet. Do you have any idea what the girls' ages are?"

"Counting back, I would guess my child would be around twenty-eight or nine," Charles replied.

"Under the Freedom of Information Act, you should be able to find out when your child was born. Have you tried the Social Security Administration? Every citizen in the U.S. is registered with them. Your daughter has to have attended a grade school, a high school, perhaps even college. Do you mean to tell me she has never had a job in her entire life?"

"You don't understand, Mr. Knight. Records have been found. However, they aren't believable. Toni was part of the subculture. She lived in a commune near San Francisco for a number of years. When she got around to registering them with the Social Security Administration, she had their births listed on the same date, no doubt to confound me. Toni Shaw hates me. She would do anything to keep me from my daughter just to punish me for being an absentee father. I won't let her stand in my way," Charles ended, sounding determined.

"Exactly what would you like me to do when I find her?" Clay asked.

He was certain locating Waters' heir would be an easy enough task. He was curious to know just what Waters' plans were.

"I want to know where she is. I want to know what kind of life she's leading. If she's married, does she have any children? I'd like photographs. Once I have your report, I'll decide where to go from there."

"I suppose it has occurred to you that she may already know about you and has chosen to avoid you?" Clay felt compelled to warn him.

"Yes, I've thought of that," Charles said wearily. "I wouldn't blame her if she hated me. After all, I abandoned her when I could have claimed her. However, I've got to try, Mr. Knight."

Clay had to admire Waters' tenacity. But what he really wanted to know was why it had taken him so long to come forward. If memory served him well, Waters' wife and son were killed over five years ago. Why did he want to claim his daughter *now?*

"I believe I have everything I need in order to get started," Clay said, offering Waters his hand. "I should tell you that my standard fee is two hundred dollars an hour, plus expenses . . ."

"Whatever it takes," Charles said. "I didn't tell you where Toni lives. She's . . ."

"She lives in New Orleans," Clay supplied effortlessly. "She moved back there around five years ago to be near her parents. She makes her living as a romance novelist and uses the name Serena Kincaid. I've kept up with her over the years. This case will be a pleasure to solve. I'm looking forward to working on it."

Charles pumped Clay's hand. "It seems I've hired the right man for the job."

"Since you've corresponded with Miss Shaw, you would have her current address, wouldn't you?"

Reaching into his coat pocket, Charles produced a slip of paper which he handed to Clay. "I took the liberty of writing it down for you."

Accepting the paper, Clay met Charles' gaze. "I take it all communication between us should be direct and not through your secretary."

"You're very perceptive, Mr. Knight. Yes, I would like to keep this strictly between you and me."

"Understood," Clay said. "One more thing, I intend to go to New Orleans as soon as possible. Would you like a daily accounting of expenditures or do I have free rein?"

"Like I said," Charles reiterated. "Spare no expense. I leave that up to your discretion."

* * *

Marie Shaw, a retired teacher at sixty-eight, took one look at the tall, handsome stranger at her door and welcomed him into her home. James, her husband of forty-nine years was out back weeding his garden. She could use the company. She knew she would pay dearly for her hospitality when her daughter, Antoinette, got wind of the latest exploits of her too-trusting mother, but she didn't care.

Marie had a nose for trouble and would have detected it the moment this young man stepped onto her front porch if he had been bad news. Her inner alarms weren't sounding; therefore, he was good people.

Clay stepped into the neat living room of the southern-style bungalow and handed Marie his wallet so that she could peruse his credentials: his Massachusetts driver's license and a business card presenting him as Clayton Knight, contributing editor of *Black Life* magazine.

Marie's pretty, milk-chocolate colored eyes lit up. She ushered him into her kitchen, talking all the while. "I'm preparing dinner—can't let the pots watch themselves. Sit down, young man, sit down and tell me what's on your mind."

The aromas that assailed Clay's nostrils briefly gave him amnesia. Mustard greens simmering in ham hocks, shrimp gumbo and dirty rice, a concoction of heavenly-smelling spicy sausage cooked in onions and peppers to which fluffy, white rice is added. The drippings from the browned sausage and the various spices give the rice its unique color and flavor, hence the reason it's called dirty rice. Clay was an aficionado of Cajun cooking. There were Sundays when he and Josie would spend the day in the kitchen making etouffée, jambalaya, gumbo and various other delicious recipes. Thinking of Josie made his heart ache.

Marie went to stir the greens and Clay sat down at the kitchen nook. Finished, Marie poured him a cup of coffee. She sat down across from him.

"You were saying?"

"Thank you." He added sugar and cream to his coffee and took a sip. "It's delicious."

Marie frowned. "It's not too strong for you? You know we like our coffee to go down fighting."

Clay smiled at her. "No, it's good. That's chicory I taste, isn't it?"

Marie nodded, returning his smile. "You've got good buds."

She poured herself a cup. Straight. She drank deeply. "I call it liquid adrenaline. Keeps you pumped up all day and night, too, if you're not careful. Now stop stalling, young man. What is it you want?"

Clay bit his bottom lip, reluctant to broach the subject too soon for fear that she'd think he was overly aggressive.

"An interview with your daughter?"

Marie laughed, her rich brown eyes twinkling in her heart-shaped, smooth caramel-colored face. "And you know she doesn't give interviews, so you thought you'd butter-up her mother and see if I'd intervene in your behalf."

"Something like that," Clay said, looking her straight in the eyes. "I'm a great admirer of Toni Shaw. I think our readers would like to know what has become of her. Why she dropped out of sight in sixty-eight. And now, why she uses a pseudonym when she writes those superb Serena Kincaid novels."

"You've read them?" Marie asked incredulously.

"I've read *Echoes* and *Dark River.* Her voice rings clear and true. It's as if she stepped down from the soapbox and sat down at the typewriter, but she still shines through."

"Exactly," Marie said, smiling benignly. "So why begrudge her her privacy?"

Clay turned on his stool, stretching his long legs out before him. He knew that behind those kind eyes was a sharp mind that didn't miss a thing. Role-playing wasn't his strong suit and when he was forced to deceive good people like the Shaws, sometimes armed with false credentials, he felt guilty for doing so. Still, sometimes, it was a necessary evil.

"That's not my aim, Mrs. Shaw. I want to present Toni to my readers as a renaissance woman, someone who keeps recreating herself and maintaining her innate strength and integrity. I want them to know that the sixties were not her finest hour, that she is and always will be, a woman to be reckoned with."

From the living room came the sound of the door being unlocked and of someone entering the house burdened with packages.

"Mere! Mere, I could use a little help," a feminine voice called.

"Well here's your chance. That's Antoinette now. Why don't you go help her with the groceries," Marie suggested.

Toni sat the three over-full grocery bags on the foyer floor and removed her coat, which had protected her from the chill of November in New Orleans. The misty rain didn't help matters. Her face was damp and her nose was cold. Hanging her coat on the hall tree, she breathed in the inviting smell of her mother's strong, chicory-laced coffee. She needed a cup after a harrowing day of shopping. Shopping wasn't her favorite pastime. She didn't enjoy strolling down aisle after aisle choosing just the right item from her mother's list. Marie Shaw was a picky cook and required only the finest ingredients which meant Toni, who was the family's designated shopper, sometimes spent an inordinate amount of time seeking-out some desired item.

She'd recently left the butcher shop and Hiram Anderson, who had been Marie's butcher for the past three years since his father's death, had been fresh out of the capons Marie wanted to prepare for Sunday dinner. Marie wasn't going to be happy when she heard the news. Father Dupree was coming to Sunday dinner and Marie's capon was his favorite dish. On top of that, Toni had had to fend off Hiram's advances. Recently divorced, he considered himself a Lothario. Toni didn't have the heart to bluntly put him in his place. She knew his wife, Christine, had left him for a younger man, and his ego was already bruised. So she'd smiled and gotten out of the butcher shop as quickly as possible.

At the sound of unfamiliar footfalls, Toni looked up to see a tall, very striking man enter the room. He was smiling as if in a daze as he walked toward her, his big hand outstretched.

Naturally wary of strangers, Toni stumbled back. "Who are you?"

The dark-skinned, well-dressed man simply stood there and stared at her.

At least he was no longer advancing on her. "I said who are you?" Toni repeated more forcefully.

There she was, right before his eyes. His idol. She was even more lovely in the flesh. Her brown, red-tinged skin glowed. Her black eyes flashed fire. Her tall, lithe body made the jeans and sweater she was wearing look like the adornment of a goddess. He sighed.

Her voice was that of a siren, cooing in his ear. "Wipe that stupid grin off your face and speak to me, man!"

"Clayton Knight, *Black Life* magazine," Clay managed as he came out of his trance. He bent down and picked up the groceries and carried them into the kitchen before Toni could protest.

Toni harumphed and followed close on his heels. "*Black Life* magazine? I don't give interviews. Mere! Mere, where are you? You haven't been spilling your guts to this loquacious charmer, have you?"

"What's there to spill?" Marie answered her daughter as she retrieved the cornbread from the oven.

Clay placed the bags on the counter and turned to face Toni. "Before you throw me out, give me a chance to tell you something about our magazine."

Her mouth set in a firm line, Toni regarded him. "I already know what kind of magazine *Black Life* is, we have subscribed to it for years but I do not break my 'no interviews' rule for anyone. May I see some ID?"

"I've already checked him out," Marie put in as she spread butter on top of the warm cornbread.

Clay handed Toni his wallet nonetheless.

She took her time reading his driver's license. Clayton Knight, born on October 5, 1960. That meant he'd recently turned thirty-seven. She paid little attention to his address but the city struck a nerve. Boston.

"Black Life magazine's offices are in Chicago, aren't they?"

"Yes, but I'm a contributing editor. I can work out of any city I choose. Boston is my hometown."

Toni gave him back his wallet. She stared up at him with narrowed eyes. "How did you find me?"

"I'm a computer hacker from way back," Clay joked. He attempted a smile, saw no softening in Toni's demeanor and suppressed it. "The fact is, I've got a friend in your publishing house. He turned me on to your present digs."

"And of course, you'll take the name of your source to the grave," Toni said sarcastically.

"You know us journalists," Clay replied, looking remorseful.

Toni continued to eye him with a mixture of suspicion and contempt. She was several inches shorter than he was, but she still made him feel like an interloper, which he was.

Marie came to stand between them. "Shrimp gumbo's ready," she announced. "Sit down and have a bowl, Clayton."

She took him by the arm and led him to the kitchen table. Her cherubic face was lit from within by a warm smile. She gave him a mischievous wink. "Don't mind her," she said in a low voice. "She's never in a good mood on shopping day."

"My friends call me Clay," Clay told her confidentially.

"Clay, then," Marie said and for a moment, he thought she would reach up and lovingly pinch his cheek.

"Mother!" Toni exclaimed, overhearing this exchange.

Turning back to look at her daughter, Marie said, "He's a nice boy, mon petite. If you aren't going to give him the interview, the least I can do is send him away with a full stomach. You have some, too, you look like you could use a little warming up." She paused. "I'll go call your Papa. He should be hungry by now, all that hoeing around he's been doing all morning." She smiled at both of them and walked out the back door.

In Marie's absence, Toni regarded Clay with a steely expression. "My mother has a weakness for lost children."

Clay smiled at her analogy. "I am neither a child nor am I lost."

Toni chortled. "Compared to me, you *are* a child and you are most certainly lost, Mr. Knight. At the very least, you've lost your way. Give me one reason why I should give you the intimate details of my life."

Clay observed her closely, taking in the unmarred complexion, shoulder-length ebony tresses with a streak of gray down the middle, which she wore in an upswept style. Her large eyes were the same almond shape as her mother's but darker and they weren't nearly as full of *joie de vivre*. When he finally answered her, he did so from his heart.

"Because it will keep you from sinking deeper into your personal mire of cynicism."

Toni's expression was devoid of amusement. "Cynicism? Cynicism isn't one of my faults, although I must commend you on your colossal nerve. I've always admired anyone who has the wherewithal to voice what's on his mind."

Realizing that a faint heart never won the fair maiden, Clay took her comment as a green light. He started talking. Fast.

"I fell in love with you when I was eight years old. You were my heroine. I'd see you on television leading a march, protesting the Vietnam War and I'd wonder how it would be to be your kid brother," he said.

Toni gestured to a chair at the table. They sat down, whereupon Clay continued his story. "My dad was a merchant marine. I saw him maybe seven times from the time I was old enough to recognize him as my father to age seventeen, when he was knifed to death in a bar fight in Nepal, thousands of miles from home. We never even recovered his body." He sighed, remembering the pain his mother had gone through. "Already an alcoholic, my mother began drinking in earnest after that. She died during my first hitch with the Marine Corps."

Toni found herself warming to him, in spite of her initial distrust. She leaned in closer. "No brothers or sisters?"

"None," Clay answered.

"But you did make it to college," her voice was soft, compelling.

Clay nodded in the affirmative. "After the Corps, Uncle Sam paid for my education. I'd always wanted to go to college. When I was in high school, there was this teacher, Mrs. March, who took an interest in me. She made me realize I had potential. She literally snatched me from the clutches of a street gang. Remind me to tell you about that sometime."

"That's assuming there's going to be another time," Toni said, adeptly informing him he hadn't won her favor yet. "So, you've had a rough life. Who of us hasn't? You're stronger because of it. Tell me something. You've obviously done well for yourself. Do you resent your parents because of their failures?"

Clay held his breath. She was definitely one to shoot from the hip. He exhaled slowly. "I used to," he said truthfully. "I used to wonder why other kids had normal family lives and I sometimes came home to an empty, cold apartment. Mom wouldn't come home for days at a time. I worried about her safety constantly. I thought the police would come knocking on the door in the dead of night to tell me they'd found her in a ditch somewhere."

Toni was moved by the emotion in his voice. "She couldn't cope on her own. Did you ever get the chance to ask your father why he chose such a hazardous career?" she asked sympathetically.

Clay laughed shortly. "My dad was not the sort of man you could pin down. He didn't know how to express himself. From what I gather, his father was a sailor, too. So I guess he was doing what he knew best."

Frowning, Toni said, "Your mother never thought of divorcing him and remarrying?"

"She was a devout Catholic," Clay explained. "Among my earliest memories of her is seeing her on her knees before the Virgin."

"We're Catholic, too," Toni said, shaking her head. "But I would have left a man like your father in a heartbeat."

Clay's hazel eyes were misty. "I wish she had. God knows I do. He killed her. And believe me, if he had been alive to see her end, he wouldn't have shed a tear."

Toni felt the rage coming off of him in waves of dark emotion. It was almost a tangible entity between them, fierce and overpowering. She scrutinized him with a writer's eye, taking in the undercurrents of his words. Cataloging his mannerisms, facial expressions, physical attributes. Where did he get those lovely hazel eyes? From his merchant-marine father? He was a striking man, at least six feet, two inches tall and very well-built. He'd probably made a formidable Marine. He certainly didn't look like a journalist. He looked like a cop. He was observant and thought quickly on his feet, like any cop worth his salt.

"I'll think about it," she said, breaking the silence.

"What?" Clay had been lost in a chasm of painful memories. It amazed him that talking about his dead parents could still fill him with such remorse, helplessness and anger.

"The interview," Toni said, smiling benevolently. "I'll think it over and let you know. Where are you staying?"

"The Hotel Le Pavillon, it's . . ."

Toni laughed. "I know where it is," she assured him. "This is my town, remember?"

Theirs was the last case on her honor's docket today. Knowing Judge Da Costa's propensity for impatience the closer she gets to quitting time and also aware of her honor's enormous case load, Georgette Shaw, public defender, was pleasantly surprised when Judge Da Costa's sentence was a light one. Time served, a stay in a drug rehabilitation center and community service, following rehabilitation.

The relief on Reggie Franklyn's face was heartrending. He let out a long sigh. "Thank you, your honor. Thank you!"

Ellen Da Costa's expression was implacably stern. "You can thank me by not appearing in my courtroom again, Mr. Franklyn. Court dismissed. Counselor, I'd like to see you in my chambers."

"Of course, your honor," Georgie replied, getting to her feet out of deference to Judge Da Costa. She nudged Reggie's shoulder and he rose, as did everyone in the courtroom.

No one moved until Judge Da Costa had exited, then everyone began gathering their belongings and filing out of the room.

"Reggie," Georgie said, looking into the gangly youth's clear, brown eyes. "It feels good to be free doesn't it? You don't have to go back to that smelly cell and sleep with one eye open, just in case your cellmate tries to get too friendly in the middle of the night. Remember this feeling. You're a bright kid. Stop acting dumb. Stay away from your brother. I know you love Kyle, but we both know where his lifestyle is going to lead him: either in prison, if he's lucky, or the graveyard, if he isn't." She sighed wearily. Was anything she was saying sinking in? "I care about you, Reggie. I've known you since you were using training wheels on your bike, for God's sake. Reggie, please go back to school and make something of yourself—something your mother would have been proud of. She wanted so much for her boys."

Too ashamed to meet her eyes, Reggie stared at his hands. "I know, Georgie. I *will* change, you'll see. And as for Kyle, he didn't want me to do it, but I went ahead just to prove to him that I could. It was stupid. I wanted my big brother to know I could be as tough as he is."

He raised his eyes, regarding her with a hangdog expression.

Georgie smiled at him. "I know you're remorseful now, but what's going to happen when you're back on the street? Kyle's world is very enticing. He wouldn't be dealing drugs if it wasn't." Her black eyes narrowed. "Is it true? Kyle doesn't want you in the business?"

"He says it's a dead end, and if there was any way out of it for him, he'd take it," Reggie said. He smiled suddenly. "And he says he wishes he had never lost you, Georgie."

Georgie didn't know how to respond to that. She wasn't one to dwell on what might have been. She and Kyle had taken different roads in their lives, even though, once upon a time, they'd been in love.

She absently placed a long braid behind her ear. "That was so long ago," she said with a laugh. "Listen to your brother. He should know what he's talking about."

She hugged Reggie briefly. "Go on, get out of here. Mr. Shaunessy will get you processed." She gave him a playful shove toward the waiting bailiff.

Reggie paused to grin at her. "I would've liked having you in the family, counselor."

Georgie sat back down for a minute or so after Reggie's departure. She was stunned by his revelation about his brother's lingering affections for her. It had been years since she and Kyle . . . Stop it Georgette Danise, don't start reminiscing about the past, she thought fiercely. You'll be here all day. She was grateful she'd been able to convince Ellen Da Costa that Reggie was worth salvaging. In spite of his background, his environment and the peer pressure copiously supplied by a brother who was the top drug dealer in the Bay area, Georgie felt Reggie could rise above it all and save himself. He would have to—no one could do it for him.

Georgie and Kyle Franklyn had been high school sweethearts. For the past eight years, however, they'd gone in different directions. She'd gone to law school, and he'd become the most notorious drug dealer in the state. She often wondered what had gone so terribly wrong. When they were in school, Kyle was captain of the football team and president of the Beta Club, an honors organization. He was a personable young man who'd received a bachelor's degree in Business Administration from California State University but instead of joining the ranks of the legitimate business world, he'd gone into business for himself. Now he was extremely wealthy from the suffering of his own people and unable to truly enjoy the pleasures the money could provide because there is a permanent bullseye on his forehead. If the authorities weren't gunning for him, people in his organization were trying to usurp him. In Georgie's estimation, it was a hellish existence.

She stood, closed her briefcase and began walking toward Judge Da Costa's chambers just down the corridor. She greeted several courthouse personnel, some of whom she knew quite well. Mel Espinoza, a security guard in his late fifties, called out to her: "Hey, Georgie, did you win?"

"Do I ever lose?" she said confidently, smiling at him.

"Not in my book," Mel said with a shy smile.

Georgie paused next to him. At five feet, eight, she was two inches taller than Mel Espinoza. "What are you and Consuela planning to do this weekend? Another one of those marvelous barbecues?"

"Our oldest is coming down from Carmel. Says she has something important to tell us," Mel said happily. "We think she's getting engaged."

"Then it's good news," Georgie said as she turned to leave. "Give her my best."

"Will do," Mel said. "What about you? Big date this weekend?"

Georgie laughed, showing straight white teeth in her golden-brown complexioned face. "Mel, it's been some time since I had a date, big or otherwise. My sister and I are going home to New Orleans this weekend."

"The Big Easy," Mel said brightly. "I love that city."

"What's not to love about it?" Georgie said proudly. "It's the diamond of the South. I intend to eat too much, laugh too much and get lost in the arms of my family."

"Sounds like a plan," Mel said approvingly.

They waved their farewells and Georgie continued walking toward Ellen Da Costa's chambers. Georgie had come to respect and admire Ellen the last three years she'd been with the public defender's office.

Ellen didn't mince words after asking Georgie to be seated.

"Still think you can save that kid, I see."

Of Cuban ancestry, Ellen had dark olive skin and lustrous auburn hair, which she wore in an upswept style at work. Her nose was aquiline and her dark brown eyes ran the gamut from stern when she was on the bench to passionate during more private moments. She was currently in her mentoring mode.

Georgie smiled. "You obviously think he deserves a chance, otherwise you would have thrown the book at him."

She crossed her long legs, getting comfortable in the leather upholstered chair.

"At this point," Ellen said, offering Georgie some M & M's from the crystal bowl on her desk. "He's not completely criminal, just stupid. I'll give him a couple of more years in the company of his brother, then we'll see what's become of him."

Taking a handful of the chocolate treats, Georgie popped a couple into her mouth. "Your Honor, if I didn't know you so well, I'd say you're beginning to suffer from burnout."

Laughing, Ellen propped her feet up on the desk, her eyes never leaving Georgie's face. "Hell, that happened years ago. I'm simply being realistic, my dear. Why don't you accept a plush position with that downtown law firm and let the streets fend for themselves?"

"So you know about that," Georgie said, not surprised. "If I had wanted to work for a firm, I could have done it fresh out of law school. I had plenty of offers, usually from firms looking to fill their quotas. I'm black and female—kill two birds with one stone. But I didn't want to get rich; I wanted to make a difference."

"Bob Denison's a good friend of mine," Ellen said, still bent on talking sense into her young friend's head. "He told me he made you a very generous offer. A partnership within two years. How could you say no to that?"

Georgie regarded her with a mixture of love and exasperation in her ebony eyes. "Billing clients three hundred dollars an hour and defending the rich is not my idea of practicing law, Ellen. I want to do something worthwhile with my life. Help someone who really needs help. Bob's clients can afford the very best representation. My clients can't afford anything, but I like to give them the best I can."

Ellen rolled her eyes heavenward. "Don't get me wrong, Georgie. You can still do pro bono work. I admire your idealism. I'd hate to see you become an old burnout like me so early in what appears to be a brilliant career. You're good, but you have to pace yourself. Take care of yourself as well as you take care of the Reggie Franklyns of the world. Got me?"

"I understand you perfectly, Ellen," Georgie told her, leaning forward. "But I don't see *you* downtown cleaning the noses of the super rich. You've been in the trenches since your career began, fighting for justice."

Ellen blew air between her red-rouged lips. "Yes," she admitted. "But it was a different time when I came along. We were all full of high ideals then. We were so sure we could change the world for the better, make it an Eden of equal justice under the law." She sat up straight. "Ask your mother to tell you about it sometime. The world is getting to be an ugly place full of desensitized criminals who will kill you for a dime or simply for the enjoyment derived therefrom. It's sad, but true."

"That's a strong argument for remaining in the fray," Georgie replied, her full lips curved in a smile.

Ellen returned her smile, her chameleon eyes twinkling with an inner light. "I give up." She sighed. "I'm not going to convince you to get out while the getting's good. You remind me so much of myself at your age, it's frightening."

She reached into the bottom drawer of her big oak desk to retrieve her briefcase. "Shall we get out of here?"

"What do you and Ed have planned for tonight?" Georgie asked as they stood waiting for the elevator's arrival.

Ellen's face wrinkled in a grin as she thought about the evening ahead.

She looked up at Georgie. "A quiet meal at home and a Bogart movie, probably *The Maltese Falcon*. We haven't seen that one in a while."

Ellen and Eduardo Da Costa were Bogart fanatics. Georgie wouldn't have been surprised if they dressed up in vintage costumes while they watched Bogie and Bacall.

"And you and Brian?" Ellen asked expectantly.

Georgie laughed heartily. "There *is* something you aren't privy to. Brian and I went our separate ways weeks ago. The dog was having an affair with his legal aide."

Ellen stared at her. "How did you find out?"

"I walked in on them," Georgie replied, frowning as she recalled the particulars: Brian and Heather atop his desk.

"You poor kid," Ellen commiserated, grasping Georgie's hand and squeezing it. "Was your heart involved?"

"It was difficult to totally commit to a man who admired his reflection in his BMW whenever he got out of it."

"I'm glad," Ellen said. "Because I would never have told you this if you had fallen for him, but Brian Chandler is a pompous ass. He didn't deserve you. Have you met anyone else?"

"No," Georgie returned, stepping into the elevator as the doors slid open. "And I don't miss dating." They were alone in the conveyance. She pressed the button for the bottom floor. "Men are such high-maintenance creatures. They want so much and give so little."

"Ain't it the truth," Ellen said, rummaging in her bag for her car keys. "But thank God they all aren't self-serving like Mr. Chandler. You'll meet someone who's right for you, and it'll happen when you least expect it. Take my word for it."

"From your lips to God's ears," Georgie said, laughing. "Anyway, I'm not actively looking, and I hope the next man who comes into my life will actually care about the things that are important to me."

In the parking garage, they waved goodbye, Ellen going to her late model Volvo station wagon and Georgie to her nineteen sixty-five powder blue Ford Mustang convertible.

Two

Georgie relaxed behind the wheel of the Mustang. It was a brisk, breezy picturesque San Francisco afternoon, and she took advantage of the weather by letting the top down.

She popped a Whitney Houston cassette into the player as she joined the swift flow of traffic along Van Ness Avenue. Glancing into the rearview mirror to check the traffic behind her before passing the car in front, she noticed a late model black Mercedes directly behind her. She would have thought nothing of it, but it stayed on her tail throughout several lane changes, and she was suddenly apprehensive.

Due to the nature of her profession, she'd made a few enemies, some of whom held grudges against her. Her mind searched back. One likely candidate was Jack Beltran, an enforcer for Marco Cansini, a reputed organized crime boss. Initially assigned to defend him, Georgie stepped down as his attorney after learning of his guilt. The state had then gone for the jugular. Jack had sworn he'd make her pay for the part she'd played in getting him convicted of extortion and sent to prison for five years. He couldn't be out on parole after only two years, could he? The way the justice system ran today, he could be. Cansini was rumored to be very generous to those who were loyal to him, and Jack had refused to turn state's evidence, which would have incriminated his boss. That could account for the shiny new Mercedes—a gift from Cansini.

She thought of driving to the nearest police station, but that would entail making a U-turn in bumper-to-bumper traffic. She couldn't risk it. No use trying to lose the car, anyway. There wasn't going to be a high-speed chase down Van Ness Avenue with the vast number of motorists on the road.

Seeing a shopping center up ahead, she decided to pull into the parking lot and check if her fears held water. The moment she slowed down and put on her turn signal, the Mercedes mirrored her actions.

She drove through the parking lot, her eyes on the Mercedes. Come on Georgie, she thought. Think girl, think. The wise thing to do would be to stay in a well-populated area. The shopping center was a good choice because people were going in and coming out of the supermarket and various other shops in the complex.

She parked her Mustang between a van and a fiery red sports car. She was preparing to make a mad dash for the nearest store when the Mercedes pulled behind the Mustang, blocking her in. Turning, she ran in the opposite direction.

"Georgette!" a deep male voice called to her.

With her heart pounding in her ears, she almost failed to recognize that voice. It was Kyle Franklyn.

She stopped in her tracks and slowly turned around. Kyle stood next to the luxury car, looking fashionable in an expensive suit and dark sunglasses.

Two other men emerged from the car and Kyle was sandwiched between two men who looked like linebackers for the San Francisco 49ers. They were all dressed conservatively in dark suits, reminding her of pumped-up bankers. Georgie couldn't help noticing the bulges beneath their tailored duds; they were artillery-packing bankers.

Curiously, her nerves immediately dissipated. Sure, there were three heavily-armed men approaching her, but one of them was Kyle. She walked back to her car, leaning against the door. She hadn't seen or spoken with Kyle since she graduated from law school.

He hadn't changed much. He still seemed fit, judging from the way his jacket stretched across his chest. His straight teeth flashed white in the sunshine as he grinned at her. As he got closer, she saw that his short, curly hair was expertly trimmed, the suit was by Cerruti, and the shoes were also Italian. The gold watch was probably a Rolex. He'd always had expensive tastes, even when he couldn't afford the trappings of wealth.

He continued to smile at her. Georgie smiled back. There was no use antagonizing him before she knew why he'd followed her. She was certain butter wouldn't melt in his mouth; he was so cool. How she hated, though, what he'd become. Her sweet Kyle was now all the cliches of the black drug dealer rolled into one drop-dead package. A shark in a slick suit—only he was smoother. Was there nothing left of the old Kyle, the boy who used to carry her books home from school? The boy who was too shy to kiss her cheek in the presence of others?

"Hello, Georgette. Still fighting the good fight?"

Georgie crossed her arms over her chest, a defensive movement. She eyed him coolly. "I do what I can."

Kyle signalled his men to stay where they were as he moved in closer.

"I wanted to personally thank you for what you did for my kid brother. I hope I didn't frighten you by following you," he said, his baritone well-modulated. "Reggie wouldn't allow me to get a lawyer for him. He said he wanted you to defend him. Apparently, he made the right choice."

"I was just doing my job, Kyle. You don't owe me any thanks," Georgie said. She wiped her moist palm on the skirt of the navy blue suit she wore.

Kyle, six feet tall to her five-eight, reached over and grasped her right hand in his. He removed a thick manila envelope from his inside coat pocket and firmly placed it in her hand.

"But I do," he said, his light-brown eyes boring into her darker ones. "I want to." His tone allowed for no refusals. "Thank you, lady."

He released her and Georgie opened the envelope, peering inside. There must have been ten thousand dollars in fifties in it.

Georgie sighed. Her almost black eyes narrowed. "Don't put me in an awkward position, Kyle. You know I can't accept this."

She forced the envelope back into his palm. "I don't want your money."

Incensed, Kyle moved so close to her she could smell the residue of the mint he'd just consumed on his cool breath.

"I don't like being indebted to anyone, Georgette. Take the damn money. I don't care what you do with it. Donate it to one of your many causes, Saint Georgie. Just take it."

Georgie pursed her lips and slowly smiled at him.

"If you want to give me something, then give me your promise."

"My promise?" Kyle said, puzzled. His nostrils flared. "Speak English, woman."

His muscular body was touching hers. Her bottom was pressed against the Mustang's door.

Her eyes raked over his handsome face. The years had fine-tuned his features, turning the boy she'd known into a remarkably attractive man. She was still half in love with him. But she could never be with him again, not as long as he remained in his present line of business.

"Kyle, promise me you'll keep Reggie out of your business, and you can consider your debt paid."

Kyle was watching her lips move as she talked. He remembered how delectable she tasted in the heat of passion. He longed for the silken touch of her skin against his. He would forever recall the first time they'd made love. It had been the first time for the both of them.

Their cheeks briefly touched. "Girl, you smell good. But then, you always did," he murmured dreamily. Then, he seemed to come to his senses, realizing where he was and who was watching. He straightened up, regarding her with clear eyes. "Reggie isn't in the business. Didn't he tell you what went down? He lied to my men in order to get in on a run. That fool could have been rotting in a Hong Kong prison, if he hadn't been arrested before he could leave the country." He sighed, his eyes narrowing. "Still, you have some nerve trying to tell me how to run my own family."

"Look how you live, Kyle," Georgie said, not backing down. She glanced in the direction of his bodyguards. "You can't go anywhere without them, can you? You can't have a normal life—or a woman you can trust. Someone who'll love you for you and not for what you can give her. A family? You and Reg are not a family. You live in a war zone, and you're unwittingly making him a part of your army. The boy idolizes you, Kyle. That's why he took such a risk." Her voice was low as she commanded his full attention. "Maybe you like it. Maybe you care more about the money than you do about your kid brother. If you did care about Reggie, you'd quit this life and do something worthwhile."

Kyle continued to look at her through narrowed eyelids. "Do you know what I do to women who talk to me like that?" His finger traced the outline of her strong jaw.

Georgie didn't flinch. "No. But I remember the time you cried when you thought I was dying. I had a high fever, and the doctor said it could be meningitis. You came to see me when I was in the hospital, and there were tears in your eyes, Poogie." She used her old nickname for him.

Kyle sighed, vividly remembering that day. "I thought you were unconscious."

"I was in and out. But I remember that. Are you trying to say you don't remember it?"

"Damn it, woman!" Kyle said angrily, jaw clenched.

In one swift movement, Kyle took her in his arms and kissed her hard and deep. Georgie didn't put up any resistance. For a split second, he was her Kyle, the first and only man she'd ever loved.

He released her just as abruptly. They stood, breathless, eyeing one another like adversaries, instead of two people who'd just shared a passionate kiss.

"I will undoubtedly pay the Devil his due for my misdeeds some day," Kyle said quietly. "Let it not be said that I am indebted to a certain angel. Reggie's out of it."

He turned on his heels and walked away. Georgie watched as he motioned to his men that it was time to depart. In a matter of seconds, they were gone.

She got back behind the wheel of the Mustang and started the engine. The man could still kiss, Lord.

* * *

"And . . . cut! That's a wrap, people. Bree, Patrick, you were both spectacular," The director, Eric Berensen, applauded and was soon joined by the rest of the cast and crew of "Hiding Out," Briane Shaw's new made-for-television movie.

Bree smiled radiantly, her beautiful light-brown, almond-shaped eyes tearing up. "Thanks, Eric. I'm going to miss you guys. I had a ball."

"Sure you did," Patrick Ashton, her co-star said as he bent his dark, curly head to give her a buss on the cheek. "You came out of it smelling like a rose."

Ashton, however, was covered from head-to-foot with mud from the final scene in which Jody Freeman, the private detective character Bree portrayed, had sent his character, villain, Davis McPherson, sprawling into the muck.

"Don't be such a spoilsport," Bree said, grinning at him. "I hear mud's good for the complexion."

Patrick bent dawn and scooped up a handful of the black mud. He walked purposefully toward her. Bree tried to duck out of the way, but he was too fast. Grinning happily, he smeared it all over her face.

"Now you can call your dermatologist and cancel your facial for next month," he said, rubbing it in.

Bree sputtered with laughter and promptly retaliated.

Soon, most of the cast and crew were rolling around in the pond, covering each other in mud and howling with laughter.

Eric Berensen stood on the bank, disgusted. "Break it up!" he shouted. "The company's not paying to clean everyone's wardrobe."

Two burly prop men pulled him into the pond and dunked him.

Bree slipped away in the middle of the melee, going to her trailer to take a quick shower and to phone Georgie to tell her she was flying to San Francisco a full twelve hours earlier than she'd initially planned.

As she walked to the trailer, she admired the beautiful Arizona sunset. In the distance, the sky was a deep azure, and the sun was like a huge orange ball disappearing behind the curtain of the horizon. She would miss the peacefulness of the desert.

She could hear Pierre, her black toy poodle barking as she pulled the door of the trailer open. He ran and jumped into her arms. Bree pulled him to her, allowing him to lick her face. "Watch out for the mud," she said. Peering around the room, she could spot no signs of destruction. She always checked for damage whenever she came into a room where she'd left the little devil for more than an hour. Pierre was like a spoiled child. If ignored, he found ways to remind you to pay more attention to him.

Placing him back on the floor, Bree headed toward the small bathroom in the rear of the trailer. "Guard the premises while I take a quick shower."

As she turned the corner leading into the hallway, she quickly spun around and growled at him. In response, Pierre bared his tiny teeth and yelped. "You're my brave boy," Bree complimented him. He wagged his tail happily, then he went and sat by the door where he would remain until she returned from the shower. He wasn't big and menacing-looking like a doberman or a pit bull but what he lacked in size, he made up for in intelligence.

In the shower, Bree relaxed underneath the hot stream of water. She was glad this gig was over. She could kick back and enjoy herself for eight weeks before having to report to Jamaica for her next television movie. When was she going to get her shot at the Big Screen? She supposed she really couldn't complain. She'd been a vixen on *Joy of Living,* a soap opera, for four years before her first TV movie. "Hiding Out" was her fifth. She was doing great, actually. She'd managed to earn a seven-figure income last year alone, and she didn't have extravagant tastes, no matter what her big sister had to say about it. She spent wisely, made solid investments and basically spoiled her friends and family—except Georgie. Her pig-headed big sister refused to accept anything she deemed unnecessary from her baby sister.

Last year, Bree had wanted to give her a new car for her birthday. You would have thought Bree had offered to murder her.

"A new car?" Georgie had cried. "I have a perfectly good car. It's a classic. They don't make them like that anymore. And I keep it in tiptop shape."

Which was true, Bree had to admit. The Mustang ran like a top. That did not preclude accepting a brand new BMW, did it?

Refreshed by her shower, Bree dried off and slipped into a hot pink terry cloth robe. Going back into the tiny living room of the trailer, she sat on the brown leather sofa and dialed Georgie's number. His guard-duty over, Pierre hopped into her lap and made himself comfortable.

Georgie answered on the second ring. "Hello, you've reached the Shaw residence . . ."

"Cut it out, Georgie," Bree interrupted her, chuckling. "Anyone who knows you knows you don't own an answering machine."

"I just got home," Georgie explained, "and if you were someone I didn't want to talk to, I was going to make you leave a message."

"You get stranger everyday," her sister told her, still laughing. "Listen, Sis, we finished a day ahead of time. Miracles happen. I'll be in town tomorrow morning, early."

"What airline are you flying?"

"I'll take a cab to your place. Sleep in."

"I'm getting up early anyway," Georgie told her. "I need a good workout."

"Then you'll be at Sammy's dojo when I get into town," Bree deduced. "Leave the key with that sweet Mr. Crenshaw."

Georgie lived on the third level of a quaint converted Victorian home in the Pacific Heights section of San Francisco. Her apartment was formerly occupied by Alana Calloway, a dear friend who had recently gotten married.

"Solid," Georgie agreed. She paused. "Someone's at my door, I've got to go."

"Careful," Bree advised her. "Make sure you see who's there before opening the door. There are a lot of creeps out there."

"You're beginning to sound like me," Georgie joked. "A few more years of my coaching and you'll be damn near perfect."

"See you tomorrow," Bree said. She was used to her sister's opinion that *she* was the guiding force in their relationship. "Love you!"

"I love you, too," Georgie replied, signing off.

Bree replaced the receiver and hugged Pierre. "One of these days, my sister is going to find out she doesn't know everything."

Recalling how she'd mistaken Kyle for Jack Beltran, Georgie took her sister's advice and approached the door cautiously.

"Yes, who's there?"

"Package for Georgette Shaw," came a male voice from the other side of the door. Georgie looked through the peephole and could make out only the brim of the baseball cap the man was wearing and the clipboard in his hand. A messenger.

She cracked the door a couple of inches and the man savagely shoved the door the rest of the way open, breaking the chain lock. Georgie was knocked off balance, almost tripping over the brass hat tree standing near the front door.

"What do you think you're doing?" Georgie shouted at her assailant. She backed away from him, looking around for a ready means of escape. He was blocking the door.

The man, who was perhaps two inches taller than her five-eight and built like a professional weight-lifter, didn't reply but advanced on her and threw a right cross at her chin which she blocked with her left arm, then countered with a fist to his solar plexus. He grabbed her around the waist, his breath coming in short rasps. "Don't make this harder than it has to be, lady. All I want is your money."

Georgie continued to struggle in his vise-like hold. She intentionally fell backward, her body weight propelling them to the floor. She landed on top of him, succeeding in momentarily knocking the air from his lungs. Unhurt, she scrambled to her feet, assuming the fighter's stance: arms up, ready to block and legs slightly apart for maximum balance.

The guy didn't move. He lay on the floor groaning loudly.

"I wasn't gonna hurt you," he said, his voice almost a sob. "I just needed a few bucks. I've been outta work for months now, and my kids are hungry."

Georgia sighed. Feeling sympathetic, she bent down to see if she'd actually put him out of commission. With lightning fast reflexes, he grasped her arm and pulled her down onto the floor, pinning her beneath his body. He grinned triumphantly.

She could barely breathe as she fought to free herself. However, the more she struggled, the tighter his muscular thighs closed around her midsection. "You had to be the hero, didn't you lady? Let's see you get out of this one," he said, dark eyes menacing. He smiled at her helplessness.

"That's enough," a feminine voice said from the doorway. "I swear, you two will never grow up." Sammy Chan, Georgie's best friend since the fifth grade, rolled off of her and helped her to her feet.

"You aren't pulling your punches enough," he complained lightly. "I may be sore from that first one to the ribs. Good follow through."

Their little exercise had made Georgie break a sweat. Laughing, she wiped her brow as she looked at Sammy. "What kind of an accent was that anyway?"

"That was my Spanish accent," Sammy answered, gingerly rubbing the area where she'd punched him.

Joanne Chan walked into the apartment, closing the door behind her. "Sammy, you broke Georgie's chain lock. You're going to have to repair that before we leave."

Leaving Sammy to nurse his wounds alone, Georgie walked over to Joanne and gave her a warm hug. "Hi, Jojo."

"I tried to talk him out of it," Jojo apologized for her husband's impromptu martial arts lesson. Jojo came out of her coat, shaking her straight, waist-length, blue-black hair as she did so. Georgie took it from her and hung it on the hall tree.

"Come into the kitchen," she invited Jojo. "I was just going to get something to drink, won't you join me?"

"Of course, thank you," Jojo replied.

They looked back at Sammy as though he were a little boy lagging behind on an outing. Sammy followed, sniffing petulantly. Whenever those two got together, they always treated him as though he were first cousin to Conan the Barbarian and needed everything spelled out for him. Women—where did they get the idea that they were the intellectual superiors of men?

He smiled at the sight they made. Georgie, tall and slightly muscular with her arm draped about five feet, two inch tall Jojo's shoulders. He supposed he loved those two women, along with his parents, more than anyone else on earth. Therefore, he generously overlooked their gargantuan superiority complexes.

Since he and Georgie were both ten years old, Sammy had been teaching her how to defend herself. Five years ago, she'd gotten serious about his attempts and earned a black belt in judo. It wasn't exactly what Sammy taught. The discipline he taught and practiced was passed on to him by his father and his father by his father and so on for generations. By the time Sammy decided to open his dojo two years ago, Georgie was already on her way to becoming proficient in judo.

The exercise that had just transpired between them was Sammy's way of testing her abilities. He didn't want her abilities to lie dormant for so long that she forgot how to defend herself properly should the time come when that expertise could mean the difference between life or death. Then too, he'd always gotten a thrill out of scaring the bejesus out of her.

In the kitchen, they sat at the breakfast nook drinking glasses of fruit juice.

"Okay, spill it," Georgie told them. "I can tell you two have something on your minds."

She looked at Jojo, then Sammy. She waited.

Sammy's brown face crinkled in a wide grin. "Jojo's pregnant."

Georgie knocked her chair over in her rush to hug them both.

"Oh my God," she cried excitedly. "A baby. When did you find out?"

"I've suspected I was for a couple of weeks now," Jojo said, her lovely serene face a mass of smiles. "But Dr. Sands confirmed it for us this morning. I'm about two months along."

Georgie stood back, admiring the expectant couple. Shaking her head, she said, "I can't believe it. I mean, you'll make a wonderful mother Jojo, but Sammy? How will you tell him and the baby apart?"

Joining in on Georgie's solo roast of her husband, Jojo turned her dark brown eyes on Sammy. "Yes," she said, continuing to appraise him. "But I believe that having a child will force him to grow up. At least, that's my theory. What do you think?"

"I certainly hope so," Georgie replied, her expression grave. "Lord knows you're going to have your hands full with one child. You don't need two."

"All right, all right," Sammy spoke up in his defense. "I've had just about enough out of you two. I'm going to be the best father who ever lived. I'm going to teach my son everything I know. He's going to be perfect, just like his old man."

"Who says it's going to be a boy?" Jojo said, unable to hide her amusement.

"I want a boy first, a girl second, so she'll have a big brother to protect her," Sammy said, feeling his ego being restored to health.

"Listen to him," Jojo said. "He got me pregnant, and now he's placing his order for the *second* child. He's got plenty of nerve, this one has."

"Gosh, Chan, your chauvinism is bursting out all over," Georgie said, on Jojo's side. "You'd better learn to control that before little Samantha shows up."

"Samantha . . ." Sammy mused aloud, his brown eyes twinkling. "It has possibilities."

Placing her hand over her slightly rounding stomach, Jojo said, "I'm hungry. Are you going to feed us tonight or not, Samuel Chan?"

"Mama Lou's?" Sammy suggested, looking at Jojo and Georgie for confirmation.

"Mama Lou's," Georgie assented.

"Mama Lou's," Jojo agreed, smiling.

The Royal Dragon, the restaurant Lucille Chan owned and operated, was packed with its usual Friday night crowd. A family-oriented restaurant, it was tastefully decorated with Chinese art and brilliant greenery. Lou was an avid gardener and had a knack for bringing near-dead plants back to life.

Lucille was in her element when Georgie, Sammy and Jojo arrived. She was chatting with diners at the center table, regaling them with stories about the restaurant's history. She embellished them ever so slightly.

"This was Al Capone's favorite restaurant when he was in San Francisco. He used to come in here with a different beauty on his arm each time. My mother would personally prepare his favorite dish, Peking duck. He could eat mounds of it," Lou told the rapt diners.

Sammy came up behind his mother and hugged her. "Al had a big appetite for everything. Hello, Mom."

"My son, Sammy," Lou said, introducing him to the diners, tourists from Orlando, Florida. "He teaches self defense. If someone tries to beat you up, call him. And this is his beautiful wife, Joanne. She's a flight attendant. If you should need to go someplace in a hurry, call her." Lou grasped Georgie by the hand. "Finally, this is our lovely, Georgette. She is an attorney. If you're accused of a crime, call her."

The diners laughed, pleased with the personal attention they were receiving from their hostess.

"Enjoy your meal," Lou said, excusing herself from their presence.

She hastily led Georgie, Sammy and Jojo to the family's private booth in the rear of the restaurant. Her husband, Samuel, a physics professor with the University of California, was already seated, going over some work he'd brought home.

He got to his feet when he saw his son, daughter-in-law and favorite visitor to their home, Georgie.

"What a pleasant surprise," he exclaimed, hugging first Jojo, then Georgie and finally Sammy. Samuel had the same dark brown eyes as his son. He was shorter, by three inches and had a slighter build and was greying at his temples. His smile was engaging and he used it often.

"Sit," Lou said, gesturing to the empty bench across from Samuel. She slid onto the space next to her husband, who quickly moved his papers aside for her. "Come, tell Mama what is going on. I can feel the tension in the air."

"Give the kids a few minutes to relax, dear, then they'll tell us what it is they want to tell us," Samuel said calmly. He ascribed to Zen philosophy. His wife, on the other hand, was impatient. She was always busy and seemed to do everything swiftly with little repose.

Samuel caught the eye of Julie, one of the waitresses and beckoned her over to their booth.

Julie had gone to high school with Georgie and Sammy. She greeted them before asking for their orders. "Hey you guys! How's it going?"

"Great, Julie," Georgie said. "How've you been?"

"Good. I'm back in college. Did Mama Lou tell you?"

"That's great, Julie," Jojo piped in. "What are you majoring in?"

"Cosmetology. That's the study of beauty, not the study of the universe, although, I thought about that, too. This time, I'm really going to stick it out," Julie announced proudly. She pushed her pencil behind her ear and shook her red locks. Anyone who didn't know her would think she was totally clueless.

"I'm glad to hear it," Georgie congratulated her. "You're so good with customers, you'll make a wonderful stylist."

"I know and you know some of those guys rake in the big bucks," Julie informed them. "I could even have my own salon some day."

"Go for it," Sammy encouraged her, lapsing into Julie's valley girl vernacular.

"Go for it right now," Mama Lou said impatiently. The rest of them might think Julie's incessant talking was cute, but she had to listen to the girl's chatter all day. "Just bring them the house special and extra egg rolls for Georgie. Go, go."

"Lucille, you really should practice more patience with that child," her husband chided her when Julie was out of earshot.

"She gives me a headache," Lou said. "If you had to listen to her for hours on end, even you would get testy. But don't worry, dear, her job is secure. In spite of her irritating habits, I happen to like Julie."

Turning her keen eyes on Jojo, she said, "Are you picking up a few pounds? Not that it isn't becoming on you—you were always too skinny."

"Lou!" Samuel said, aghast.

"I'm not joking," Lou insisted. She grasped Jojo's hand and squeezed it affectionately. "You know I love you, Jojo. What's going on, have you suddenly learned how to cook or something?"

"Well, she does have a bun in the oven," Sammy joked.

Silence reigned at the corner booth. It took a few seconds for the meaning of the colloquialism to dawn on his parents. Then, Lou let out a shriek that nearly burst his eardrums and threw her arms around his neck, squeezing him so hard it cut off his breath.

Every eye in the restaurant was turned on them as Lou repeatedly kissed her son's and daughter-in-law's faces and Samuel hugged the both of them, tears of happiness streaming down his cheeks.

Georgie sat quietly, enjoying the sight of the people she'd thought of as a second family for years in the throes of extreme joy. Her face was wet, too.

After a few minutes of unadulterated bliss, Lou must have realized she was making a spectacle of herself. She sat down, her legs weak. Then she did something that nearly threw the other four persons at her booth into shock: hidden behind one of the restaurant's pristine white cloth napkins, she wept.

"Mama," Sammy said, his voice filled with awe. He placed a comforting arm about her slim shoulders. "Don't cry."

"Let her cry, son," Samuel said softly. He gently held his wife's hand. "Aside from the day you were born, this is the happiest day of our lives."

Julie arrived with their entrees and taking a look at Lou, said: "Oh, Mama Lou, don't cry. You know I never take what you say to me like . . . *seriously.*"

Lou glanced up at the waitress and laughed. "Thank you, Julie. I'm happy to know that."

The others were having a difficult time restraining laughter. Julie placed the heavy platters on the table, then, as she was straightening up, she planted a kiss on Lou's cheek. "Cheer up, boss lady. I think you're super."

With that, she left them to attend to the needs of the diners at the remaining tables assigned to her.

"She may not be too quick on the uptake," Samuel said. "But you must admit she's sweet about it."

Lou could only nod as she dabbed at her tears with the napkin.

Unable to resist the tantalizing aroma of the food, Georgie picked up an egg roll and bit into it. "Delicious, Mama Lou."

"Not too much ginger?" Lou asked, seemingly concerned her chef might be losing his touch.

"Absolutely not," Georgie assured her. "It's perfection."

"I know," Lou replied. There were some things she made no apologies for. One was being conceited where her cuisine was concerned. She ran a first-rate establishment and she was proud of it.

They all ate to their satisfaction, heaping praise on Mama Lou, and at the end of their meal, Samuel passed around the basket of fortune cookies, imploring everyone to partake.

"You know I'm not superstitious, Samuel," Lou said, her hand already in the basket. She cracked open a cookie, dropping the edible part onto her plate and read, "You are blessed by the men in your life."

Smiling, she looked into Samuel's eyes. "Well, perhaps I am, if only a little bit."

Sammy opened his and popped the almond flavored cookie into his mouth. Chewing, he read, "You will receive a gift of incalculable value."

"That's true, too," Samuel said, looking at Jojo. "What does yours say, Joanne?"

"Good things come in small packages," Jojo read. She looked over at Sammy. "Our bundle will be small at first."

"But then she'll grow to be as beautiful as her mother," Sammy said, kissing her forehead.

"Shall we make it four for four?" Samuel said, looking at Georgie.

Georgie was like Lou about superstitions. Not wanting to spoil Samuel's fun, however, she obligingly read the message in her fortune cookie:

"Your life will be filled with romance and adventure."

She laughed. "Three out of four ain't bad."

"Wait," Samuel said, his brown eyes alight with amusement. "I haven't read mine yet."

He held the slip of paper aloft in his hand as though he was trying to build the suspense in those looking on. After a moment, he read, "To the lovely maiden . . ." He smiled at Georgie. "That would be you, my dear. Everyone else is married." He cleared his throat for effect. "To the lovely maiden, beware—a tall, dark stranger brings danger."

"You're putting me on, Samuel," Georgie said, laughing. "It doesn't really say that."

Samuel placed the tiny sliver of paper in her hand. It did indeed express exactly what he'd read.

"Now you see why I don't believe in that nonsense," Mama Lou reiterated. "Georgie will be wondering about every tall, dark man she meets from now on."

"No," Georgie disavowed. "I'm not that gullible."

But her stomach muscles had constricted painfully when Samuel had read the message.

Samuel reached across the table and grasped one of Georgie's hands.

"It's nonsense," he said reassuringly.

Three

Toni glanced in her mother's direction as Marie sliced tomatoes to go with the collard greens they were about to sit down and enjoy. Her father, James, was in the garden gathering scallions. The tiny green onions were his favorite accompaniment to collards. Toni wondered what her life would be like if she hadn't moved back to New Orleans four and a half years ago. Her father had just had a stroke, and she knew her mother needed help with him, despite her fervent protestations to the contrary. The one thing she and her mother had in common was stubbornness. In any event, Toni had never regretted the move. Her father was fully recovered now, and Toni was happy being so close to her parents.

"The girls are coming home for a few days," Marie said, opening the conversation. "I'm glad. They don't come home often enough."

"Their careers don't allow them to, Mere. I'm sure they'd like to."

"How long are we going to be graced with their presence?" Marie wanted to know.

"A week, maybe two for Georgie and several weeks for Bree. She doesn't have another movie for a few months. She'll go to Jamaica next," Toni said, with more than a touch of pride in her voice.

"Did you tell them about that nice reporter who wants to interview you for his magazine?" Marie inquired sweetly.

"No," Toni replied, wondering what was on her mother's mind.

If Marie wanted information from her, she was simply taking a roundabout route getting it out of her. "I haven't decided if I'm going to give him an interview."

"He was nice, Toni. A good boy, very decent," Marie said cajolingly. "Why wouldn't you want to let your many fans know you're still kicking?"

"Toni Shaw doesn't have fans, Mere. A few people might remember her fondly. Others probably remember her as a rabble-rouser. But fans? Now there's a misnomer if I've ever heard one," Toni said thoughtlessly.

Pulling herself to her full five feet, two inches, Marie rounded on her. "Level with me, young lady." Whenever she referred to Toni as "young lady," it always made Toni feel all of three years old. "What's the *real* reason why you don't want to do any interviews?"

"I don't like dredging up the past, Mere," Toni hedged. "You know that. And another thing, I don't like the way Mr. Knight insinuated himself right into your good graces when I wasn't at home. By the time I returned, he had you in his hip pocket, for God's sake."

"Leave God out of it," Marie said. She thought using "God" in a sentence utilized for any communication other than prayer was blasphemous. "The boy is trying to do you a service. He wants to bring you into the nineties—then maybe you will stop hiding. Besides, he liked my gumbo."

Sighing and turning to look her mother squarely in the eyes, Toni said, "Everyone likes your gumbo. I simply don't trust anyone who can blend in so easily with anyone, anything. He wants something."

With a sigh heavier than her daughter's, Marie smiled slowly. "Yes. He wants you to speak up and let people know you're more than Toni Shaw the sixties activist. You went on to have a normal life like everyone else. You have a family and good friends, and your life didn't end in nineteen sixty-eight when you disappeared from the public eye."

"I know, Mere," Toni said, sounding exasperated. Her mother was like a bulldog when she wanted to make a point. When she sank her teeth into a problem, she wasn't likely to give up. "Isn't that enough that I have millions of readers who know I'm alive and well?"

"You have millions of readers who know you as Serena Kincaid. It's just another facade to hide behind," Marie said accusingly.

"That's just the way I like it," Toni returned stubbornly. "I don't want to be thought of as larger than life. That should be my prerogative, Mere. It's my life, after all."

"I believe only good would come from this interview," her mother persisted. "If nothing else, than at least Charles Waters would know what a fine woman he gave up all those years ago."

Relieved that her mother had finally come to the point, Toni smiled.

"So that's what you've been getting at. All that talk about my hiding. You think I'm still in love with that snake. Well you couldn't be further off base. Charles Edward Waters is old history."

"Hah!" Marie said, calling her daughter's bluff. "If he's old history, then why aren't you married with several other children by now?"

Frowning, Toni busied herself by washing the colander Marie had used to rinse the tomatoes in. "I never met the right man," she offered weakly.

"You weren't looking," her mother stated. "You play at love, mon petite. Poor Spencer Taylor. He adores you, but you use him as a convenience. You don't have an escort for some function? Call Spencer and the lovesick fool comes running." Marie paused, going to take the colander from Toni's hands and dropping it into the sink. She wanted to make certain what she was saying was being heard. "You're a beautiful woman, Toni. It's not too late for you to experience love. But, because of your unresolved feelings for Charles Edward Waters, you've allowed real love to elude you. There, I've had my say."

"Love is not an option for me," Toni said, as if by rote. Her mother had heard this spiel before. "No one is ever going to

get close enough to me to cause the kind of damage the girls'
father did."

She forced a smile. "I have all the happiness I want or need,
Mere. I have two wonderful children. You and Papa. I have a
career that some writers would kill for. I date interesting, attractive men. What more could I possibly want?"

Marie sighed and regarded her daughter with sympathy.
"Amour, mon petite, amour. A love affair. That's what you need.
You haven't given anyone else your heart. Charles Waters, alone.
Now what does that tell you?"

Toni stared at her mother. She was at a loss for words. Sitting
on a stool, her mouth agape, and all the bravado extinguished,
she recognized the truthfulness of her mother's words. She *had*
allowed the past twenty-nine years to slip by her. Could she have
somehow harmed her daughters by presenting to them the image
of a woman who didn't need a man, a woman who did not trust
men and consequently, abhorred the male sex? All because she'd
once been deceived by Charles Edward Waters?

Her vision was blurred by tears when she looked up into her
mother's sweet face. "Have I really allowed that man to ruin my
chance for happiness?"

Marie went to her, grasping both her hands in her own. "It
isn't too late. I just want you to wake up, Toni. Be aware of what
you're doing." She smiled at her daughter. "Sweetheart, I know
about the letters."

Toni's heart was in her throat. "How could you know?"

"I went into your office one day. I was looking for something
to write with. You know I can never keep up with a pen. You had
recently gotten a letter from him because you had crumpled it
and tossed it into the waste basket. I fished it out and read it,"
Marie said with regret. "I'm sorry. You know I'm not a snoop.
But, when I saw the name on the letterhead, curiosity got the best
of me."

"It's okay," Toni said softly. Actually, she was relieved someone else knew about Charles Edward's recent harassment of her.
"I would have eventually told you anyway."

"When are you going to tell them about him?" Marie asked, her dark eyes meeting Toni's.

Toni frowned. Even the thought of revealing the true identity of their father to her daughters caused her to experience a searing pain in her gut.

"How do I tell them their father isn't dead? All their lives, they've believed he died a hero in Vietnam," she said, her voice quivering with emotion.

"Sit them down and tell them," Marie said succinctly. "Don't beat around the bush. Give them the facts as you know them. They're mature enough to take it."

"I lied to them, Mere. I have been lying to them all their lives," Toni moaned.

"I believe, under the circumstances, they'll understand the reason you resorted to subterfuge. They will forgive you. You were only trying to protect them."

"I couldn't bear it if it poisoned the closeness, the richness of our relationship. It would kill me, Mere."

"That isn't going to happen, baby," her mother assured her. "It would be far worse if he somehow got in contact with them before you had the opportunity to explain."

Toni's face was wet with tears. She breathed in deeply and released with a groan. "I suppose I'll have to tell them soon," she said, resigned to the inevitability of it. "His letters are becoming more and more urgent all the time. He isn't going to give up. I wonder if he's actually grown a backbone."

"There could be a fight brewing," Marie said sagely.

Toni pooh-poohed the idea. "Hah! The girls are adults. He can't sue me for custody," she said with derision.

"He's a wealthy man with endless resources at his disposal. He could make life miserable for you."

"No more than he already has," Toni replied, wiping her tears on the back of her hand. "Let him try." The expression in her ebony eyes served to relieve some of her mother's anxiety. Her daughter was ready to do battle with Charles Edward Waters, if it came to that.

The doorbell rang.

Marie looked into Toni's eyes. "You okay?"

"I'm fine," Toni replied stoutly.

Marie went to answer the door. Seconds later, Toni was running from the kitchen to the living room to investigate the reason behind her mother's shrill screams of delight.

Her girls were home. Fresh tears sprang to Toni's eyes as she hugged first Georgie then Bree. She was once again amazed by how much they resembled her when she was their age. The same warm, brown skin, tinged with red and, in Georgie's case, almost black eyes that were thickly fringed. Bree had her father's eye color, light-brown, reminiscent of good cognac. However, both of them possessed similar heart-shaped faces with delicate bone structure and impossibly high cheekbones surrounded by mounds of thick, jet-black hair.

They had their father's nose—not too long, but aquiline in some respects. No matter how hard she tried not to, Toni could still see their father in them. She thanked God that attributes like honor were taught and not inherited. She would have been greatly disappointed if they shared their father's sense of right and wrong. As far as she was concerned, Charles Edward Waters had a deplorable character.

"You devils," Marie accused them. "Why didn't you tell us you were arriving today? We could have met you at the airport with a brass band."

"We wanted to surprise you, Gran," Georgie replied, easily reverting to a southern accent. When at home, it became an involuntary habit.

"Well you did," Marie said affectionately as she hugged her. "Mon Dieu, I nearly keeled over when I saw you standing on my gallerie."

Bree placed Pierre on the floor, and he immediately ran for Marie, avoiding Toni, who did not suffer the tiny dog gladly. Marie, however, doted on him.

"Here is my dear grand doggie," she said now as she bent over and picked him up. "Did you have a pleasant trip, darling? Did they make you ride with the baggage, or did Mommy hide you in her carry-on bag?"

"The last time I did that," Bree said, "they threatened to toss us both off the plane in midair. He rode with the rest of the baggage." Looking around, she added, "Where is Paw Paw?"

"Where indeed," Marie said, laughing. Pierre's tongue was tickling her face. "In his garden, where else?"

Toni hated to see them go, even the short distance between the house and the garden. She was feeling quite sensitive what with the guilt she had carried for so long. She looked longingly after them.

Observing the woebegone expression her daughter wore, Marie shook her head sadly. "Twenty-nine years old. They're twenty-nine, Toni. The time has come to set the record straight. Like my mother used to say: the melon is ripe, you'd better cut into it and devour it before the flies start in on it. There is no telling what kind of an explanation Charles would give them about his absence. He could tell them you didn't want him to be a part of their lives, making you the heavy. You must tell them now, Toni. Tell them the first chance you get. I beg of you!"

"I don't know what to do!" Toni cried, rubbing her temples as though she had a migraine. "I need some air."

She went outside to join the girls and their grandfather, hoping to find solace, but the instant she saw her daughters laughing delightedly at something their grandfather had said—he was somewhat of a jokester—she knew she had no alternative but to finally come clean with them.

She smiled at the sight of her tall, dark and lanky father taking such pleasure in the company of his granddaughters. James Shaw was a retired railroad car inspector. Seventy years old, he was a self-educated man who had always been there for his family, no matter how rough times got. He had been a splendid role model for his granddaughters. So, Toni thought, I was able to provide them with one example of what a good man is. Perhaps I haven't been totally remiss in my duties as a mother.

Tonight, after the interview. She would give Clayton Knight

his interview then she would return home and tell them everything. Not leaving out one minute detail. Everything.

She knew her decision to go ahead with the interview was just an excuse to postpone the inevitable. She needed time to buck up her courage. You've already wasted twenty-nine years, she thought critically. What difference will a few more hours make?

Clay paced the floor in his room at the Hotel Le Pavillon. Five minutes earlier, Toni Shaw had phoned to say she would meet him downstairs in the lobby in an hour. He had been wearing the carpet thin with his size twelves ever since.

Toni was willing to grant him the interview as long as he didn't inquire about her family.

"My children and my parents may be mentioned in the article, but absolutely no photographs of them," was her stipulation.

He'd readily agreed to honor her wishes.

His conscience was bothering him big time now though. He didn't enjoy lying, especially to someone he respected.

His meeting Toni yesterday had done nothing to lessen that respect. When she'd started asking him personal questions, he had intended to ad-lib something, anything. However, one look into Toni's deep brown eyes, and he'd spilled his guts.

So that was his dilemma. This case was already too close to the bone for him. He liked Toni Shaw. He liked Marie Shaw. They were the type of people he wished he'd had for family. Deceiving them would be the most difficult moral dilemma of his career.

His indecision grew by leaps and bounds a few minutes later when he spotted Toni sitting on the Louis the Fourteenth-inspired settee in the lobby, flanked by two young women whom he knew had to be her daughters, Georgette and Briane.

Toni had not mentioned her daughters were accompanying her. Normally, Clay would be congratulating himself on his fantastic stroke of luck. But he knew that whenever everything fell into place too easily, something was bound to go awry. This case couldn't be such a breeze.

The three women rose as he approached. Clay had an unusual reaction when he could see them clearer. The young woman on the left was a dead ringer for Briane Shaw, the actress who starred in those hilarious detective movies on television.

However, it was her sister, the one with the braids, that made him do a double-take. While Briane was wearing a mini skirt that displayed her shapely legs to perfection, Georgette was attired in button fly jeans and a billowing white poet's shirt. Here was a woman who didn't need to advertise. Her confidence shone through like a lighthouse beacon to a sailor who desperately needed to be led through dangerous waters.

Clay was instantly smitten, a condition that had, heretofore been entirely foreign to him. He thought he'd developed an immunity to crushes years ago.

Her mane of hair was all her own, he knew instinctively He liked the way the baby-fine curls framed her heart-shaped face and the braids spilled down her back in a dark waterfall.

She met his gaze dead-on. No coyness in her demeanor. Her eyes were so dark, they were like obsidian with amber lights buried deep within. And the well-shaped nose beneath them was turned up at the moment. She didn't trust him. He could read that much from her expression. Her full lips were set slightly apart, as though she wanted to moisten them but decided against it because he was watching her too intently. He lowered his gaze, but then, her body came into view and his heart was off and racing again. Briane had the physique of a Hollywood actress: fit, trim, delicately sculpted. Georgette, however, had a voluptuous figure—full breasts, hips and good muscle tone. He could tell she worked-out. There was nothing weak about her physical being. And, baby had back . . . a fact the fit of her jeans attested to.

Toni stepped forward, offering her hand in greeting.

"Good evening, Mr. Knight. I'd like you to meet my daughters." She gestured to Briane. "Briane."

Bree shook his hand, her sharp eyes giving him the once-over.

"It's a pleasure, Mr. Knight. I hope you'll go easy on Mom. She isn't accustomed to giving interviews."

Clay smiled down at her. "Miss Shaw. The pleasure's all mine. I've seen your work. You're very talented."

"Thank you," Bree replied, genuinely flattered. She gave him the benefit of her most brilliant smile.

"And this is Georgette. She's an attorney with the public defender's office in San Francisco," Toni continued.

Georgette had a firm, no nonsense handshake.

"How do you do, Mr. Knight?" Her dark, unwavering eyes met his and Clay had to remember to breathe.

Her voice was deep, melodious. Clay thought he could listen to it for the rest of his life and never tire of it.

He held Georgie's hand as he looked into her eyes and something miraculous happened. In his mind's eye, he fast-forwarded to the future . . . and, in it, they were together. A couple. It was then that he realized that if he did not watch his step, he could easily fall for this woman. Therefore, he mustered up all his willpower and ordered his rampant libido to settle down. He was *not* in the market for a relationship.

He heard himself say, "Miss Shaw. How do you do?"

Georgie, for her part, found the manner in which he was staring at her faintly amusing. She'd previously witnessed that expression (a cross between dazed and dazzled), on the faces of her sister's many admirers, but she was not used to such open admiration.

There was no denying he was a good-looking man. Clayton Knight's dark brown skin was smooth and made her think of chocolate that had been left at room temperature—gleaming, warm and inviting. His deep eyes were piercing, the kind some women found acutely compelling—bedroom eyes. And the brown-green color was intriguing and lent an air of mystery to them.

He was a tall drink of water. Under different circumstances, she would find him extremely attractive. She looked at his clean-shaven face. She'd never seen a chin that square and determined. Or lips quite so uniquely curved. They were full and wide and imminently kissable. His nose complemented the rest of his face nicely—not too long, nor too short. Quite a memorable package.

Her eyes moved upward. His black, naturally wavy hair was closely shorn, tapering at the back of his strong neck. A conservative cut, which was unexpected. When he was approaching them, she thought he had a cowboy's swagger—a little cocky, deliberately sexy. Or maybe it was the black jeans, boots, denim shirt and long duster he wore. It all fit his muscular body as though he was most comfortable riding the trail. He moved like a man who was ready for whatever came his way. Totally at home in his skin.

"It's a pleasure to meet both of you," Clayton Knight said, drawing his eyes away from Georgie's face. "But, if you'll excuse your mother and me for a moment, there's something I should tell her in private."

"Of course," Bree said at once. "We'll wait for you in the lounge." She took Georgie by the arm and led her away. "Isn't he a dream?" she said when there was little chance of the reporter overhearing them.

"He's up to something. What could he have to tell Mom that we couldn't be a party to?" Georgie said cynically. She looked back at her mother and Clayton Knight. She'd had run-ins with unscrupulous newshounds before. The last one only a few weeks ago when a television reporter had shoved a microphone under her nose and insisted she tell her viewers why she was representing the brother of a known drug dealer. "Because in this country, every citizen has the right to legal representation. Haven't you ever read the Bill of Rights? They were adopted in 1791. Check out the fifth amendment."

"Loosen up girl," Bree told her as they entered the busy hotel bar. "He likes you."

"He doesn't even know me," Georgie countered. "But apparently, I'm his type."

"You noticed," Bree said, smiling. She often wondered whether her sister was cognizant of the mating signals men sent her way. If she were, she chose to ignore the bulk of them. Georgie didn't suffer fools gladly.

"I'm not blind," Georgie commented drily.

Bree laughed as they sat on stools at the bar and ordered mineral waters with a twist of lemon. Their mother and Clayton Knight shouldn't be long.

"Why is it I get the feeling you aren't being completely honest with me, Mr. Knight?" Toni asked when she and Clayton Knight were alone.

"Because you have good instincts," Clay stated frankly.

"Please explain yourself, Mr. Knight," Toni said, her brows knitted together with concern.

They were standing near the row of public phones adjacent to the lobby, away from the general flow of traffic.

"This is going to come as a shock to you, Toni, but you've got to listen to me closely. I am Clayton Knight. And I am from Boston. But I don't represent *Black Life* magazine. I'm a private investigator and I was hired by Charles Waters to find his daughter."

Toni's dark eyes narrowed to slits. She knew he had had something up his sleeve all along. She just hadn't been able to pinpoint it.

"And I have foolishly handed her over to you," she angrily cried. "Is that why you've suddenly decided to come clean?"

Clay sighed wearily. "No, Toni. I don't like deception any more than you do. The only reason I took this case was because I wanted to meet you. I had misgivings from the beginning. Why did Waters take so long to try to get to know Georgette? What's his purpose behind wanting to find her at this late date?" He paused, looking into her eyes. "Then, when I saw you with your daughters just now, I felt like a total louse. If you won't answer Waters' letters, I'm sure you have a good reason for it."

"Nearly thirty years of reasons," Toni said darkly. She had calmed down somewhat, although she continued to look at him as though he was the stuff you wiped off your shoe after taking a walk in a park frequented by well-fed dogs.

"I'm grateful to you for one thing: you confessed to me in private. Chuck had his chance to know his child. He turned his back on me, on us! He's had too many years to get to know his offspring. Tell me, Mr. Knight. Why now? Is he dying? Did he have a spiritual awakening? Does he dream dreams, or have visions? Tell me!"

"I believe he simply decided he was man enough to face you, Toni. He'd already lost the only reason he had for not acknowledging his child over five years ago when his wife and son were killed in a freak accident. It was you he couldn't bring himself to confront, not his child," Clay told her.

"This wouldn't have happened if Georgie hadn't insisted on accompanying me tonight," Toni muttered more to herself than to anyone else. She frowned at Clay. "You don't think I should just turn my daughters over to a father who ignored them all their lives?" Her voice was becoming shrill with rage.

"You mean both Georgette *and* Briane?" Clay said incredulously.

"They're twins," Toni informed him shortly.

"But they're so different."

Toni looked around them. "I'm leaving."

Clay caught her by the arm. "Is it so wrong for him to want to get to know his children?"

"You may know a few facts, Mr. Knight, but you'll never understand the dynamics of what's going on here. There is too much pain to get through in a matter of minutes. Your employer knows that. That's why he hired you to face me instead of doing it himself. You can go back to him and tell him his latest plan failed miserably, as will any future plots he may cook up. You tell him that for me."

"He thinks he fathered only one child," Clay said, not giving up.

"He didn't give me the chance to set him straight," Toni told him, her voice low. "When I tried to tell him, he hung up on me. I vowed never to speak to him again after that." She regarded Clay with curious eyes. "Why should I be the one to be magnanimous about this?"

"Forget him," Clay said dismissively. He took her by the shoulders, turning her around to face him. "Toni, don't you think Georgette and Briane should have the opportunity to know their father? Take it from someone who had one hell of a set of parents. They should have that choice."

Toni seemed to sag within his grasp. "They believe their father was killed in the Vietnam War."

"You lied to them?"

She looked him in the eyes. "Yes. Your hero lied," she said, her voice harsh. "The great Toni Shaw has a chink in her armor." Her eyes flashed angrily. "Don't be naive, Mr. Knight. I *protected* them. I don't know if you're capable of understanding that he gave me no choice. I told them that their father and I fell in love, that he got drafted, and they were conceived the night before he shipped out. There was no time for a wedding. My protests against the war, I told them, were mainly inspired by their father's involvement in it. In my heart, I figured it was better for them to believe he'd died than that he just didn't want anything to do with them."

Clay released her, his eyes sympathetic. "You have some serious thinking to do," he said. "I'll tell you what, I won't report back to Waters with what I've learned for twenty-four hours. That will, I hope, give you time enough to make up your mind whether or not you want to talk to him."

"I don't need time to think," Toni firmly said. "I know I don't want to talk to him."

"You loved him once," Clay began earnestly.

"I was barely eighteen. Little more than a child."

"You had two beautiful children together . . ."

"You're wrong there," Toni corrected him. "I had them with my two best friends at my side in a cold-water walk-up in Haight-Ashbury. Those girls and I are lucky to be alive."

Clay looked shocked. "Why didn't you go home to have them? Did your parents disown you?"

"I was too ashamed," Toni replied, evenly meeting his gaze. "My parents always put me on a pedestal. I am their only child. And I went away to college, got infatuated with an immature rich boy and got myself pregnant. When I finally went home, they cried because I'd endured it all without them. I was doubly ashamed for causing them additional pain. It wasn't a pleasant time in my life, Mr. Knight."

"Clay, please."

Toni sighed, the fight gone out of her. "I suppose I should thank you for coming clean about who you are and giving me a grace period, but I have nothing but contempt for Chuck. If he'd wanted to see his girls so badly, he's always known how to find me. I'm sure he could have gotten his company's jet to fly him here. You can tell him for me he can go straight to hell."

"I don't see why you can't run him up a flagpole and see if he'll salute," Bree was saying to her sister as they sat at the bar sipping their drinks.

Neither of them noticed a dark man of average height in a black leather jacket sit down next to them, or the interest he took in their conversation.

"Because I'm not casual where men are concerned," Georgie said, a bit miffed by her sister's suggestion, but still patient. She never took Bree's flippant comments seriously.

"Did you notice his hands? You know what they say about men with big hands," Bree said suggestively. "And those eyes. Girl, you would be a fool not to try that."

"You sound exactly like they do when they're discussing us," Georgie observed, a smile on her full lips.

"Good," Bree said, tossing back her drink as though there were spirits in her glass instead of mineral water. She set the drink down. "They're always treating us like sex objects." She turned to look her sister in the eyes. "Truly, Georgie, when was the last time you were held in a man's arms?"

Georgie sighed. She didn't want to think about it. "Let's see, that fiasco with Brian doesn't count, does it? I'd say it's been *too* long."

Bree nodded sympathetically. "Don't you miss the feel of a

pair of masculine arms wrapped around you? I know I do. Pierre, that rat, broke my heart into tiny pieces."

Georgie held back a string of unladylike words at the mention of Pierre St. Martin's name. She knew it was a bad sign that he and Bree's toy poodle shared the same name. He turned out to be a human "canine" in disguise.

"He was riding your coattails," she told her sister. "The minute someone offered him a role in a film, he was off like a shot. You need someone who's already established, someone confident enough to withstand your strong personality and above all else, someone who's going to love you unconditionally." Georgie laughed suddenly. "And yes, in answer to your question, I do miss having a man hold me but that doesn't mean I'm going to fall into the arms of the first handsome stranger who shows a little interest, Baby Sis."

"So, you do like him," was all Bree had to say. She'd made her point.

The man in the black leather jacket got to his feet, paid his bill and walked from the lounge to the nearest telephone.

The person he was phoning answered on the second ring.

"I've made her," he said into the receiver. "She has a younger sister, were you aware of that?"

"Toni Shaw is some piece of work. Two bastards," the voice on the other end hissed.

"You want me to do them both?"

"No. The first-born only. The kid sister's no threat to anyone."

"How do you want it done?"

"What do I care? Just do it, and quickly."

"You're the boss."

"Good evening, Mr. Kovik." The connection was abruptly severed.

Eddie Kovik replaced the receiver and hurried back to the lounge. He did not want to wind up missing the target when she was irrevocably in his sights. She was his now. White pawn takes black pawn en passant. His opening move. She would be his masterpiece.

An uncontrollable smile twisted his thin lips, transforming his

average face into a macabre mask. She was pretty, and she had
a lush figure. He liked the feel of a woman with a little meat on
her frame.

He assumed his post on a chair directly across from the
lounge's entrance. Then, he waited.

Four

Georgie and Bree were perplexed by the change in their mother's demeanor when she returned from her chat with Clayton Knight. Formerly cheerful, she appeared disturbed by something. Looking at both of them, she insisted that they leave the hotel at once.

"What happened, Mom? What did he say to you?" Georgie asked as they made their way to the exit.

"Leave her alone, Georgie. Can't you see she's upset?" Bree interjected anxiously.

Georgie stopped walking and grasped her mother's arm. "Mom, you've always been straight with us. What gives? A few minutes ago you were prepared to give that reporter an interview and now, all of a sudden, you want to go home? Something happened."

Toni met her daughter's eyes. "You've got to trust me on this, Georgette. Nothing's the matter. We've simply decided to do the interview tomorrow. I really would like to go home now."

"He said something to upset you," Georgie said insistently. "Where did he go? I'd like a word with him." She looked around, her dark eyes blazing with anger.

Toni's heart lurched. If her persistent daughter got Clayton Knight alone, it could be disastrous. She tried to keep her voice calm when she turned to Georgie and said, "He didn't say anything to upset me." She forced a smile. "I'm just postponing the interview, I've suddenly gotten a splitting headache, and I need to go home and lie down for a few minutes. Mr. Knight understood, and we're going to talk tomorrow instead of tonight. So, shall we go?"

Ignoring her mother's comments, her eyes on her sister, Georgie pursed her lips. "Take Mom home, Bree. I'll get a cab."

"But Georgie . . ." Bree whined, her face a mass of frowns.

"Georgette Danise, I forbid you to talk to that man," her mother said in her most imperious voice.

But her mother's attitude only made Georgie more determined. She disappeared around the corner, heading in the direction of the last spot she'd seen Clayton Knight. Bree took her mother's hand and they reluctantly left the hotel. She had never thought of her mother as the type of person who needed support. However, looking at her now, with her downcast eyes and the troubled expression she wore, Bree was frightened that something truly *was* wrong. The night's occurrences had left her with a strong feeling of foreboding. She hoped her headstrong sister wasn't about to make matters worse.

Clay was sitting at the bar, nursing a beer when Georgie caught up with him. She sat on the bar stool next to him.

"Proud of yourself?" she said, looking at him accusingly.

Clay's initial reaction was to smile at her. He couldn't help it, she elicited that response from him. Then, he saw the thunderous expression in her dark eyes and he knew he was in trouble.

"Why should I be proud of myself?'' he asked as casually as he could manage.

The muscles worked in her strong jaw as she coolly regarded him. She reminded him of Toni when she looked at him in that way. "What could you have said that would make my mother beat a hasty retreat? She isn't easily frightened off. Was it something about Bree and me?"

"It isn't my place to tell you what your mother and I talked about, Miss Shaw. Why don't you ask her?" Clay said as he got to his feet. He left money for the beer on the bar. "I'm sorry to have upset your mother. It wasn't my intention."

Georgie rose also, never taking her eyes off him. For a few seconds, their eyes met and they simply stood there sizing each other up.

Clay cleared his throat and said, "Good night, Miss Shaw. I have an early flight back to Boston in the morning."

Georgie followed him from the lounge. "I want to know what it was you said to my mother, Mr. Knight," she said again.

Clay kept walking, thinking she would give up if she saw he really didn't want to pursue the conversation. But Georgie wasn't ready to relent. They stopped in front of the bank of elevators in the lobby. Exasperated, Clay looked down into her inquisitive, upturned face.

"Well?" Georgie prompted him.

"Under more amenable circumstances, I'd tell you just about anything you want to know, Miss Shaw. And you wouldn't have to use Gestapo tactics to wring the information out of me. But I made a promise and I always keep my promises."

"It must be the boy scout in you," Georgie said sarcastically. "You can't prove that by me. Fifteen minutes ago, when we were introduced, you seemed nice enough. I thought you possessed a certain raw charm, and then you proceeded to devastate my mother. You tell me, Mr. Knight. Exactly what am I to make of you?"

"You thought I was charming, huh?" Clay said, grinning.

"I want an explanation!" Georgie promptly reminded him.

"You're probably an excellent trial lawyer," Clay said, no longer smiling. His hazel eyes held amusement in their depths. "You get on a point and will not let up. I have nothing to tell you, Georgette."

Another hotel guest walked up and pressed a button on the elevator's control panel.

Georgie thought he looked vaguely familiar but shrugged it off. She'd probably seen him walking past while she was in the lobby earlier that evening.

Clay, on the other hand, observed that the man seemed to be hanging on their every word. And if years of law enforcement experience served him well, the guy was packing a gun under his sharp leather jacket. Judging from the size of that bulge, a cannon.

Clay's mind was racing. Maybe the guy was a cop. He didn't look like a cop. He had a seedy, hardened appearance about him. Around five-ten and one hundred and sixty pounds. Lean. Dark hair, dark eyes, unremarkable features. He'd be hell for a witness to describe at the scene of a crime because he was so average-looking. Still, his instincts told him you wouldn't want to meet the guy in a dark alley.

Clay had always trusted his instincts. They'd kept him alive on more than one occasion.

"Go home, Miss Shaw," he said, his tone making it more of an order than a request. "Please. This discussion isn't going anywhere."

Georgie's eyes pleaded with him to talk to her but she refused to beg.

"Fine. I'm going. But I want you to know that if what Mom tells me does not satisfy me, I'll be back in your face."

"I'm sure you will be," Clay said without a trace of malice. "I look forward to our next meeting."

Frustrated, Georgie tossed back her braids, blew air between full lips, fixed him with an angry expression, then turned and strode off.

Clay chuckled. "Women," he said, drawing the other man into a conversation.

"Yeah, you can't live with 'em and you can't puree 'em without having to go to jail for the rest of your life," the man joked in a gravelly-voiced Boston accent.

That did it for Clay. His danger antennae were at full alert.

The man pulled out a packet of cigarettes, shook one out into his hand and made an obvious attempt to locate his lighter. "Damn it, I must've left it on the bar."

He left Clay standing in front of the elevators while he went in the same direction Georgie had a minute earlier. Clay followed at a discreet distance.

Out on the street, Clay spotted Georgie's tall, curvaceous form a few yards ahead of the man. She'd apparently decided to walk off some steam. The hotel was on Poydras Street, perhaps a mile from her grandparents' home. The night was cool and breezy, and she was wearing low-heeled shoes. New Orleans was a town that slept late, coming to life at sundown. Pedestrians were commonplace, so she had plenty of company on the well-lit streets, and from the look of her confident stride, she knew precisely where she was going.

The man in black was nervously looking around him. Clay pegged him as an amateur. An amateur *what* though? Why was he following Georgette Shaw? And if his intentions were sinister, who had hired him and why had they targeted Georgette? The suspect having a Boston accent was too coincidental. Was there someone close to Waters who wanted his daughter out of the way?

The man suddenly stopped in his tracks and looked behind him. Clay ducked inside a shop's entrance way to avoid detection. After one more furtive glance, the man increased his pace, intent on closing the distance between himself and his quarry.

Clay saw Georgie stop and chat with a street musician, a guitarist. She was laughing at something the old guy had said. A crowd was gathering around the two of them and as he got closer, he realized Georgie was singing. It was the Irish folk song, "Danny Boy."

Clay could have easily gotten distracted because her voice was hypnotic. Her low, melodious instrument in conjunction with the lyrical sound of the guitar strings was breathtaking, mesmerizing. "Oh, Danny Boy, the pipes, the pipes are calling . . ."

All the other sounds of the night receded into the background as her voice carried on the breeze. She sang with such passion, Clay wondered whom she was thinking of when she voiced the words of the song and, surprisingly, he wished he could be the recipient of those smoldering emotions.

The song ended and enthusiastic applause was immediate. Georgie bent down and gave the old guy a peck on his wizened cheek. "Nobody plays like you, Hank."

"You could go to the top with pipes like those, Georgie," Hank returned the compliment. "If you ever tire of Frisco . . ."

"You'll be the first to know," she said, smiling happily. They'd obviously been over that ground many times before. "Take care, Hank." She bid him farewell with a wave of her hand.

The people who'd been drawn by the beauty of her voice moaned in unison.

"Sorry," she said, bowed and kept walking. Hank launched into a classical piece reminiscent of Andres Segovia and soon his audience was caught up in the music's magic.

The man in black fell in behind Georgie once more and Clay resumed his surveillance.

A few blocks later, the man quickened his pace. Then, he was running toward Georgie in a headlong rush. The only thing Clay could figure was that the guy had cased this area earlier and knew of an alleyway close by. There were practically no pedestrians in this section of Poydras. The streets were not as generously illuminated. He was going to grab her and pull her into the darkness and tomorrow, in the papers, the assault would be described as a tragic mugging.

Clay couldn't allow that to happen. Head tucked in, he ran toward the man, intending to tackle him from behind. Hearing the heavy footfalls behind him, the man in black turned. Uttering an expletive, he swiftly reached inside his jacket. However, before he could withdraw his weapon, Clay was on him, pinning the offending hand behind him and ramming him, head first, into the brick wall of the building to the right of them with the force of a tractor-trailer. The man was mercifully knocked unconscious, falling onto the pavement with a sickening thud.

Georgie stood, transfixed, mouth agape as she watched the magazine reporter dispense with an armed man using moves Sammy Chan would have been envious of.

She knelt with him as they checked the unconscious man's vital signs.

"Strong pulse," she said after locating it. "Do you think he's all right?"

"He just tried to assault you, do you care?" Clayton Knight

asked as he riffled through the man's pockets for some form of identification.

He found a battered black leather wallet. The Massachusetts driver's license identified him as Bruno Smith, as did the round-trip airline ticket stashed in his jacket pocket.

"Unlikely," Clay commented derisively. "If he's a Smith, I'm a Kennedy."

After donning a pair of leather gloves, he relieved Bruno Smith of his weapon, a Browning 9mm. It wasn't the preferred piece of your common everyday mugger, for a certainty. Unless airport security had become extremely lax, "Smith" had apparently acquired it in town from an illegal gun trader. He definitely hadn't brought it with him from Boston.

Clay deftly removed the cartridge and pocketed it, then he returned the gun to its holster strapped around the man's chest. No use leaving a gun in the alley where a curious kid could find it and get into mischief.

"You're giving the gun back to him?" Georgie protested sharply.

"He doesn't have any more cartridges on him. It's useless without ammunition," Clay explained.

He bent and unbuckled the snoozing Bruno's pants, unzipped them and pulled them off him.

"What are you doing?" Georgie asked.

"A man walking around in his shorts gets noticed, even in New Orleans," Clay replied. "The last thing this guy wants to do is draw attention to himself. If he comes to and leaves before I can get back with the cops, it will be more difficult for him to blend in with everyone else on the street."

"You're not a reporter, are you?" Georgie said, looking at him with a mixture of awe and irritation.

Clay ignored her question, choosing instead to finish his task of stripping Bruno, rolling the slacks into a ball and tossing them as far into the pitch blackness of the alleyway as he could.

Finished, he stood, taking Georgie by the hand. "Come on, I'll walk you home."

Georgie allowed herself to be led along but she'd already made a silent promise to herself that before the night was over *someone* was going to fully enlighten her as to what was going on.

"You just happened to be coming this way?" she asked as they quickly walked away from "Bruno Smith."

"I saw him following you, and I was curious as to why he was interested in you," Clay said simply.

"So you took it upon yourself to be my protector?"

"Can you say anything that isn't a question?" Clay Knight said, his voice rising with irritation.

Squeezing her hand impatiently, he said, "Would you walk a bit faster? I want to get back to Mr. Smith before he decides to skip town."

Georgie stopped walking altogether and glared at him. "Just who the hell are you? What did you want from my mother? Why was she so upset after talking to you?" She wrenched her hand free of his hold. "Come on. Speak!"

Looking down into her angry face, Clay sighed wearily. "When you get home, tell your mother what almost happened to you tonight. I think you'll get all your questions answered."

Georgie fell silent. *What almost happened to her.* A chill came over her but she mentally shoved it aside, replacing it with a red-hot feeling of rage. Her body fairly shook with anger and frustration. Someone wanted her dead and this man—this stranger!—standing before her was being close-mouthed.

"I want answers now!" she cried, stomping her right foot on the pavement for emphasis. "You knew that man was tailing me for a reason. The question is: How did you know that?"

They stood glaring at one another, with Georgie impatiently shifting her weight from side-to-side. Clay thought she looked like a boxer about to throw a punch. He took a step back, just in case.

"I'm not at liberty to tell you anything, Miss Shaw," he said. He then spun on his heels and resumed walking, hoping she'd see reason and come along with him.

"Is my mother in some kind of trouble?" she asked directly

behind him. "Is that it? Do you work for the government? The FBI? You're *not* a reporter."

"You've already said that," Clay reminded her.

"It bears repeating," Georgie said huffily. "You're not saying much of anything. How do I know you can be trusted? You could be waiting for your chance to take a crack at me."

She didn't really believe Clay Knight was of the same ilk as "Bruno Smith," however, she hoped her accusation would get a rise out of him and thereby loosen his lips.

Clay humphed deep in his throat and looked around them. "Then this would be an ideal time, wouldn't it? We're alone in a dark alley. You don't seem to be in much of a hurry to reach the relative safety of your mother's house."

Disappointed by his reaction, Georgie sighed. "All right," she conceded. "You mean me no harm, but you have to admit, since you showed up, my life hasn't been lacking in excitement."

"Then you feel it too," Clay said, placing one big hand over his heart and smiling seductively at her. His hazel eyes raked over her.

It was Georgie's turn to humph derisively. "Listen," she told him, turning narrowed dark eyes on him. "I'm grateful to you for preventing whatever 'Mr. Smith' had in mind for me, but let's not get crazy."

Clay chuckled and continued walking.

"Could we continue this conversation at your mother's home, Georgette?"

"We can go to my mother's home, 'Clay,' however, this conversation, for all intents and purposes, is over."

And she walked ahead of him, demonstrating her desire to keep some distance between them,

Clay smiled to himself. Against his better judgment, he felt drawn to Georgette Shaw. He even liked that bold stubborn streak she displayed so boisterously. Yes, this was proving to be an interesting case, indeed.

Georgie walked swiftly. The sooner she got home, the faster she'd get to the bottom of this mystery and get rid of the infuriating Clay Knight.

* * *

Bree heard Georgie coming into the house and ran downstairs from her bedroom to interrogate her about her encounter with the handsome reporter. She was certain Georgie had read him the riot act.

Her questions froze in her throat when she saw Georgie's face, however. And then Clayton Knight, who walked into the house behind Georgie and secured the door. He peered through the window next to the door before turning back around to face them.

"Georgie! Girl, what happened to you?" Bree cried, going to Georgie and wrapping her arms around her.

They held each other for mutual support.

"I'll tell you everything in a few minutes," Georgie promised. Looking at Clay, she said, "If you'll excuse us, Clay . . ."

"Sure," Clay said. "I'd like to use your phone if I may."

"It's right through there," Georgie told him, pointing in the direction of the den. "On the desk by the French doors."

Clay disappeared into the den.

Bree jerked on Georgie's arm in her excitement. "What's he doing here?"

Georgie began walking upstairs, Bree on her heels. "I can't believe the goings on of this night," Bree said worriedly. "Mom came home and went straight to her room. A few minutes later, Gran went upstairs to talk to her and I heard them in a heated argument. You know them, they rarely argue. Now you come in looking like you've been frightened by the Devil. What's going on?"

"I think someone has put a gris gris on this family," Georgie said cryptically.

"A hex?" Bree said, with a nervous laugh. "Don't be melo-dramatic, Georgie."

Georgie paused on the staircase to look her sister in the eyes. "Bree, some guy tried to shoot me tonight." Her voice was quivering with pent-up anger. After getting over her initial fear, she was mad. Mad at whomever had hired "Bruno Smith" to take her out. Because that was precisely what Mr. Smith was, a hired assassin. What other possible reason would he be stalking her, his wallet full of fake ID and armed with an illegal weapon? It was the Boston connection with Knight that puzzled her.

Bree was suddenly dizzy. She held onto the railing for support. Georgie reached out, catching her by the shoulders, steadying her.

"I'm sorry," she said. "I shouldn't have blurted it out like that. I'm just so mad. I'm not thinking straight."

She slipped her arm around Bree's waist as they continued upstairs. "Something's going on, Bree; something that Mom's involved in."

"How do you figure that?" Bree asked.

"Clayton Knight wouldn't answer any of my questions. He apparently promised Mom he wouldn't talk to anyone about this. However, he told me I should tell her about the attempt on my life tonight. He thinks that will encourage her to open up."

Bree's normally healthy skintone had gone ashen. Her light brown eyes were filled with dread. "No wonder she behaved the way she did tonight. She's sick with worry, Georgie. I've never seen her like this before."

Georgie stopped in front of her mother's bedroom door. She went to turn the doorknob and Bree stayed her hand.

"She's still upset, Georgie. Can't this wait a while longer?"

Georgie shook her head. "No, it can't. Mom knows what's going on. She's the only person who can help me figure out why 'Bruno Smith' wanted to harm me."

Standing with her back to the door, Bree said, "You told me you mistook Kyle for a stalker. Couldn't that man have been working for someone who's holding a grudge against you?"

Exasperated, Georgie blew air between her lips. "No, he couldn't be. I'm positive Mom is involved in this somehow. Look at how she tore out of the hotel after her chat with Clay." She thought she'd take a different tack. "Don't you understand, Bree? Mom must be in some kind of trouble. Maybe someone wants me dead because they know it will devastate *her*. Some sick, depraved man whose affections she once spurned."

Bree laughed shortly, eyeing Georgie in disbelief. "A man? Mom hasn't been seriously involved with a man since I don't know when."

"All right," Georgie conceded, losing patience. "Maybe it isn't a man, but we aren't getting anywhere by standing in the hallway. I'm going in."

Toni wasn't sleeping. She was lying in bed staring at the ceiling, wondering how she was going to tell her girls their father had been miraculously resurrected. What had she been thinking all those years ago when she'd invented the lie anyway? Did she actually believe a deception of such magnitude would go undiscovered indefinitely?

She'd always told herself she'd done it in order to protect her daughters' feelings. Knowing they had a father who refused to acknowledge his paternity could ruin their delicate developing psyches. Was that the real reason? Or was it out of anger and spite? Charles Edward had hurt her, and therefore she wanted to hurt him in return by forever severing him from his children's lives.

Even now she could feel anger welling up within her. She hated him for his cowardice. She detested his lack of conviction, sense of duty and responsibility. Even if he didn't want *her* anymore, the girls were his flesh and blood. They deserved his support. Why didn't he try to see them in twenty-eight years? And what happened to change his mind? Even when he lost his family in an auto accident years ago, he didn't try to contact the girls. Why now?

When someone knocked on her door, she was pleased by the interruption, even if it was her mother, back for round two. She smoothed her elegant white caftan as she hurried to the door and swung it open. Georgie and Bree smiled nervously. She briefly hugged both of them.

"Tell them," a little voice in the back of her mind urged her. "Tell them now."

The anguish in her face made Georgie and Bree anxious. They didn't want to cause her further worry. They stood motionless, staring at her.

Toni attempted a weak smile to put them at ease but it didn't work, she wound up grimacing instead. She would have to be direct. Her mother had been right all along. "Sit down," she said, her voice cracking. She cleared her throat. "I, um . . . I have something important to tell you."

"Mom," Georgie said hesitantly.

"Let me go first, Georgie," her mother begged her. "This is difficult for me to say and it's best said in a hurry before I lose my nerve."

Georgie clamped her mouth shut. She took Bree by the hand and they went to sit on the settee near the fireplace. After sitting, she tried to release Bree's hand but her sister nervously held onto her with a vise-like grip.

Toni paced the room like a caged tiger.

"I should have told you both this years ago, when you were children. You should not have had to grow up with a lie."

Bree's grip was getting tighter.

"Oh God, Georgie," she whispered. "We're adopted."

Georgie shooshed her. "We're not adopted. Be quiet."

"I lied to you about your father," Toni said quickly. "His name wasn't David Warren. He wasn't an orphan and he didn't die in Vietnam." Tears were flowing down her cheeks. "Your real father is alive. His name is Charles Edward Waters and he lives in Boston."

Georgie and Bree were instantly on their feet. "What?" they both cried. The look of shock and disbelief on their faces tore at their mother's heart. She took a step toward them and thought better of it. She didn't deserve their comfort. She would never be able to fully explain her course of action, not with any credibility. Still, years of hidden secrets began to spew out of her mouth.

"We met at Berkeley. I was still seventeen, he was twenty. He was the first man I ever loved. The only man. I thought we would be together forever, but it didn't turn out that way. He was wealthy, very wealthy and his parents hated me on sight. I was too poor for them, too common, too dark-skinned and too opinionated. In short, I was their worst nightmare. They gave him an ultimatum—either drop me or there would be no inheritance. He chose the money. I was already pregnant with you by then, but I was too proud to tell him."

Her eyes narrowed and both hands sat on her hips as she continued. "I didn't want him giving me a hand-out and sending me on my way—just another poor girl used by a rich kid who was sowing his wild oats." She looked into her girls' faces for some reaction to her woeful tale.

Georgie and Bree broke into tears and fell on her, hugging her tightly and kissing her tear-stained face.

"You were only trying to protect us," Georgie said analytically. She was attempting to remain calm under the weight of the recent revelation.

Toni nodded, grateful that they weren't vilifying her. "When you were around two or three, he married and had a son. Then after he lost his family in an accident and he still didn't come forward, I figured he never would."

"You mentioned he has money?" Bree inquired, raising her head from her mother's bosom.

Toni smiled. "He owns a food processing company. Waters Foods, Incorporated."

"Oh my Lord, they're huge," Georgie said. She met her mother's eyes. "After practically twenty-nine years he is just getting around to finding us? Why?"

"I don't know why," Toni replied, apparently peeved by the fact. "All I know is Clayton Knight is a private investigator hired by your father to locate you. I can't truthfully say I would have ever told you about him otherwise. I'm sorry, but I hated what he did, and I still detest him. But, if you choose to go to him and let him into your lives, I'll try to understand. Mere has been telling me for years now that I needed to tell you about him."

She backed away from them, holding on to one hand each. Looking into their faces, she said, "You don't hate me for keeping you from him, do you?"

"Of course we don't hate you, Mom," Bree said, sounding all of five years old. Tears sat in her light brown eyes.

Georgie smiled. "You have been everything to us—a mother, a father, a friend. We could never give you anything less than our total love and devotion. We will always adore you, Mom." Her smile faded and her voice was more serious as she went on. "And I can fully appreciate the position you found yourself in and why you thought it best to tell us he was dead. You thought Bree and I would be harmed by the knowledge that he'd rejected us. You aren't responsible for your actions. He shares the blame."

"My daughter, the attorney," Toni said, smiling through her tears. She affectionately squeezed Georgie's hand. Her eyes moved to Bree's face. "And you, Bree. What do you think of your mother?"

"I think you should have hit him with a paternity suit. He owes me a few convertibles by now, the cheapskate," Bree said without cracking a smile.

"My daughter, the realist," Toni said, laughing. "Well, dears, what are you going to do about it all?"

Toni could practically see the wheels turning inside Georgie's head as her firstborn pursed her lips and fixed her with a serious gaze. "Oh, we've got to have a long chat with Daddy Dear," she said. "Because his sudden rush of sentimentality has made someone in his camp extremely nervous. Nervous enough to want his heirs out of the way."

Frowning, Toni gripped Georgie's arm. "Someone tried to harm you?"

"Ma," Bree spoke up, "someone tried to assault Georgie tonight. He was armed and if it wasn't for Clayton Knight, something terrible could have happened!"

"Sweet Jesus," Toni said quietly. Purposefully walking over to her desk, she opened the top drawer and pulled out her address book. She'd kept Charles' number just in case she succumbed to her mother's constant badgering and broke down and told Georgie and Bree of his existence. She quickly dialed.

"Yes, Carson, you can help me," she said brusquely. "This is Toni Shaw. Put your employer on immediately."

Sounding a bit breathless, Charles picked up the receiver. "Toni, thank God you've decided to see . . ."

"Reason?" Toni said angrily. "Listen to me, Chuck, and listen closely. Because you've suddenly gotten religion, my daughter's life was threatened tonight."

"What?" Charles said, his voice rising. "Toni, calm down. What possible reason would anyone have for harming our daughter?"

"Your bank account!" Toni spat out. "Chuck, you sent Clayton Knight down here, and someone close to you sent the person responsible for the near-attack on my daughter."

"I—I simply can't believe it," Charles sputtered on the other end. Her news had his usually ordered mind in chaotic disarray. Someone close to him? No one close to him would be a party to murder. "Well how is she?" he inquired. "Where is she? Where is Clayton Knight?' "

Downstairs, the doorbell rang, and Toni looked up at her daughters before answering Charles. "Would you get that?" she asked Bree.

Bree left the room and Georgie went to sit down on the edge of her mother's desk, listening intently.

"She's right here," her mother said to the father she'd never met. "Clayton Knight? How would I know where he is?"

"He's downstairs," Georgie offered. "He walked me home after the incident."

"Georgie says he's downstairs," Toni related the information to Charles.

Bree burst back into the bedroom, her breath coming in short intervals from her run up the stairs. "Mom, Georgie, Captain Bragg of the police is downstairs." She looked at Georgie. "They're getting ready to go back to see if they can apprehend the man who tried to attack you."

"I'll call you later," Toni told Charles. "The authorities have arrived."

"Toni? Toni!" Charles cried.

She hung up on him. Let him fret for a change. She'd worried over their children, solo, for nearly thirty years.

* * *

The authorities' plans to arrest the would-be assassin turned out to be a bust. By the time they returned to the alley, "Bruno Smith" was long gone.

Captain Bragg, a twenty-year vet of the New Orleans police department stood next to Clay and Georgie shaking his big, square head. In his early fifties, he was six-feet tall, solid with a head full of salt-and-pepper hair. A native Louisianian, he spoke with a French Creole accent. "Too bad," he said, clearly disappointed. "But don't you worry, Miss, we'll get him. I'll put an APB out on him. I'll have my men at every departing point in this city: the airport, bus stations, car rental outfits." He regarded Clay with steely eyes. "You're certain he had a Boston accent?"

"I've been listening to that accent all my life," Clay said. "Yes, I'm certain."

"Well," Captain Bragg said, offering Clay his hand. "I'm real sorry we couldn't be of more help. But if he's still in the city, we have a chance of apprehending him. We'll get on it."

He tipped his hat to Georgie. "Miss Shaw."

"Thank you, Captain Bragg," Georgie said.

After the police departed, Clay and Georgie walked back to the house at a leisurely pace. She filled him in on her conversation with her mother.

"So," Georgie said. "Tell me everything you know about Charles Edward Waters."

"Your father," Clay said.

"That still hasn't sunk in," Georgie said, looking sideways at him. "I'll give it a few days. About Charles Waters. Did he remarry after he lost his family in that accident? And whom could he have told about his search for his children?"

Clay saw no reason to keep what he knew from her now. "No, he never remarried. He is somewhat of a recluse, if you want to know. I hear he runs his business from his home. His nephew, Benjamin, is his second-in-command."

"So he has a brother or a sister?"

"His brother is dead. I believe Benjamin is his only living relative, aside from you and Briane, of course."

Georgie considered that bit of information. "Do you think Benjamin could have hired an assassin?"

"As far as I know," Clay replied, "Charles hasn't told anyone else about you or Briane, I don't believe *he* is even aware he is blessed with two daughters, instead of one."

"Perhaps we ought to keep that a secret until we find the person behind the attempt on my life," Georgie suggested. "Bree could be in danger as well, if it's known she's my twin sister."

"Great minds think alike," Clay said, smiling at her. "I was just thinking the same thing."

Five

Charles Waters' brows were deeply furrowed with worry when he got off the phone with Toni and Clay later that evening. Fear had gripped his heart as Toni related the account of Georgette's close call.

He sat down behind the oak desk in his study. He had a daughter. He couldn't even savor the idea at the moment because, according to Clay Knight, she was in danger. And it was probably his fault. If he hadn't sent the investigator to locate her, then whomever wanted her killed would not have shown his hand so precipitously. It was difficult to believe that someone close to him could be behind the plot. Benjamin stood to gain the most, should Georgie become the victim of foul play. But he refused to think badly of Benjamin.

The culprit would have to be flushed out, however. Therefore, he'd instructed Clay Knight not to let Georgette out of his sight. And tomorrow morning, the Waters Foods company jet would bring them here to Boston. Clay had convinced him that if there was a chance the assassin could still be in New Orleans, it would be wise to get Georgette out of the city. Then, too, Clay was almost certain that "Bruno Smith" had followed him from Boston. Consequently, the search for the culprit who had ordered the hit should begin in Boston.

There was a knock at the study door and Carson came into the room with slow, measured steps.

"Excuse me, sir, but Miss Germaine is here."

Charles looked up into the tired, dark brown face of his butler who'd been a family retainer for at least forty years. The old fellow was beginning to develop a stoop. Charles had thought seriously of retiring him, but every time he'd broached the subject, Carson began putting more pep into his step, proving there was still life in the old boy yet. To prevent Carson from working himself to death, Charles stopped hinting at retirement. He figured they would have to take Carson out of Greenbriar feet first.

"Show her in, Carson," Charles said. "And you may retire for the night. I won't be needing you."

"Yes, sir. Thank you, sir. Good night, sir," Carson said, backing out of the room.

A moment later, Lillie Germaine, forty-two, glided elegantly into the room. She and Charles had been seeing one another a little over two years.

Charles had politely risen from his chair when she entered the room. He was always happy to see Lillie. He smiled at her. "Lillie, to what do I owe the pleasure of this surprise visit?"

Lillie, splendidly attired in a winter white pantsuit with every raven tress in place looked at him sultrily. "I've come to try to convince you to change your mind about escorting me to the fund-raiser tomorrow night, Charles. Won't you reconsider?" She batted her thickly-lashed eyes at him and pouted seductively.

As far as she was concerned, theirs was a match made in cash heaven. To Charles, she was a winsome diversion at best. He was emotionally detached. He'd informed her from the beginning that he wasn't looking for a love-match. Marriage wasn't even a possibility. Lillie was content with what he *did* give her—attention in the form of monetary rewards. Save Benjamin, he had no one to leave his money to therefore he reveled in indulging her, whether it was with a bauble from Cartier or a trip to Jamaica. Charles was a generous man, and she was a grateful woman.

Lillie's full red lips formed a smile.

"Charles, I'm beginning to feel neglected. Have I done something to displease you?" Her cognac-colored eyes were demure.

Charles laughed softly. Her intense sexuality invariably had a heady effect on him. "I'm sorry, my dear, but I have an important business appointment I can't forego. Benjamin has agreed to serve as your escort."

"Benjamin is no substitute for you, Charles," Lillie cried reproachfully.

She put her arms around him, laying her head on his shoulder. She was only five-three to his five-eleven, so she fit nicely in his arms. "I don't know what I'm going to do with you, darling. You don't take me anywhere anymore."

"Come now, I'll have none of that," Charles said, sounding as though he were chastising a child. "You knew I was no social gadfly when we met."

"For a while, I thought I'd rehabilitated you. We were becoming quite the pair on the social scene," Lillie said regrettably.

Charles smiled down into her pretty, pecan-tan face. "Be patient, Lillie. I'm very busy now, but I won't always be."

"What is it, darling? Talk to me. I thought you were turning over the reins to Benjamin."

"That is the plan, my dear. However, there are many things I need to finalize. The transition isn't as simple as signing my name on a piece of paper."

"Oh, very well," Lillie said, sighing heavily. "If I must attend the fund-raiser with your nephew, I will, but I want you to know I'm doing it under duress."

She kissed his chin. "Do you want me to stay the night, darling?"

"No," Charles said, trying to sound disappointed at the prospect of spending a night without her. "Go home, my dear. I'll be working late tonight."

Charles was relieved to see Lillie depart. He wasn't in the frame of mind to cajole and soothe her wounded ego. At the moment, he could think of no one except the person behind the attempt on Georgette's life.

He'd made his share of enemies on his way to the top, but he could think of none who would resort to murder in order to claim one-upmanship over him.

He didn't want to admit it, but the only person who stood to benefit from Georgette's death was Benjamin. As his brother's only child—Charles and Benjamin, Sr. being the sole offspring of the founder of Waters Foods—Benjamin stood to inherit everything upon his death. That is, before Georgette came into the picture.

As the senior brother and CEO of Waters Foods, Charles' share of the company was substantially larger than his deceased brother's. Therefore, Georgette would inherit a great deal more than her cousin, Benjamin.

At thirty, Benjamin was president of the company. He was a corporate attorney and had an MBA from the Massachusetts Institute of Technology. Though he was born wealthy, he had worked hard and earned his place at Waters Foods. Charles would never ask Benjamin to step down in order to make room for Georgette. His position wasn't something he'd give up easily, certainly not without a fight. There was the possibility that Georgette would have no interest in the family business. It could be a delicate situation, but somehow Charles would convince Benjamin that he had no cause for concern now that he had a legal heir.

Walking to the large picture window that overlooked the greenhouse that housed his beloved roses, Charles drank in their beauty. The sight of the garden Mariel had so tenderly cultivated usually served to render him momentarily stress-free. It wasn't working tonight.

Looking at his reflection in the glass of the enclosure, he smiled suddenly. Toni had told him in no uncertain terms that she was accompanying their daughter to Boston. The prospect of seeing her again excited him immensely.

He should be quaking in his boots perhaps. But he wasn't nervous any longer. He just wanted to make amends. Make things right with Toni and their daughter while he had the chance. Admittedly, it wasn't the right time. He should have stepped forward years ago. But, by God, he was doing it for all the right reasons.

* * *

Clay awoke to the sounds of the rest of the household preparing breakfast. He'd spent the night on the couch in the den and went to the adjacent bathroom and washed his face before following his nose to the kitchen.

In the kitchen, the Shaws were engrossed in their various tasks. Marie was at the stove, scrambling eggs while James stood next to her flipping his special pancakes on a griddle. Briane was at the breakfast nook squeezing oranges while her sister caught the juice in a pitcher and prepared the glasses. At the microwave, Toni was busy making certain the bacon was nice and crisp.

Marie was the first to notice Clay. Her warm brown eyes lit up. "Well if it isn't our Mr. Knight. How are you, sweetheart?"

Clay actually blushed at the genuine kindness in her voice. "Good, thank you, Mrs. Shaw." Looking around the room, he added, "Good morning, everyone."

"Good morning, young man," James said, neglecting his griddle momentarily. "I hear you saved my grandbaby last night. I reckon that makes you a hero in my book."

"I'm no hero," Clay said. "I figure if it wasn't for my snooping in your lives, the man who tried to harm Georgette wouldn't have found her. I'm very sorry for bringing this trouble down on you. I had no idea someone had followed me." He finished with his eyes on Georgie's face.

Georgie felt her cheeks grow hot under his scrutiny. "You were just doing your job," she managed to say. She looked down. "Excuse me, I need to make a phone call."

She had to get out of his presence. She didn't know what was wrong with her. Why should she feel so self-conscious around him now after they'd gone through a life or death situation together last night?

Toni went to the coffee maker and poured a cup of coffee. She handed it to Clay. "Sit down, Clay, I want a word with you."

"This isn't laced with arsenic, is it?" Clay joked.

"I'm fresh out," Toni said, laughing. Clay thought she looked quite pretty this morning, even though, like the rest of them, she hadn't slept well.

They sat at the table. Bree went to sit next to her mother, afraid she'd miss some vital piece of information.

"What do you know about Chuck?" Toni asked without preamble.

"Only what I've read," Clay said, taking a sip of his coffee. "What is it you want to know?"

"I don't care about his business, or what he's worth . . ." Toni began.

"I do," Bree said quickly. "What *is* he worth?"

"Briane Marie . . ." her mother warned.

Bree sat quietly.

"Specifically," Toni said, looking into Clay's hazel eyes. "How is his health?"

"He looked fit to me. He's trim, healthy-looking. I don't know much more than that, Toni," Clay answered truthfully.

Toni frowned. "I simply can't figure out why he has forced himself back into our lives. I don't get it."

"Like I said," Clay put in. "I believe he's just got up the nerve to face you."

"It's got to be more than that," Toni said, unconvinced. "People don't just wake up one morning and change their whole mindset. Something happened to him. Perhaps he's had a scare. A close-call. But definitely something life-threatening."

"You think so?" Clay said, thinking she might be on to something.

"I know it," Toni replied confidently.

Bree pulled her chair a bit closer to Clay's and said in conspiratorial tones, "Tell me, Clay, are you married, engaged, committed to, involved with, or otherwise attached to anyone?"

Clay met her eyes. In them, he recognized a latent sense of humor and not romantic interest, which pleased him. He liked Bree, but it was her sister that intrigued him more.

He chose his words carefully, nonetheless. "Not at the moment, but there is someone I'm interested in getting to know better."

"Let me guess," Bree said with a mischievous gleam in her light brown eyes. "Would she be an attorney, say five-eight, soulful brown eyes, bountiful black hair and a killer bod?"

"You don't miss much, do you?" Clay said, grinning. He pushed his chair back, preparing to rise. Bree reached out and grasped him by the arm. "I didn't mean to embarrass you," she said apologetically.

"Am I that obvious?" Clay asked. "She must think I'm a fool."

"Don't be ridiculous," Toni chortled. "Georgie is as transparent as you are. She finds you tempting. But there's something you should know about our Georgie—she routinely resists temptation. It's that strong streak of self-discipline that runs a mile deep in her. I don't know where she gets it from."

"Maybe she gets it from Daddy," Bree suggested, laughing along with her mother.

Georgie returned and began putting the food on the table. "What are you guys talking about?"

"Daddy," Bree said.

Georgie frowned at her sister's use of the appellation.

"Is there something I should know?" she asked, looking at the three of them.

"No new developments," her mother told her. "We were just trying to figure out why Chuck chose this time to find you two."

"And he still believes he has only one daughter," Bree said. "I'll be a big surprise to him."

"Remember, Bree," Georgie admonished, going to sit across from her sister and clasping one of her hands in both of hers. "No one must find out that we're twins. No one."

"Eat now, discuss business later," their grandmother said, coming to the table with a platter of eggs and bacon. "Anything but pleasant talk is bad for the stomach, no?"

A fine mist of rain fell as Charles stood on the tarmac next to the limousine. The weatherman hadn't predicted snow this morning, but he knew that if the rain kept up, they'd probably have a snowfall before night. So far, autumn in Boston had been fairly mild, only three snowstorms in the last month.

He recognized Toni the moment she stepped from the plane. The years had been more than kind to her. She was as lovely as ever, perhaps more so because time had molded her features, producing a woman out of the girl he had once known.

The young woman on her left was vaguely familiar. He knew he'd seen her somewhere. The young woman on Toni's right had to be Georgette. She was as Clay Knight had described her—really quite lovely. Charles rocked back on his heels in his excitement. He couldn't wait to meet her.

Clay led the procession, being solicitous of the women, ever the vigilant bodyguard. Charles moved forward, feeling nervous about the type of reception he would get from the three women.

"Toni, you look wonderful," he said, knowing he sounded too effusive. "I am grateful that you decided to come."

He held out his hand to her in greeting. Toni took it, grasping it tightly, her grip growing painful as she fixed him with a steely glare. "God help you, Chuck, if you have done anything to endanger the lives of my children by interfering in our lives."

She released his hand and Charles shook it to encourage the blood flow.

Looking into her eyes, he said, "It's good to see you too, Toni."

"We should be going," Clay suggested diplomatically. The last thing they needed was for Toni and Charles to get into a shouting match out in the open, where they were presently standing.

Charles ushered them into the limousine. The women sat on one plush seat while the men sat on the other, facing them.

"I can assure you, Toni," Charles said once they were settled in, "to my knowledge, I have done nothing to cause an assassin to go after our daughter. And I can also promise you that we will get to the bottom of this mystery with all speed."

"Still long-winded I see," Toni stated, with a short laugh. "An 'I'm innocent' would have sufficed."

"Excuse me," Clay put in impatiently. "But would you instruct your driver to take us to my office downtown? There are some things we need to discuss and I know my office is bug-free."

"You think my limo . . ." Charles began, outraged.

"Put a sock in it, Chuck," Toni said derisively. "We live in a technological age. It isn't inconceivable that *you* are bugged, let alone your car. Do as the detective suggests."

"Carrington, take us to Mr. Knight's offices," Charles ordered the driver.

"Very good." Toni commended him as though she were offering praise to a recalcitrant child. "Now, Chuck, I'd like you to meet your daughter, Georgette Danise."

Georgette had been silently observing her father. Yes, she could see the resemblance. She had his nose and her skin color was somewhere between his light golden brown and her mother's darker, red-tinged skin. It gave her a funny feeling in the pit of her stomach sitting across from the man who'd fathered her after assuming for nearly thirty years that he was dead.

"Sir," she said politely, her eyes on his face.

Charles stared at her. "Georgette . . ." He cleared his throat of the lump that had formed in it. "I don't know what to say."

He grasped both her hands in his and tears sprang to his eyes. Then, he was out of his seat hugging her to him. "Oh, Georgette, Georgette, you're absolutely beautiful."

Georgette, trying to purge negative thoughts, was more stiff than she would have liked to have been upon meeting her father for the first time. She looked into his eyes, noting the sincerity and sheer happiness in them, and she found herself questioning his motives even more. What kind of man refused to acknowledge his blood? He was just a stranger to her.

Her father's hand was in her hair, gently stroking it. "Dear Georgette—I've imagined your face so many times. Wondered what your voice must sound like, and now I know. You're perfect."

"Sir . . ." she said again. She didn't know what to call him.

Charles released her and Bree switched places with him without being asked, sensing her father's need to be close to Georgie whom he thought to be his only flesh and blood.

She sat, fascinated. She and Georgette, indeed, had his nose and what was more, she had his eye color. All her life, she had wondered why her eyes were light-colored whereas her mother and Georgie both had very dark eyes.

A few minutes later, they were seated in Clay's comfortable private office at the Knight Detective Agency offices. His assistant, Alma, an African-American woman in her early fifties, brought them coffee and pastries. As she placed Clay's cup before him, Georgie noticed a look of concern for her employer in her eyes. Clay hadn't taken the time to shave this morning. Georgie could imagine what was going through Alma's mind at the moment.

Alma held her curiosity in check though and left them alone in the office. Clay gave her a parting smile as she closed the door behind her.

"Shall we begin?" he said, looking at Toni.

Toni placed the cheese danish she was consuming on her plate and regarded Charles.

"Chuck, may I also introduce you to your daughter, Briane Marie."

Toni relished the look of shock on Charles' face.

"How can this be?" he cried, springing to his feet to pull Bree into his arms.

Taking another bite from her danish, Toni sighed. "There were two fertilized eggs instead of one," she said drily. "It happens quite often."

Charles was too happy to take offense with Toni's droll attitude. He hugged Bree repeatedly, pausing to kiss her forehead and look into her eyes. "Oh my God, you've got my eyes."

Bree laughed. "Yes, I suppose I have."

Charles pulled Georgie to her feet for a group hug. "I'm the luckiest man alive," he exclaimed.

"You could have been lucky thirty years ago," Toni commented with a mouthful of danish. She swallowed and drank some of the black coffee to wash it down. "Chuck, you and the girls will have plenty of time to get acquainted after we've apprehended whomever wants them out of the way." Looking at

Clay for support, she continued. "Charles Edward, are you listening to me?"

"So that's why you wanted to make certain we had no listeners," Charles said, unable to pull his gaze from Georgie's and Bree's faces.

Getting to his feet, Clay spoke up. "We have reason to believe the person behind the attempt on Georgette's life thinks she is your sole heir. Therefore, you must not tell anyone, and I can't stress this enough, not *anyone,* that Briane is also your daughter."

"I understand," Charles said gravely. He held tightly to his daughters' hands.

"Good," Clay said, going to sit on the corner of his desk.

Charles sat on the leather couch, his daughters flanking him. He still had not let go of them.

"Where do we begin?" Charles asked Clay. He was more anxious than ever. Now he had more than wealth and position to protect, he had a family.

"You will have to tell us about everyone close to you who stands to gain anything should you lose your daughters," Clay stated seriously. "And you must be candid, sir. Don't hold anything back."

For the next few minutes, Charles told them about Benjamin, his nephew, all of the household staff, including Anne Ballentine, his personal assistant of ten years. When he was finished, he looked to Clay for further guidance. "Is there anything else you need to know?"

"You didn't mention any personal relationships," Toni noted with interest. "Was that an oversight or do you simply deem it none of our business?"

Charles sighed. "I didn't think it was important." He raised his eyes to Clay's.

"No one should be left out, sir," Clay said.

"I've been seeing a woman for two years now. Her name is Lillie Germaine, she's forty-two and works as an interior designer. That's how we met. She redecorated my study at the house."

"How much do you know about her?" Clay inquired, walking around his desk and sitting on the leather swivel chair behind it.

"I haven't had her investigated, if that's what you mean," Charles replied defensively. "I don't make it a point to create dossiers on personal friends. I don't believe what Miss Germaine did in her past is any of my business."

Shaking her head, Toni sighed. She sniffed derisively. "We don't care about your personal life. However, anyone close to you is suspect. You can't live in this world with your head in the sand, Chuck."

"She is divorced. She has no children. She told me her ex-husband has had a few scrapes with the law. Petty theft, that sort of thing."

"Okay," Clay said. "My staff should have no trouble finding information on Miss Germaine and her ex."

"Then we're ready to go on to the house," Charles suggested hopefully.

"We're not staying with you," Toni protested, getting to her feet.

"Toni," Clay said quietly. "I think it would be a good idea if you stayed at the Waters Mansion. It could serve as our base of operation. And it has an excellent security system."

"But what if the killer is someone on the premises?" Bree said. "I'm with Mom. I think we ought to go to a hotel."

"I agree with Clay," Georgie said, going to stand beside her mother and sister. "A hotel has people coming and going all day. At the mansion, traffic can be controlled. We'll know whom we're dealing with. Clay is the professional here. We should listen to him."

"Oh, very well," Toni agreed. Logic had always been Georgie's forte. "But just for the record, I'm not convinced that this man," she pointed accusingly at Charles, "didn't hire 'Bruno Smith' to frighten Georgie so that we'd react just as we have."

"I would never do such a thing!" Charles vehemently stated as he abruptly got to his feet to face Toni. "And if you'd cooperated with me and let me see my children, none of this would have happened."

"That's just like you," Toni cried, thrusting her chest forward. "Passing the buck. Never wanting to take responsibility for your actions . . ."

Stepping between the two of them, Georgie said, "Come on, we're all wound a little too tight. Arguing among ourselves isn't going to help us solve our problems. We need to cooperate. Please . . ."

Breathing hard, Toni turned her back to Charles. He hadn't changed one iota. But she had. She was mature enough to forego a battle with him until Georgette and Briane were out of danger. She could stomach his presence for that long.

"All right," she said to Georgie. "Your mother will behave herself." With that, she walked from the office, leaving the others following close behind.

Six

The Waters mansion was in Beacon Hill, Boston's exclusive residential area where the wealthy resided in spectacular brick homes passed down from one generation to the next. The streets were cobblestone, and as the limousine rode over them, its suspension afforded its passengers an undisturbed ride. Georgie peered out the window at the expanse of lawn beyond the gate and saw acres of manicured grounds, then a house that was as large as any European castle. With its gables and turrets, it reminded Georgie of a Swiss chalet.

Frowning, she sat back on her seat, refusing to behave like a tourist. She looked up at Clay and their eyes met. He gave her a questioning look. He seemed to sense her inner turmoil. Her father was undeniably a very rich man. What possible reason did he have for not supporting her and Bree over the years? Even if he didn't want anything to do with them, it didn't take much to put his signature on a check each month. There were times, when she was growing up, that her mother had a difficult time keeping her and Bree in decent clothes. Toni had been too proud to ask her parents for money. A few dollars monthly from their father would have been a godsend. She sat stiffly the remainder of the ride, looking straight ahead while Bree chattered away with their father, as if he were the most fascinating man on earth.

They were met at the door by Carson and a young maid whom Charles introduced as Maggie. She had the red hair and freckles of a fresh-faced Irish girl. She shyly curtsied to them as she took their coats.

"Carson, would you and Maggie get Miss Shaw's and her daughters' bags? Take them to their rooms and unpack for them," Charles ordered.

"Of course, sir," Carson said, bowing. To the guests, he said, "Welcome to Greenbriar. We will try to make your stay as comfortable as possible."

"Greenbriar?" Georgie asked, looking at her father for elucidation.

"It's what my mother named the house," he explained. "When they cleared the property to build it over fifty years ago, the land was overrun with wild roses."

He gestured toward the great room which sat a few feet past the staircase. Their footfalls echoed throughout the house. Looking at her sister's face, Georgie could see she was impressed by the quiet elegance of the mansion—their father's home. Only, up until this moment, they'd never set foot in it.

"It's beautiful," Bree gushed.

Charles beamed his thanks. "I'm so happy you like it. Georgette, what do you think of your home?"

"You have a lovely home, sir," she replied.

Recognizing the tightness in her daughter's voice, Toni reached out and grasped her hand, squeezing it reassuringly.

"I'm sure you all must be famished," Charles said. He couldn't wipe the smile off his face. He was delighted that his daughters were finally in their home. He wanted to show them everything in one afternoon, tell them about their grandparents, Charles and Honore. He had volumes and volumes of family photographs to share with them.

He took a deep breath. He sensed a good deal of reticence in Georgette, but Briane was like a child in a candy store. They had an instant rapport. He prayed that he would eventually be able to win their trust. He knew he didn't deserve it, but he wanted it more than anything

In the great room, Toni sat apart from the others lost in her own thoughts. Charles and Bree sat on the sofa in front of the fireplace talking and Georgie and Clay paired off on the window seat that looked out over the grounds.

Clay gently touched Georgie's chin, tilting her head back so that their eyes met. "What's wrong?" he asked, his smile reaching his lips but not his hazel eyes.

"All this," Georgie said, looking around them. She sighed, her eyes on Clay's face. "Why didn't he want us? Why didn't he even try to help support us? Was it because Mom didn't come from *this?*" Her voice broke.

"I'm sure he'll explain everything to you when the time's right," Clay said. He wanted to pull her into his arms and hold her close to him. But this wasn't the time or the place. His finger trailed along her strong jawline. "Georgette . . ."

"Call me Georgie, all my friends do."

"I prefer Georgette—it suits you," Clay said, his voice tender.

She smiled, her dark eyes raking over his square-chinned face. "Oh? You don't see me as a Georgie?"

"Nah," Clay said, his light eyes filled with humor. "Too masculine. You, Georgette, are all woman."

Georgie laughed shortly and moved closer to him. "You'd better keep your mind on the case, detective."

Clay bent his six-foot-two-inch frame to whisper in her ear, "You are the case, Georgette, and my mind is fully on you."

Georgette found herself blushing profusely. "If I get out of this alive we'll talk, Boston."

"You will get out of this alive, Frisco. I promise you that," Clay returned, his green-brown eyes boring into hers.

"Good afternoon, everyone," a deep male voice said from the direction of the entrance.

"That must be Benjamin," Georgie said to Clay in a low voice.

Benjamin Waters, was impeccably dressed in a dark blue double-breasted pinstriped Brooks Brothers suit. He looked as though he'd come straight from a board meeting. He was around six feet tall, trim, with the physique of a runner: lean, sleek lines. His short, black, curly hair formed a widow's peak at his wide forehead. He had the good looks of his uncle, only with twenty years shaved off. His light-brown eyes took in all the inhabitants of the room, however they lingered on Georgie as his uncle made the introductions.

Afterward, they all went into the dining room where Maggie and another young maid served them a delicious lunch of grilled salmon on endive and lemon sorbet for dessert. Georgie sat between Clay and Benjamin. Benjamin monopolized the conversation at every turn, appearing quite eager to get to know his cousin.

"You are a refreshing addition to the family," he told her. "I don't know why Uncle felt it necessary to keep you a secret all this time." He smiled, revealing straight, white teeth in his honey-colored face. Georgie wondered if all the Waterses had that honey-colored skin. Probably. There were undoubtedly a gallery of family portraits hanging in the hallway with nothing but honey-colored Waterses in them.

Clay finished his sorbet and rising said, "If you will excuse me, I have a few calls to make."

"Of course," Benjamin said dismissively.

"You don't mind, do you, Benjamin? I need to discuss something with Mr. Knight," Georgie said, feigning regret. She pushed her chair back and Clay held it for her.

Benjamin looked put out. But he smiled, nonetheless. "I'll try to carry on without you," he said pleasantly.

In another corner of the mansion, Toni and Charles were finally alone together.

In the muted splendor of the library, they faced off. Charles felt the air around them charged with angry energy.

He met Toni's eyes from across the room. "Go ahead, Toni. Let me have it before you explode all over my Persian rug."

"If it were up to me," Toni hissed, her dark eyes sparking fire, "the only thing exploding around here would be you."

"I suppose I deserve that," Charles allowed, lowering his gaze. His eyes fell on her legs. Toni was wearing a tailored suit whose skirt fell a couple of inches above her knees. Like her daughters, she had long, shapely legs.

Charles regrettably drew his attention away from them. He wasn't going to succumb to that old cliche of falling for a past love, was he? He looked into her eyes. This woman hated him.

He felt the heat that had arisen so unexpectedly beginning to turn to a nice chill.

"Oh, you deserve much more than that," Toni said, lowering her voice and moving closer to Charles in case there were, indeed, listening devices at strategic points around the mansion. "But I'm done with being angry with you, Chuck. I can only pity you now. You've met your daughters, after nearly twenty-nine years, but you missed out on everything in-between."

"I know . . ." Charles began contritely, following Toni's lead and keeping his voice volume nearly at a whisper.

"You'll never know what they were like as infants or toddlers. The mischief they got into during their terrible-twos. You weren't there on their first day of school, and you missed seeing Georgie play Little League baseball. Yes, she played with the boys. She threatened the coach with a lawsuit if he didn't allow her to play, and then she was voted MVP when they won all-city."

She laughed suddenly, remembering.

"And you missed Briane's ballet recitals. For a while, she dreamed of becoming a ballerina . . ."

"I know, Toni. I know," Charles cut in. He went to her, grasping her by the arm. "All those years are lost, like tears in the rain. I'll never be able to retrieve them. I wish I could relive the last thirty years of my life. Believe me, I'd do things differently. But I can't. All I can do is try to make amends and go on from here."

Toni wrenched her arm free of his hold, moving away from him and going over to the French doors to peer out at the waning overcast day.

"Just tell me one thing," she said. "Did you ever love me, or was I just a bit of poor trash you amused yourself with?"

She turned back around. She wanted to see his face when he answered her.

Charles walked over to her and grasped her by the shoulders. "I loved you, Toni. I loved you for years after we broke up. But I was weak and afraid of being penniless. I was spoiled by wealth. I'd known nothing else." He smiled at her, recalling their youth and how idealistic they had both been. "Do you remember how you and my parents reacted to one another?"

"Vividly," Toni replied sardonically. "They detested me."

"And you thought they were snobs."

"Was I wrong?"

"No. But what you didn't know was that I was a bigger snob than they had ever been. Oh, I went to Berkeley in hope of finding myself, and what I found was that I was an elitist. I liked the finer things in life. I liked thinking of myself as superior to others, especially to other blacks."

"Your parents were color-struck," Toni remembering the discovery she'd made the weekend Charles had brought her home to meet his parents. "I think that's what shocked me the most when I met them. They were like these white, Anglo-Saxon Protestants."

"They lived in a color-conscious society and behaved as they'd been taught to," Charles said regrettably. "I'm not proud of their behavior. That was another time, Toni. Do you suppose I could have converted them?"

"I suppose not," Toni admitted.

"He was a brilliant man," Charles said of his father. "And he did the best with what opportunities he had. Yes, he and mother were elitist in their views, but they did quite a bit to help the black community. Father made certain key people on his team were black. They also donated money to black colleges. In many ways, they were decent people, Toni."

"I'm sure they were," Toni said calmly. "They simply couldn't have their son destroy the gene pool by marrying a brown-skinned woman."

Charles released her, turning away. He was still ashamed of the way he and his parents had treated Toni. Now it was time to face the music.

"It's true, they threatened to disown me if I continued to see you. But do you believe for one minute that they could have kept me from you if I had possessed any strength of character? No Toni. *I* am the one who kept us apart. I thought that trading love for wealth and power was a bargain. I'm the one who hung up on you when you tried to tell me that we had a child together. I was spineless. I made the choices. Now, I must pay for them."

"And you will," Toni told him. "You see, I lied to them over the years, telling them their father was killed in Vietnam."

"An understandable ruse . . ." Charles said.

Toni nodded. "Yes. They know why I lied. But you, Chuck, you have no excuses. What could you ever say to make them understand why it took you nearly three decades to come forward and claim them?"

"I'll tell them what I've told you," Charles said. "I was a coward who possessed no integrity. I didn't know what was truly important in life. I made money my God. Instead of making love and family a priority, I went after power and self-gratification."

"And what will you tell them when they ask, why now, Daddy dear? Why do you want us to be a part of your life all of a sudden?"

Charles paused. Seemingly without an answer to her query. Then, he looked her in the eyes. "I recently had a cancer scare, Toni," he said quietly.

Toni frowned. "What do you mean by a scare?"

"My physician thought I had prostate cancer, but he's since found he was mistaken. I had a benign cyst removed. It was really quite minor."

Toni was visibly relieved to hear his prognosis.

Charles smiled down into her upturned face.

"Toni . . . For a second there, I thought I read a look of concern in your expression."

Toni humphed. "I was concerned for my girls. Here they are with the chance to get to know their father, and he's dying? Talk about irony."

"Of course," Charles said, secretly elated that she'd shown a flicker of human feeling for him. "I was hoping beyond hope that perhaps you don't hate me as much as you let on."

"Don't be deceived, Chuck," Toni said, waving her finger beneath his nose. "You and I will never be friends again. After this mystery is solved, I'll go back to New Orleans and I hope our paths will never cross again. I'll never forgive you for abandoning your daughters. Whether they do or not is up to them. But to me, you will always be a coward." She turned to leave.

"Toni?"

"Yes?" She didn't bother turning back around.

"You've done a wonderful job bringing up those girls."

"You don't know the half of it, Chuck," Toni said, her lovely eyes sad.

She departed.

Charles sat down on the nearest chair available, his legs suddenly weak. The charisma Toni had possessed as a woman-child was now more powerful than ever. Could it be he had never stopped loving her?

Outside the library, Toni paused to catch her breath. Damn the man for being so devastatingly handsome and charming after thirty years. One would think he would have had the decency to develop a paunch like any self-respecting fifty-one-year-old man. But no, he had to be trim and muscular, impeccable in every way. Her mother was right. She was not over him. It didn't matter, though. She would stop entertaining thoughts of being back in Charles' arms because even if her emotions were treacherous, her stubbornness and pride were both intact. He'd hurt her once. He'd never get the chance to do it again.

After wandering around the mansion a few minutes following lunch, Bree turned a corner and found herself in her father's study. She went to sit at his desk and picked up the phone. It had been forty-eight hours since she spoke with Ari Sanchez, her best friend and agent. And the last number she'd given Ari, should she need to contact her, was her mother's in New Orleans.

She was lucky to find Arieanna Sanchez at home. She usually got her answering machine. "Hi Ari, how're things in L.A.?"

"Bree!" Ari said excitedly. "Your grandmother told me you were in Boston. What are you doing there? No, don't tell me. You met a fly brother, didn't you?"

"As a matter of fact, I did," Bree said, laughing. "But unfortunately he's taken with my sister. No, I'm here on family business. I'll have to fill you in later."

"Unsecured line, huh?" Ari said. There wasn't much Bree kept from her. Hence, she knew Bree simply wasn't at liberty to discuss the particulars with her at the moment.

"Right," Bree said.

"Well, I'm glad you phoned anyway," Ari said breezily. "I've got great news for you. Dominic Solomon wants you to read for him. He's going to be in San Francisco for a symposium on film next week, on Friday. Peter Hogan will be there, too. Dominic wants you to audition with Peter for a role in his upcoming film . . ."

"Not *Dark Universe,*" Bree said hopefully. "Every actress in Hollywood is vying for the role of Romalia, the warrior princess."

"Then you've heard about it," Ari said, laughing.

"How did he even hear about me?" Bree asked. "Is he a fan of movies-of-the week?"

"You have Peter to thank for that," Ari informed her. "Peter saw you in your last Jody Freeman film and was blown away by your ability to combine action and comedy. Plus, you're the physical type they're looking for. You're tall and fit. You'll need to add some muscle though. I've already lined-up José to be your personal trainer for the next few months. He'll help you pump up." As always, Ari had it all figured out.

Bree laughed into the receiver. "Hold on. Are you saying they're looking for a black actress for the role of Romalia?"

"No, it wasn't expressly written for a black actress, but that doesn't mean a thing. You are going to nail this audition, girlfriend. I know it. Peter already wants you opposite him in the film. He and Dominic are tight. You have a real chance at stardom with this vehicle. Why do I hear doubt in your voice?"

"This is a big step for me. What if I'm not ready?"

"You spent five years on a soap, girl. You're ready for anything. The soaps are the best training ground for an actor. You've gone through the grueling schedules. You're the queen of the small screen. Now it's your turn to grab the brass ring." Ari's Spanish-accented voice rose. "You're a pro."

"Peter Hogan is the biggest box-office draw in the world," Bree said timidly.

"You're a pro," Ari repeated more forcefully.

"I'm a pro," Bree said as though she were chanting a mantra. "I'm a pro. Thanks, Ari. I needed that."

"That's why you pay me," Ari told her with a laugh. "Before I get off, give me your address, I'll FedEx a script to you. You can rehearse your lines. I've read it, it's truly wonderful. The writing's lyrical and your character is the heroine. She's a cross between the Ripley character in the *Alien* films and Princess Leia in *Star Wars*."

"So it's a science fiction/fantasy," Bree surmised.

"I predict it'll be the biggest release of ninety-eight," Ari said optimistically.

Ari went on to give Bree the plot of the film while Bree sat with her feet up on her father's desk, imagining how thrilling it would be to be the star of a Dominic Solomon blockbuster. In his ten-year career, he had yet to produce a flop at the box office. She would make that audition the day after Thanksgiving if it killed her. And if the assassin who'd targeted Georgie found out she was her twin sister, it just might.

A frown creased Clay's brow when he got off the phone with Captain Bragg. There had been no sign of "Bruno Smith" in New Orleans. Captain Bragg assumed he'd somehow slipped through their fingers. They had covered all the bases but, conceivably, Smith could have stolen a car and driven out of the city and taken a connecting flight out of another town nearby. Smith could be back in Boston right now.

Standing at Clay's side at the antique secretary where the phone sat in the living room of the mansion, Georgie waited patiently to hear his report.

"It looks as if 'Bruno' is back in business," he said, meeting her eyes.

Georgie looked alarmed. "They didn't catch him?"

"I didn't hold out much hope that they would," Clay said from experience. "Characters like 'Bruno' can be pretty slippery."

"Then that means he could be right here in the city, just waiting for his chance," Georgie said.

Not wanting to frighten her further, Clay smiled at her. "Georgette, you're perfectly safe here. I've checked the security system. The entire mansion has been swept for electronic listening devices. And I or someone from the agency will be with you at all times until 'Bruno' and the person who hired him are behind bars."

"Now," he continued. "I've got to go to the Back Bay police station to look at some mug shots. The sooner we identify 'Bruno,' the better."

He grasped her by the shoulders, pulled her into his arms and hugged her briefly. Holding her at arms' length, he said, "You stay here and have a chat with Benjamin. Ask him if he knows of any business rivals your father may have who would want revenge for some past grievance. Would you do that for me?"

"You're giving me an assignment to keep my mind off 'Bruno,' aren't you?" Georgie accused him. "I can talk to Benjamin anytime. I'm going with you. I can identify Bruno's mug, too."

Sighing, Clay shook his head in the negative. "No. You're safer here."

"But you just said that either you or someone from your agency would be with me at all times," Georgie protested strongly. She looked around them. "I don't see anyone here to take your place when you leave. I'm going with you."

"I can have someone here within fifteen minutes," Clay told her, thereby nullifying her reasoning.

Georgie's eyes narrowed. "Listen, Boston, I'm not some wimp who's afraid of her shadow. I'll have you know I have a black belt in judo and, although I hate guns, I have a certificate from the San Francisco police department stating that I'm qualified to use a handgun. I've spent a total of fifty hours practicing to become proficient at it."

"I'm impressed, Frisco," Clay said with a wry smile. "Unfortunately you're not licensed to carry a weapon in the state of

Massachusetts, and unless I'm misinformed, I've never known judo to stop a bullet yet. So be a good kid and stay here."

Georgie was preparing to throw down the gauntlet when they were interrupted by Benjamin.

"Georgie," he said, as he strode into the room. "Uncle wants you to come meet the staff."

Georgie glanced at Clay. She was just beginning to enjoy their altercation.

"Go," he told her. "I'm going to get on the phone with the agency and ask Alec O'Hara to come babysit you for a while."

"You can be the most infuriating man," Georgie began in a low voice.

Benjamin stood near the entrance, tapping his foot impatiently on the hardwood floor.

Georgie turned on her heels and left the room.

Clay watched her sublime hip action as she walked away with one angry glance tossed over her shoulder at him before she disappeared into the hallway with Benjamin.

He wondered what had happened to his former resolve to stay clear of Georgette Shaw. It must have been lost somewhere between here and New Orleans. Now he couldn't wait to kiss her.

Georgie felt as if she was in the middle of a gothic novel in which a young heiress arrives at a distant relative's castle and is introduced to the household staff.

Her father, obviously used to being lord and master, proudly put his progeny on display before his servants, seven persons in all. Carson, being the senior member of the staff, informed them that Maggie was to act as their personal maid for the remainder of their visit. He was too mindful of his place to inquire how long they would be staying.

Besides Carson and Maggie, there was the head maid, Mrs. Webb, and another young girl, Kate, whose main task was the upstairs. Then there was Mrs. Hughes, the cook, whom everyone referred to as 'Cook'. Mr. Carrington was the chauffeur. And, finally, Mr. Soo was the gardener.

"And this," their father said, gesturing to an attractive African-American woman in her late forties, "is my personal assistant, Anne Ballentine. If you need anything outside the house, whether it is the name of the best Italian restaurant in town, or where to find a rare volume of poetry, Anne is the woman to ask."

Anne shook both their hands. She was of medium height, five-four, and on the plump side. Her smile began in her brown eyes and encompassed her entire rosy-cheeked face. She was wearing a tailored skirt suit in blue linen and her fragrance was Chanel No. 5. There were streaks of grey in her short black hair which was swept back from her high-cheekboned face.

"Miss Shaw, a pleasure," she said warmly as she grasped Georgie's hand. "Miss Shaw, I've seen your films. I enjoy your work," she told Bree.

Both Georgie and Bree liked her immediately.

Charles dismissed all the staff except Anne, whom he asked to meet him in his office.

Bree excused herself, saying she wanted a word with their mother, leaving Georgie alone with Benjamin.

Benjamin stood smiling at her. "Have I done something to offend you?" he asked.

Georgie smiled at him. "No, why do you ask?"

"I get the distinct feeling that you're not comfortable in my presence. Uncle told me of the situation you find yourself in. I must say, it's exciting." His keen eyes watched her face for some reaction to his comment. "I suppose you wouldn't agree, since you're the target in someone's twisted game."

He had removed his jacket and tie. Georgie thought he looked rather relaxed in his shirtsleeves, blue pinstriped slacks and black wingtips.

"You suppose correctly," she said, meeting his gaze dead-on. "I haven't been having fun the last twenty-four hours. First, some guy tries to kill me in an alley, then I find out my father is none other than Charles Waters, possibly the wealthiest black man in

America. Do *you* have any shocking information for me, Cousin?"

Benjamin laughed. "You're just as I imagine your mother was when she was protesting the Vietnam War—strong, vocal and full of spirit. I remember reading about her in history class in college. I never dreamed she and Uncle were involved and produced a child together."

"That's life," Georgie said dryly. "Full of pleasant surprises."

Benjamin continued to smile at her. "I overheard the detective mention that you should enlist my help in the investigation." He stepped forward and placed a hand under her elbow. "I'm eager to get started. Shall we go to my office? We can surf the Internet and see what we can come up with."

Georgie assented to his suggestion, but as they left the library, she wondered what other sort of subterfuge Benjamin was guilty of. He'd just admitted to eavesdropping. Clay had asked her to talk to him *before* Benjamin had interrupted them in the living room. He had apparently stood outside the door listening at least a couple of minutes before entering. What had he hoped to hear?

In his office, Benjamin invited her to sit at the desk and man the computer, while he supplied the names of his uncle's business rivals. He accessed the file then stood back. "Daniel Youmans," he said.

Georgie typed in the name, pressed enter and waited. "Isn't he CEO of Green Fields?"

"Correct," Benjamin replied, seemingly pleased she knew something of the food processing business. "Green Fields is our closest competitor. When we developed a more efficient flash-freezing method, they copied it. Still, they remain so far behind us in production that they aren't a real threat."

On the screen, there appeared a run-down of Green Fields' assets and liabilities. What's more, there was information about the company's CEO that Georgie thought was too personal to be floating around the Internet, including the fact that at age nineteen he'd been arrested for possession of marijuana.

Looking up at Benjamin, she said, "Do you have information like this on all of your competitors?"

"You never know when something of this nature may come in handy," Benjamin said simply. "Joseph Powell."

Georgie typed in the name and pressed enter. She had no idea who Joseph Powell was. The information that came on the screen was more like a rap sheet than the life history of a captain of industry.

Joseph Powell had served five years in the Massachusetts State prison system for forgery. He was on probation and lived in a halfway house in Boston.

"Who is this?" Georgie asked. "He definitely isn't one of my father's rivals."

"Oh, I wouldn't say that," Benjamin said. "He's the ex-husband of Miss Lillie Germaine."

Georgie was losing patience with his bourgeoisie attitude. Throwing her tidbits as if she were a pauper begging on the street. "And exactly why did you want me to know about Joseph Powell?" she asked, her voice rising in anger.

His cool facade impenetrable, Benjamin straightened up and pursed his lips.

"Uncle and Miss Germaine have been seeing one another for over two years now. I believe she expects a proposal. If they eventually marry, she stands to inherit quite a bundle should something happen to Uncle. Lillie Germaine has millions of reasons to want you out of the way."

"So do you, Cousin," Georgie said. "As the only son of my father's brother, you will be a very rich man when your Uncle dies."

"I'm already a very rich man," Benjamin informed her. "My parents left me more money than I'd be able to spend in two lifetimes."

"But you have reason to believe that Lillie needs money so badly, she'd be willing to kill for it?" Georgie said.

Benjamin sighed. "Let me put it this way—the lady has extravagant tastes that her income cannot support. She's a gold-digger."

"I can see why you may resent Lillie. You think she's

using my father for what he can give her. So, you believe her ex-husband is involved, too?"

"He's an ex-con," Benjamin said. "There can't be that big a leap from forgery and theft to attempted murder."

"I'll be sure to inform Clay about his record," Georgie said. "It shouldn't be that difficult to get information on him—and maybe a photograph."

"If Lillie wanted to hire a hit man, who better to turn to than her ex?" Benjamin concluded.

"What I'm wondering," Georgie said speculatively, "is through what means did the culprit find out about me? My father assures us he didn't tell anyone about his search for me."

"Maybe he talks in his sleep," Benjamin said with a grin.

Georgie laughed. "Shall we get back to the business rivals? And nothing else from left field, please. If you want to tell me something, just come out with it, Benjamin. No more games."

"Okay," Benjamin said, leaning down so that his face was inches away from hers. "I find you deliciously attractive, Cousin."

Georgie sat up straight in her chair. Frowning, she laughed shortly.

"Get real, Benjamin. We're blood kin."

"Here's another secret for you, Cousin," Benjamin replied smugly. "I was adopted."

"But your resemblance to the family portraits is uncanny," Georgie said incredulously.

"My parents searched until they found an infant who could pass for a Waters," Ben explained. "What can I say? I aced the paper bag test."

"Oh Lord," Georgie said, shaking her head. "This family is rife with secrets."

Seven

"Clay, damn, where have you been keeping yourself, man?" John Bendini said, his rich Boston-accented voice booming.

The two men hugged, slapping each other on the back in the usual greeting of the ex-partners. John, a barrel-chested Italian, was several inches shorter than his good friend. He looked up at Clay now with a questioning expression on his dark, mustachioed face.

"Sit," he said.

"How is Margarite?" Clay asked.

"Fine, fine," John said, grinning.

"The kids?"

"Fine," John said again. "What's up, buddy?"

Clay filled him in on the Waters case. John was leaning back in his chair, shaking his head in amazement when he finished.

"You do get some dillies, don't you? Charles Waters. He must be richer than Midas. So you go looking for the daughter and wind-up protecting her from an assassin. What's she like, this Georgette?"

"She's an attorney. Around thirty. Smart, sassy and beautiful," Clay replied, giving John the short version.

John nodded knowingly. His friend was leaving out some salient point, he was certain of it. "You attracted to her?"

Clay shook his head. "Come on, John, I came here to get your help, not to have you play matchmaker."

John laughed. "There's no rule that says I can't do both. I bet you do find her attractive." He went on in contemplative tones.

"I'll bet you're both attracted to each other. It's about time, buddy. I haven't seen that look in your eyes since Josie left us."

Clay grimaced. "That's a nice way of putting it, Johnny, but we both know that I killed Josie."

John rose from his seat behind his desk and pointing his thick finger at his friend, shouted, "The hell you did! After three years, even a stubborn, thick-headed dolt like yourself should realize that even *you* couldn't be in two places at once. You were delayed. Police work is like that. Josie understood. That's why she went on to the play without you."

"If I'd been at her side, like I was supposed to be, she would be alive today," Clay said for the thousandth time. The anguish was as fresh as the first time he'd spoken those words.

"You would be dead, too," John said bluntly. "That piece of crap who shot Josie wasn't after the money that night. For God's sake, he only got twenty bucks! He meant to kill and that was his only purpose. You are not psychic, my friend. There was no way you could've known what would happen to Josie, and you couldn't have prevented it. We got the guy, and because he thought he was in Dodge City, he's no longer walking this earth." He reached over and grasped Clay by the shoulder. "Put your guilt to rest, buddy. Josie would want you to go on. She wouldn't put up with your attitude."

"Those sessions you've been having with the department shrink are really paying off," Clay said half-jokingly.

He knew his friend was only trying to make him see reason, but some part of him didn't want to be absolved. Josie was gone, and he didn't want to make peace with it. He wanted to suffer. He wanted to be punished for not being there for her when she needed him most. He could never forgive himself for that.

"You could use a little time on the couch yourself," John replied seriously.

"I'll think about it," Clay said. "For now though, I need to borrow your computer and look at some mug shots."

"Help yourself," John said. "My office is your office. I've got to go take a statement from a shop owner over on Boylston who swears that a customer walked off with a ten thousand dollar diamond bracelet."

"You've got the cushy beat, huh?" Clay said admiringly.

"Nah," John said. "The chief is punishing me because I was insubordinate. The louse says I didn't follow procedure when I arrested a drug dealer. I told him I did. Of course, he got his way."

"He's the boss," Clay said sympathetically.

"That son of a b . . ." John began. He didn't finish because Chief Kowalski appeared in his doorway.

"Bendini," he bellowed, "didn't I tell you to get over to Boylston?"

Noticing Clay, he said, "Knight, what the hell are you doing here? I hope you're giving Bendini a few pointers. He never got into trouble when you were around to wipe his nose for him."

"I'm going, I'm going," John said in frustrated tones.

"Well, let me see some movement," Chief Kowalski, a tall, gaunt man in his late fifties said loudly. He smoothed his thinning, white hair back from his hook-nosed, angular face. "And I don't want to hear any excuses this time, Bendini. Follow procedure."

John backed out of the office, pulling on his shoulder holster with his weapon in it as he did so. "See you, Clay. Good luck with the case."

"Move it, move it," Chief Kowalski cried, not letting up. He gave Clay a little salute as he also turned to leave. "Don't you miss the excitement of the force?" he asked with a rueful smile.

Not with a nut like you in charge, Clay thought. "I regret leaving every day of my life," he said aloud.

After more than two hours of poring over the photos of nearly three hundred known offenders on the computer screen, Clay recognized Georgie's stalker.

His name was Eddie Kovik, age thirty-eight. He'd served time in a Massachusetts prison for armed robbery. Before that, he'd spent time in a Florida prison for assault and battery on his ex-wife. The file read that he'd beaten her within an inch of her life.

Clay read further down. Kovik had been released from the

Massachusetts prison a year ago. Since then, he'd stayed out of jail. His probation officer was listed as Sharon Pileggi. Clay wrote her number down. If he needed to, he'd go see her. First, he was going to check out the last known address of Eddie Kovik. It was in Roxbury—not far from his old neighborhood. He hadn't been back there in years, not since his mother passed away.

"That's it?" Georgie asked, looking up at Benjamin.

"Uncle is a rarity," Benjamin said. "He's a man who hasn't made many enemies on his way up the ladder. He really is a decent fellow."

Georgie smiled. "You sound as though you're fond of him."

Benjamin reached down and shut off the computer. "Yes, I am. My father died in a boating accident when I was sixteen and Mother succumbed to cancer two years later. After that, Uncle brought me here. He's always been keen on keeping the family together." He winced, thinking how insensitive his statement must have sounded to Georgie. "Sorry," he said lamely.

"Forget it," Georgie told him. She rolled her chair back from the work station, still looking up at Benjamin. Crossing her legs, she said, "I'm sure he had his reasons for not wanting to be a part of my life. Maybe one day he'll tell me what they were."

Benjamin sat on the edge of the desk, his light brown eyes trained on her face. "Are you bitter about it?"

"Bitter?" Georgie said with a laugh. "Too much has happened in the last few hours for me to gauge my feelings accurately. At this point, I feel like an onlooker. My mother and father will have to work their problems out first. Until then, I'm trying to remain objective. Let's talk about you, Ben. May I call you, Ben?"

Ben smiled at her, admiring the way her hair, like a thick, black glistening crown framed her heart-shaped face. "Of course," he said easily.

"What do you do for the company?"

"I'm second in command. I make certain all our plants are operating efficiently. I visit all of them periodically to check on operations. There are thirty-six plants, and approximately a hundred thousand employees."

"That must not leave you much time for a social life," Georgie said, encouraging him to fill her in.

Ben grinned. "I'm a man, not a workhorse. I make time for socializing. For the last few months, I've been seeing Cassandra Morelle. Cassie's a geneticist. She works with recombinant DNA technology."

"Oh, making monsters in the lab," Georgie joked.

Ben laughed heartily. "Cassie would crack up if she heard you say that. No. Actually, they're developing ways to control, or destroy viruses that are detrimental to humans. You've heard of Ebola, E. coli and other potentially deadly strains of viruses?"

Georgie nodded in the affirmative.

"Yes, well, Cassie is working on activating genes that produce certain proteins that can prevent the replication of a virus."

"Sort of stopping it in its tracks," Georgie commented.

"Right," Benjamin said, pleased that she'd understood the concept.

"She sounds interesting," Georgie said. "So, why were you flirting with me when you've got Cassie?"

Sighing, Ben stood and walked over to the window, peering out into the garden beyond. "We're growing apart. Nothing short of dynamite can blast Cassie out of that laboratory."

"I bet when you met, her ambitious, dedicated nature was what attracted you to her," Georgie said, swiveling in her chair so that she could see his face.

"Do you always read people so well?" Ben asked.

"It's a curse."

"Okay, I love Cassie. But I'm getting tired of being pushed aside for a cell."

"Then do something about it."

"What?" he asked.

"You're the big executive, Cousin. Think of something. What does Cassie like to do when she isn't splicing genes?"

"Eat," Benjamin said.

"Eat? Everyone likes to eat."

"Not like Cassie. She isn't overweight or anything, but she devotes so much time to work that when she takes the time to eat a meal, she gives it her full attention. Watching Cassie eat is a sensual experience unto itself."

Ben continued to look out across the grounds as he imagined Cassie tearing into a filet mignon.

A glare, like the sun reflecting off a mirror caught his attention. There was something in the brush surrounding the property. He squinted, trying to make out the source of the glare. Then, it occurred to him what he was seeing and in that split second, he lunged for Georgie, throwing her to the floor. The computer monitor exploded and Georgie looked up at the screen, which she'd been sitting in front of only moments before, as shards of glass rained downward. Someone was shooting at them.

The barrage ended as abruptly as it had begun. Georgie and Benjamin cowered flat on the floor. A moment later, a hefty stranger burst into the room, doing a tuck and roll, landing beside Georgie.

"Alec O'Hara," he said. "Clay sent me."

"And none too soon," Georgie said.

"Follow me," Alec said as he slithered toward the door on his belly. Georgie and Ben mimicked his movements as best they could and when they were in the hallway, they sat with their backs against the wall, staring at each other with shock and disbelief in their frightened expressions.

"Did you see anything?" Alec asked.

"No," Georgie replied.

Ben had his arms around her, trying to quell her shaking and hopefully stanch his own. "I was standing at the window when I saw a glint. It reminded me of a movie I recently saw in which an assassin killed someone using a high-powered rifle with a scope." He laughed nervously. "Thank God I didn't react with my usual logic and try to reason my gut reaction away."

Alec got to his feet. "You two stay here. The police are on the way. I'm going to have a look outside."

He quickly checked his handgun, an automatic. There were

fifteen rounds in the clip and fifteen more in the gun strapped to his right leg.

Alec O'Hara was, by nature, a non-violent man. He was an ex-cop who truly believed in the edict, "protect and serve." And he had single-mindedly followed his inclination to do just that all his adult life—first, as a Marine, where he'd met Clay Knight in boot camp at Parris Island, South Carolina.

He and Clay were rivals, at first, because in all competitions during eleven weeks of physical training, they were equally matched. Then, after a brawl in a bar in nearby Port Royal while on leave, they became the best of pals. After the Corps, Alec had become a New York City police officer. By the time he turned thirty-three, he was suffering from burnout, and Clay offered him a partnership in the agency. He'd jumped at the chance. That was three years ago. Since then, he'd met and married a beautiful woman, Dian, a dark-haired Irish lass who at times melted his heart and at others incited his anger. Either way, they remained completely in love. And now, Dian was expecting their first child. No, Alec O'Hara was not a violent man—but it was his duty to serve and protect. Therefore, he searched the grounds.

"Your hand is bleeding," Ben said.

Georgie glanced up. Her heart was beating so fast, she felt as if she would pass out. Bree and her mother were at her side. Bree had run in the direction of the commotion, her mind so focused on her sister that she'd stepped on a piece of glass in her stockinged feet. She had a deep gash on the bottom of her left foot.

Ben saw Anne entering the hallway, followed by his uncle.

"Anne," he said. "Would you get the first aid kit? I think Cook keeps one in the kitchen."

"Yes, of course," Anne said, turning on her heels to do as he'd asked.

Charles stooped to survey the damage.

"It's not bad," he said of Georgie's cut. He frowned when he saw the blood flowing from the wound on Bree's foot. "However, we may have to get you to the emergency room, young lady."

Toni sat on the floor beside Georgie, holding her uninjured hand. Her eyes were riveted on Charles. It was the second time in less than twenty-four hours that someone had tried to take her child's life and it had also contributed to her other daughter's injury. She wanted to punch Charles' lights out.

Anne returned with the first aid kit and Benjamin cleaned Georgie's cut with an antiseptic and bandaged it.

Anne worked quickly on Bree's cut, applying pressure until the bleeding stopped, then spraying on an antiseptic and bandaging the wound.

Bree smiled at her. "Thank you, Anne."

"I'm glad I could help," Anne said. She gave Bree's hand an affectionate squeeze. "Come on, I'll help you hobble back to the living room. The police should be arriving shortly."

There was no sign of the shooter on the grounds—save for a few divots left in the lawn, evidence that he'd beat a hasty retreat.

Alec squatted to examine the holes. He was stumped as to why the shooter would risk getting this close to the house. If his weapon were adequately outfitted, all he needed was to have accurate sights. This smacked of amateurism. Alec had tracked enough professionals to recognize sloppiness.

He followed the divots to the edge of the lawn where it met the driveway. A professional wouldn't even have left the divots behind as evidence.

He was standing on the black surface, still pondering the kind of mind they were up against, when a bright red late model Mercedes convertible careened around the sharp curve leading to the house and almost hit him. He leapt out of the way just in time. The car came to a halt and the driver, an attractive black woman in her early forties, got out.

"What were you trying to do, get yourself killed?" she shrieked at him.

Alec wasn't taking any chances. He moved swiftly, going to her and, none too gently, forcing her to assume the position against the hood of the car. He patted her down. She wasn't carrying a concealed weapon.

"Are you insane?" she fairly screamed at him. "I've got to get to Charles. I just saw a man running away from the house. I think he was carrying a rifle."

Alec let go of her and turned her around to face him.

"Who are you?"

"I'm Lillie Germaine. Charles Waters and I are close friends."

The name checked out.

"May I see some form of identification?"

Lillie grudgingly reached into her purse and produced her wallet. She flipped it open, showing him her driver's license.

"California?"

"My home state. I'm back and forth a lot. I didn't see a need to change it. Who the hell are you, anyway?"

"You're free to go, Miss Germaine," was all Alec said. He opened her car door for her.

Lillie slid onto the seat with cat-like sensuality. "I could have your job for this," she said contemptuously.

"You wouldn't want my job, ma'am. The hours stink and the people you meet are the dregs of humanity," Alec said politely.

Lillie put her foot down hard on the accelerator and the Mercedes shot forward.

Eddie Kovik's last place of residence was a shabby walk-up on the south side, sandwiched between a twenty-four hour Laundromat and a liquor store. The neighborhood was home to various street elements: drug addicts, pushers, prostitutes, thugs. The law-abiding folks who were left behind because of poverty rarely ventured out of their locked apartments and did not dare allow their children the privilege of playing outdoors. Fear was a palpable thing in this part of the city. Clay knew it well. He'd been brought up only a few blocks away.

He buttoned up his duster against the cold as he stepped out of the Ford Explorer. Harve Sussman, his associate, followed him. Harve was twenty-seven and had been with the agency for three years. He was around five-eleven, wiry, with dark skin and hair and brown eyes. Intelligent and introspective, he was a competent investigator and someone Clay trusted to always have his back, no matter what went down.

The buildings were dilapidated, save one brownstone, that Clay supposed was a part of the city's urban renewal plan he'd been hearing so much about lately. Trash littered the streets. Pedestrians didn't seem to notice. Their faces were locked with expressions of apathy.

He waved Harve around back. Many suspects tried to flee via the fire escape when he came knocking on their doors. He gave Harve a few minutes before ascending the rickety stairs two at a time.

At the door of Kovik's apartment, he stood listening for a minute or so. He heard no sounds of life within. Knocking didn't produce a response. He tried the doorknob. It was unlocked. He quietly turned the knob and cautiously entered the apartment, his hand on his holstered weapon should Kovik be waiting inside.

Empty. Clay knew it the moment he stepped into the cesspool of a domicile. The smell of decay was what hit him first—the odor of dead rats left to ferment in their traps. He placed his handkerchief over his nose in order to remain in the apartment. As he moved about, he was careful not to trip over debris. Trash covered the floor. Roaches scurried for their hidey-holes when he kicked it aside.

The one-room apartment had only three pieces of furniture in it: a cast iron bed along the far wall with a stained mattress atop it, a tattered armchair next to the sole window and a bureau, the drawers missing. Not much to search for clues as to where Kovik might have gone.

Clay searched the bed first, flipping the stained mattress over. Nothing was under there except dust bunnies and more debris. There was a tapping on the window and he looked up to find

Harve standing on the fire escape. He walked over and unlocked the window. Harve climbed inside.

"Anything?" his associate asked.

"Nah, he hasn't been here in a while."

"This place is a sty," Harve said, pulling the corner of his jacket over his nose.

Clay was removing the cushion of the armchair and checking down in its sides. He came out with empty cigarette packs and match books.

"He smokes Camels," he said, holding up one of the packs.

Digging down again, he came up with several slips of paper. Taking a closer look, he laughed. "It seems our Mr. Kovik has a gambling habit." He handed the ticket stubs to Harve.

"The dog track," Harve said. "You want me to do a bit of surveillance at the track?"

"Couldn't hurt," Clay replied. "He may be in hiding, but compulsion is a nasty habit to break. Check it out, Harve."

"You want me to take a cab out there?"

"No," Clay told him. "You can take the Explorer. I'm going to knock on some more doors, then I'll get a cab back to the office."

"Right," Harve said, turning to leave. "Don't stay in here too long, you might get cooties."

Clay acknowledged his partner's warning with a nod as he went into the kitchenette to check the cabinets.

Eddie Kovik anxiously paced the floor of the hotel room where he'd been staying the past week, ever since he'd been given the first part of the payment for the job: five thousand dollars. It wasn't the Ritz, but it was much nicer than that rat hole he'd formerly lived in.

He pulled on the cigarette he was smoking, held the smoke in his lungs for a few seconds and blew it out. Why didn't she phone? She always phoned at six o'clock every night. The black queen—that's what he called her. He didn't know her name. He'd only seen her once, and that was in a smoky club. She'd been wearing dark glasses and a scarf that covered her entire head and part of her face. All he knew about her was that she was a woman, and she was black. Hence, the black queen.

Bored, he flopped down on the bed, next to the phone, picked up the remote from the nightstand and channel-surfed until he found a basketball game. He nearly swallowed smoke when the phone rang.

Coughing, he snatched the handset up. "Mmm, sorry."

"You missed your target, Mr. Kovik. I'm very disappointed in you," the feminine voice said acidly. "You had your chance, and you blew it. I have a good mind to call the whole thing off. I cannot abide fools."

"I won't miss next time," Eddie promised. A trickle of sweat slowly rolled down the side of his thin face. "You just tell me where she'll be and I'll do the rest."

"One final opportunity, Mr. Kovik," the black queen said menacingly. "A certain market makes deliveries to the Waters mansion each Saturday morning. What you need to do is . . ."

Listening intently, Eddie pulled deeply on the cigarette. One final opportunity. He would succeed this time—he had to.

After Harve left, Clay made a thorough search of Kovik's apartment, coming up with nothing except clues to what a slob Kovik was. However, he wasn't discouraged. Grunt work was the nature of the business. Contrary to what many people thought detective work was like, he spent an inordinate amount of time doing legwork. The glamour and excitement depicted in books and movies happened only in a blue moon. As he left the apartment, closing the door behind him, he resolved to come away from the building with at least one clue.

He got no response after knocking on the first couple of doors. However, at the third, he heard someone stirring around inside.

A grizzled black man of indeterminate years opened the door just far enough to stick his bulbous nose out. "I ain't buyin' nothin'. I ain't payin' for nothin' and I ain't donatin' nothin'. What you want, boy?"

"I'm looking for one of your neighbors. Eddie Kovik. Do you know him?"

The nose wrinkled in distaste, then the door opened wider.

"You the law?"

Clay held his ID under the nose.

"The name's Clay Knight. I'm a private investigator. I'm looking for Eddie because I have a few questions that only he can answer."

The door opened all the way. A trim, wiry body went with that nose. A pair of laughing brown eyes were above it. "Come on in and sit down, Mr. Private Investigator."

The apartment was small but neat. The man, who introduced himself as Joe Jackson, lived alone except for his tomcat. The cat insisted on sitting in Clay's lap throughout their conversation.

"Kovik ain't been around here for at least a week, I'd say," Joe said, settling back on his brown plaid couch. Clay sat on the matching chair across from him. "Don't know where he is. Sally, that's the girl who lives next door to him—she does a little candy selling on the side. Not the sweet kind, mind you. Anyway, Sally was bragging as how Eddie gave her two hundred for some candy, and she had never seen such a roll. He must have gotten lucky at the track. He likes the dogs. Aside from chess, I guess gambling is his favorite pastime."

"Chess?" Clay said, interested.

"Yeah. The way Kovik tells it, he was quite the prodigy when he was a kid. His parents, both nut cases, according to him, had him on the tournament circuit. He flipped out. Never played in another tournament. But he likes to play with a friend every now and then." He gestured to the chess board set up on a card table near the window. "We played sometimes. He beat me every time."

"Do you have any idea where he likes to hang out?" Clay asked Joe.

"Have you tried Clancy's?" Joe said. "That's where Eddie's

WE INVITE YOU TO JOIN THE ONLY BOOK
CLUB THAT DELIVERS HEARTFELT ROMANCE
FEATURING AFRICAN AMERICAN HEROES AND
HEROINES IN STORIES THAT ARE RICH IN
PASSION AND CULTURAL SPICE...
And Your First 4 Books Are FREE!

Arabesque is the newest contemporary romance line offered by
Pinnacle Books. Arabesque has been so successful that our
readers have asked us about direct home delivery. We
responded to your requests. You can start receiving four
bestselling Arabesque novels a month delivered right to your
door. Subscribe now and you'll get:

✧ 4 FREE Arabesque romances as our introductory gift—a value
   of almost $20! (pay only $1 to help cover postage &
   handling)
✧ 4 BRAND-NEW Arabesque romances
   delivered to your doorstep each month
   thereafter (usually arriving before
   they're available in bookstores!)
✧ 20% off each title—a savings of
   almost $4.00 each month
✧ FREE home delivery
✧ A FREE monthly newsletter,
   Zebra/Pinnacle Romance News that
   features author profiles, book previews
   and more
✧ No risks or obligations...in other words, you can cancel
   whenever you wish with no questions asked

So subscribe to Arabesque today and see why these books are
winning awards and readers' hearts.

After you've enjoyed our FREE gift of 4 Arabesques, you'll begin
to receive monthly shipments of the newest Arabesque titles.
Each shipment will be yours to examine for 10 days. If you
decide to keep the books, you'll pay the preferred subscriber's
price of just $4.00 per title. That's $16 for all 4 books with
FREE home delivery! And if you want us to stop sending books,
just say the word...it's that simple.

See why reviewers are raving about ARABESQUE
and order your FREE books today!

WE HAVE 4 FREE BOOKS FOR YOU!

ARABESQUE

FREE BOOK CERTIFICATE

Yes! Please send me 4 *Arabesque* Contemporary Romances without cost or obligation, billing me just $1 to help cover postage and handling. I understand that each month, I will be able to preview 4 brand-new *Arabesque* Contemporary Romances FREE for 10 days. Then, if I decide to keep them, I will pay the money-saving preferred subscriber's price of just $16.00 for all 4...that's a savings of almost $4 off the publisher's price with no additional charge for shipping and handling. I may return any shipment within 10 days and owe nothing, and I may cancel this subscription at any time. My 4 FREE books will be mine to keep in any case.

Name _____

Address _____ Apt. _____

City _____ State _____ Zip _____

Telephone ( ) _____

Signature _____ ARO697
(If under 18, parent or guardian must sign.)

Terms and prices subject to change. Orders subject to acceptance by Zebra Home Subscription Service, Inc. .
Zebra Home Subscription Service, Inc. reserves the right to reject or cancel any subscription.

bookie does most of his business. If anyone's seen him lately, it's his bookie."

Clancy's was the kind of dive men came to in order to get blitzed out of their minds. The smoke-filled air reeked of stale beer and liquor and was so thick it looked as if Clay would require searchlights to spot anyone in the melange.

Not a place to come to meet people like some of the trendier bars in the city. Clancy's bleary-eyed denizens nursed drinks at the bar or in booths. No one seemed interested in conversation, just in the spirits in the glasses before them. The juke box played a selection ranging from B.B. King to John Lee Hooker—all designed to soothe the blighted soul.

Clay expected a bar that went by the name Clancy's to be a hangout for Irish Americans, but most of the patrons were blue-collar African-American males.

He sat at the bar between two men who appeared to be diehard regulars. Neither of them looked up when he sat down.

"Be wid ya in a minute, buddy," the bartender, a burly fellow of Irish descent called from the other end of the bar.

A couple of minutes later, he was drawing a draft beer for Clay.

"Two bucks and four bits," he said, as he placed the brew in front of Clay.

Clay handed him a twenty.

"Where can a guy place a bet around here? I feel lucky tonight."

The bartender looked Clay up and down. "And you came in here?"

"Someone told me a bookie hangs out in here. Would you point him out to me?"

"You mean Moe. That's him in the corner booth. You can't miss him, he's the one with the cellular phone growing out of his ear."

Clay stood, taking his beer with him. "Thanks. Keep the change."

The bartender swept the twenty off the bar and pocketed it. "You really *are* in the mood to give your money away. Moe's your man."

Kieron McPherson went back to drawing drafts for his regulars.

He watched the generous stranger as he made his way across the room. He smelled like a cop to him. Kieron wasn't usually so forthcoming with information, but he was getting tired of Moe using his bar as his office without paying any rent. He hoped the stranger *was* a cop and put Moe so far under the jail he'd only have earthworms for cell mates. He'd like to get rid of a few more of these losers, too. He hated this place. He wished he'd never inherited it from his old man, the original Clancy. The neighborhood was going to hell. This street was populated by vermin. He wished he had the guts to torch the bar and collect the insurance. But, with his luck, he'd end up in prison for arson.

"Give me another one, Clance, and put it on my tab," a bar regular demanded, slapping his hand on the counter top.

"How many times do I have to tell you, I ain't Clancy, and you don't have no damn tab!"

Kieron drew another tall one for him nonetheless. The old coot was one of his best customers.

Eight

After a minute in the bookie's presence, Clay developed a genuine dislike for Moe Wilson. But then he'd never met a hustler he did like simply because they were continually looking for your weak spot, trying to judge at what point they could run a con on you.

Moe eyed him suspiciously until Clay flashed a wad of bills big enough to choke a horse, whereupon Moe waved him to the seat across from him.

"Keep talking, Jolly, I'm listening," he said into the cellular phone's receiver. "What can I do you for?" he said to Clay.

"You can tell me where I can find Eddie Kovik," Clay said, straight from the hip. "You're a busy man. One sentence and I'm out of your hair."

Moe sucked his teeth and grinned, revealing gold crowns on his two front incisors.

"Eddie's a good customer. What do you want with him? He in some kind of trouble?"

"Maybe you'll be in some kind of trouble if you know where he is and refuse to tell me," Clay said, meeting Moe's pale blue eyes.

"Who do you work for? Mr. Domenico?"

"That's none of your business," Clay said, his voice hard.

Perspiration had broken out on the bookie's forehead.

Clay knew what must be going through his mind. Jake Domenico was an organized crime boss. Clay knew him from his cop days. Domenico was unusually cruel to those who crossed him. The Atlantic was probably the final resting place of several of Jake Domenico's enemies, although no one would ever be able to prove it.

Moe hung up the phone and ran a hand through his limp, mousy brown hair.

"If I tell you where Kovik's hiding, you'll put in a good word for me with Mr. Domenico?"

"That can be arranged," Clay said, his gaze relentless.

"Okay, okay," Moe said hurriedly. "He's staying at the Barstow Hotel over in Dorchester. I know 'cause he just won a bet, and that's where I went to pay him off."

"He's on a lucky streak, huh?" Clay said, his smile sinister.

Moe swallowed hard. "That's all I know, pal. Now, if you'll excuse me, I'm working here."

Clay got to his feet. "Mr. Domenico will be in touch."

Moe reclaimed his cocky veneer. "Whatever," he said dismissively.

"I'll be sure to tell him how grateful you were to hear of his interest," Clay said.

"Hey, my man, can't you take a joke?" Moe cried.

Clay walked off, letting the bookie stew in his own juices. That ought to give him a few sleepless nights.

Upon his return to the mansion, Clay found the household in an uproar over the second attempt on Georgie's life. Everyone was vying for his attention at once, however his first concern was for Georgie. He took her by the hand and pulling her along with him, abandoned the rest of them. Alone in Charles' study, he closed and locked the door behind them.

"That's the last time I leave you," he promised as he pulled her close.

"That's the last time you leave me," Georgie said at practically the same moment. She relaxed for the first time since the incident.

"Perhaps you should call someone else in on this case," Clay said, looking into her brown eyes. "I'm getting too personally involved."

Georgie stared up at him. Her pulse sounded like a drum in her ears. Was it adrenaline from her latest brush with death, or was his nearness the cause? Admittedly, she'd wanted to kiss him since he'd rescued her in Louisiana, and not just out of gratitude. It was a chemical attraction—a very strong one. She'd known he would be a hard man to resist the moment he'd walked into the hotel lobby. Even her long-practiced reserve was no adequate weapon against his magnetism. She would be lost if they didn't soon solve this case and allow her to return to her sedate life in San Francisco.

"Oh, why not?" she said suddenly. "Who knows if I'm even going to be alive tomorrow!"

She tiptoed and kissed him squarely on the mouth. Caught by surprise, Clay stumbled backward under the assault but quickly recovered. His strong arms enveloped her and the kiss deepened. She tasted sweet and clean and her womanly form molded itself perfectly to his male hardness.

"Sorry, Boston," Georgie said when she came up for air. "You just looked so imminently kissable. Forgive me?"

"Only if you'll forgive me for this," Clay said as he bent his head and kissed her again.

Georgie's knees buckled when he released her. She was slightly dazed but still wanted another taste of those soft, pliant lips.

She tiptoed and planted another one on him.

Afterward, she smiled and said, "Now we're even."

Clay grinned. "You call that getting even? *This* is getting even."

He began with a gentle nuzzle to the curve of her neck and worked his way up to her chin and finally to her soft, inviting lips that parted eagerly to receive his kiss.

Georgie felt a warmth invade her body like none she'd ever experienced before. She pressed closer until Clay was maneuvered against the wall of her father's study. The impact must have jarred the awards hanging on the wall because a couple of them came crashing down.

Someone knocked on the door of the study. "Clay, Georgie," it was her mother's anxious voice. "Are you all right in there?"

Clay and Georgie parted, laughing quietly. They didn't want those on the other side of the door to know they hadn't been discussing business behind closed doors.

"I'll get the door while you straighten your clothes," Clay suggested.

"Wait a minute," Georgie said, going to wipe her lipstick off his mouth with a tissue from the dispenser on her father's desk.

Everyone from the living room strode into the study. Ushering them in, Clay told them to be seated. He had something to tell them. "Probably as we speak," he told them, "the police are arresting Eddie Kovik. I got a tip that he was staying at a Dorchester hotel, and John Bendini is following up on it. John promised to phone as soon as it's over."

Across town at the Barstow Hotel, the police were breaking down the door of room 361. There was no sign of Eddie Kovik. John Bendini ordered two of his men to stake out the hotel until further notice, then he went to the nearest phone and dialed Clay's number.

"I'm sorry, Clay," he said. "The clerk identified Kovik. Said he was paid up for a week, but he isn't here. And with all of us milling around, he isn't apt to show his face any time soon."

Mrs. Adelaide Hughes, "Cook," had a tried and true routine she followed in the operation of her kitchen. And she didn't like straying from it. So when a strange man appeared at the back door of the Waters mansion Saturday morning, saying he was from Spencer's Market and that Tim, the regular delivery man, had been in an accident, she was instantly suspicious.

For one thing, she didn't like the surly look he was giving her.

Anyone coming into her kitchen had to respect her as the authority. She stood in the door, blocking his entrance. The bundles of meat, which were presumably in the bags he was holding, appeared quite heavy.

"Can I come in, lady?" he said, trying to force his way past her.

Mrs. Hughes was five-ten and two-hundred and sixty pounds. She made an imposing figure.

"Not until I see some identification," she said, dark eyes narrowing. "I don't have time for your nonsense, so out with it."

The man shifted the heavy bundle in his arms. "I don't think I'll be able to go in my pocket with this. Would you hold it for just a second?"

Mrs. Hughes sighed and reached for the packages. When her arms were full, the man removed a gadget about the size of a remote control from his back pocket and quickly zapped Mrs. Hughes with it. Mrs. Hughes didn't even have time to utter a scream. The electrical system in her amazonian body short-circuited, and she collapsed to the floor.

The man kicked the packages out of the way and taking Mrs. Hughes underneath both her sizable arms, dragged her outside behind a clump of evergreen shrubbery near the back door. Alert, but unable to control her muscles, Mrs. Hughes had to silently endure this indignity.

The man then went inside and locked the door behind him. He checked his watch. It was 7:15 a.m. He had ten minutes in which to find the Shaw woman, deal with her and get back out. He estimated it would take about fifteen minutes before the effects of the Taser wore off that bull of a woman. He wanted to be long gone before she regained her senses.

He touched the stock of the silencer-equipped 9mm concealed beneath his leather jacket. Stealthily, he left the kitchen and entered the hallway.

Upstairs, Pierre had grasped Bree's nightgown between his sharp teeth. He yanked on it, trying to awaken her. When that didn't work, he barked once and waited. She stirred and he pounced on her. Bree opened her eyes and the first thing she saw was the back end of Pierre as he jumped down off the bed, heading for the door.

"You want to go out now?" she moaned, sitting up in bed. She rubbed the sleep from her eyes and felt for her slippers with her feet. "Did you move my slippers, rug rat?" she asked. She got down on her knees and peered underneath the bed. At that instance, the door opened. Bree spied a pair of men's boots. They were scuffed and covered with mud. Heart hammering, she quickly scooted under the bed.

Pierre, who'd been rudely pushed aside by the door when the man had entered the room, was now yelping his head off.

Bree saw the boots advance, turn around and head for the door. Pierre's barking apparently made him nervous. He pulled the door shut behind him. Bree waited about thirty seconds before she felt it was safe to come out of her hiding place, then she crawled out from beneath the bed and went to the phone on the nightstand. Each phone in the house was connected to all the other phones. She quickly perused the directory and pressed the button for the bedroom next to Georgie's, the room Clay had spent the night in.

Clay picked up on the first ring. "Yeah?"

"Clay," Bree whispered. "Someone's in the house. A strange man was just in my room."

"Okay, you stay put," Clay told her, hanging up.

Clay was dressed and cautiously leaving his room within twenty seconds. As he walked into the dimly-lit hallway, he looked to his right. Not a soul. Then, he peered to his left. No one.

Leaving the door ajar, he moved to the left. Georgie's bedroom was only a few feet away. He had instructed her to lock her door. He tried the doorknob, it was securely locked. He had to know she was safe though, so he knocked softly.

"Who's there?" came Georgie's voice.

"It's Clay, are you all right?"

Opening the door, Georgie looked concerned. "Yes. Why? Is something wrong?"

Before Clay could reply, the sound of furniture being overturned came from down the hall. Knowing the layout of the house, he thought it sounded as if a herd of elephants was stampeding through Charles' suite.

Flinging her door open, Georgie followed.

"Get back in your room and lock the door," Clay tossed over his shoulder.

"I'm going with you," Georgie said, ignoring his orders.

As Clay sprinted around the corner, a man ran from Charles' room. He paused in his tracks long enough to get off a round in Clay's direction. The bullet lodged in the molding beneath a portrait of one of the Waters ancestors.

"Halt!" Clay warned, recognizing Eddie Kovik.

Eddie ran for the stairs, descending them in leaps. Clay ran after him, loath to use his weapon for fear of injuring an innocent bystander.

Georgie went into her father's room. Stepping around an overturned cherry-wood bureau, she found Charles in a heap on the floor. She ran to him and turned him over. He was conscious, but there was a fresh wound in his right shoulder.

"He shot me," he croaked.

Georgie cradled him in her arms. "You're going to be all right, Daddy."

"You—you called me Daddy," Charles said. He smiled, a tear trickled down the right side of his face. "Georgie, I'm so happy you're here now."

"Me too," Georgie said, smiling down at him.

Toni appeared in the doorway.

"What happened here?" Spotting Georgie on the floor with her father's head cradled in her lap, she entered the room. "Did you dial 911?"

"Not yet," Georgie told her.

Toni went to the phone and calmly dialed the number.

"You'll do anything to get into my good graces, won't you, Chuck?" she said with a straight face.

Charles laughed. "It hurts when I laugh, Toni."

"Then don't laugh," Toni advised him.

Clay had followed Eddie Kovik downstairs to the kitchen. He

cautiously entered the kitchen, thinking it would be an ideal place for Eddie to suddenly spin on his heels and get off another round.

Peering into the room, he saw the door standing open. He entered in a crouched position, his weapon drawn. He heard footsteps, then a moan. Standing, his weapon at the ready, he pointed and aimed. Just then, Mrs. Hughes stumbled into his sights.

Clay uttered an expletive and quickly moved forward and caught the woman in his arms before she could fall, head first, to the floor. Eddie Kovik had eluded him again. At least he'd gotten a good look at him.

"He electrocuted me," Mrs. Hughes babbled, once again coherent. "He would not have gotten past me if I'd seen it coming."

"I'm sure he wouldn't have, Mrs. Hughes," Clay said. He gently laid her down on the spotless black-and-white checkerboard floor. "Don't exert yourself. Help is on the way."

Benjamin entered the kitchen. He knelt to clasp one of the beloved cook's hands in his. Formerly no fan of the wealthy businessman, Clay had to grudgingly respect him for this gesture.

"There, there, Cook," Benjamin said consolingly. "You've been brave beyond your job description, I should say."

Rising, Clay said, "You'll stay with her?"

"Of course," Benjamin assured him.

"Mr. Knight," Mrs. Hughes said. "I got a good look at him."

"So did I," Clay said. "It was Eddie Kovik. The question is—who told him you take deliveries every Saturday morning?"

"It could have been anyone," Mrs. Hughes said. "I have my schedule posted on the bulletin board for all the world to see."

Clay looked up at the aforementioned bulletin board on the wall next to the back door. She was right, anyone could have gotten that piece of information. Anyone living in or anyone who had access to the Waters mansion.

Eddie was out of breath by the time he made it to his car, a nondescript dark Chevy. He'd driven it right up to the house. After all, he was supposed to be a delivery man. Three strikes—

he knew he wouldn't be able to talk the black queen into giving him another chance. He'd bungled the hit three times. The Shaw woman must be the luckiest woman alive.

He would have had her this time except for two drawbacks: he'd forgotten to bring the drawing of the layout of the house with him. After years of abusing his body with drugs and alcohol, clear thinking was a thing of the past. Plus, he hadn't counted on the toughness of old man Waters.

When he had gone into Waters' bedroom by mistake, the smallest sound had roused the old guy. Then, even after he'd pointed the gun at him and warned him not to move, Waters had lunged at him. The gun went flying out of his grip, landing on the floor beneath a straight-backed chair. As he and Waters struggled on the floor, each of them trying to subdue the other while attempting to keep the gun out of reach, they'd overturned several pieces of furniture.

Eddie was sure they'd awakened the entire household with the racket they'd created. By some stroke of luck, he'd gotten in a good punch and while Waters was trying to shake off the effects, he'd recovered the gun and shot him in the shoulder.

Then, as he ran from the room, there was that detective with the Shaw woman close behind him. He shot one round at the woman, not waiting to see if he'd gotten her.

By the time he ran out the back door, he heard the cook hoisting herself up from behind the bushes. She bellowed at him like a bull moose. She scared him so badly, he thought he'd have a heart attack right then and there, and they could save the cost of a bullet.

But, somehow, he'd made it out by the skin of his teeth. He slowed the car. It wouldn't do for him to be stopped by a cop now. Looking around him, he realized he was further north than he'd wanted to be. Think, he thought. I'll have to find another hotel. The other place was probably crawling with cops by now.

He was on Columbus Avenue in Roxbury before his heart had returned to its normal rhythm. He would find another hotel, and then he'd phone the black queen and apologize for his foul-up.

* * *

"Joseph Powell is not even in the state of Massachusetts," Alma told Clay over the phone later that day. "He's in Bethel, North Carolina, burying his mother. I got the information from his landlord who says Powell is doing his best to go straight."

"And what did you find out about Lillie Germaine?" Clay asked. He and Georgie were alone in Charles' study. He was sitting at the desk, and she was perched on the desk top, listening to his side of the conversation. Every now and then, they'd give each other smoldering looks, but since yesterday, they hadn't succumbed to their feelings.

"She was born here in Boston and left when she was seventeen. She lived in San Jose, California, up until three years ago. She has a special needs child in a health care facility in San Jose. Costs a pretty penny to keep him there. Anyway, Miss Germaine is somewhat of a groupie. You know how women follow rock stars from concert to concert, hoping to land one of them? Well, it says here that she latched on to a millionaire, Malcolm Devers, three years ago, and that's how she got the capital to open her interior design business. He recommended her to all his influential friends."

"Charles did say he met her when she redecorated his study," Clay said. He looked around him. "And she did a hell of a job."

Alma laughed on the other end. "You're going to have to tell me all about that place when you wrap this case up."

Clay laughed affectionately. In some ways, Alma was more of a mother to him than his birth mother had been. Eight years ago, when he'd opened the agency, Alma was a fifty-year-old divorced mother of two grown sons with no marketable skills. He'd hired her as his receptionist and now, she was an indispensable part of the agency.

"Will do," Clay said finally. "Gotta go, Alma. Let me know if Harve reports in and don't forget to close the file on the Galloway case and bill Jack Galloway. I'll be at the Waters mansion if you need me."

"All right," Alma replied. "Tell Miss Shaw hello for me. She seems real nice."

He looked up into Georgie's inquisitive face. "Alma says hello."

Georgie smiled. "I bet she asked you if you were eating right. Has she always treated you like her child?"

"Alma has lots of love in her heart. She's the type of woman who adopts everyone she likes. She treats all of us at the agency as if we're hers."

"So," Georgie said, swinging her legs around so that she could face him more comfortably. "Where do we go from here?"

"We wait," Clay told her. "We wait for whomever hired Kovik to make his next move. My theory is: he's fed up with Kovik. Three tries. Three misses. He definitely isn't happy about it."

His hazel eyes rested on her long legs. She was wearing a jean skirt and a white peasant blouse. Her golden-brown skin glowed as though she'd recently been on the beach soaking up the sun's rays. His eyes rested on her pristine pair of white Nikes. "Do you ever wear heels?" he asked, amusement apparent in his green-brown depths.

"Not if I can help it," Georgie said, smiling at him. She posed her legs so that he got an eyeful. "You don't like my legs in sneaks?"

Clay laughed. "You couldn't possibly lose in that area since you're your mother's daughter."

Georgie looked at him, her head cocked sideways. "You've got a crush on my mother," she stated. "That's so sweet."

"I've been in love with Toni since I was eight years old," Clay told her, not trying to deny how he felt about her mother. "But I'm not eight any longer, and what I feel for her daughter coincides with my more mature outlook."

Georgie smiled slowly and slid right down onto his lap where Clay wrapped his strong arms around her and held her close.

She kissed his cheek. "If someone wasn't trying to kill me, I'd be having quite a good time right now." She met his gaze. "Why couldn't I have met you last week? You could have been having dinner in my favorite restaurant, and I walked in and our eyes met across the room. You would've sent a drink to my table with a note and I would've invited you over."

"I would've asked you out," Clay said, picking up the story.

"I would've politely declined."

"What?"

"I would've had to check you out first," Georgie explained, laying her head on his chest. "A girl can't be too careful these days. But after that, I would've phoned you and asked *you* out."

Clay laughed softly. "So that's how it's done. I haven't been a part of the dating scene in quite a while."

"Oh?" Georgie said, sitting up to look into his eyes.

"My wife, Josette, was killed by a mugger three years ago," Clay said, his voice low.

Georgie suddenly felt her behavior was too frivolous. What must he think of her?

She went to get off his lap and Clay pulled her back down. "It's okay," he said. "I can talk about it without breaking down."

Georgie settled comfortably on his lap, her arms around his muscular neck, her cheek pressed to his. "Tell me about her."

"She was twenty-seven . . ."

"My age."

"Yeah, she would have been thirty now," he said. "Josie taught second grade. She adored kids. We wanted to have a house full. She was warm, giving and smart . . . you would have liked her."

"Do you have a picture of her?"

Clay reached into his coat pocket and retrieved his wallet. He flipped it open to a small snapshot. Georgie took the wallet and looked into the smiling face of an attractive African-American woman with shoulder-length curly brown hair, dimples in both cheeks and dark brown eyes, eyes not unlike her own. The resemblance she saw probably had something to do with the contrast between the golden-brown of Josie's skin and the darkness of her eyes. They had that in common.

She returned the wallet to Clay. "She was beautiful. You must miss her terribly."

"I think I'll always miss her," Clay said. He put the wallet away. "I told you about her because I want you to understand something about me, Frisco. I know what love is. I've been lucky enough to have experienced it. I'm no good at playing games." His gaze held hers. "Since Josie died no other woman has warranted my interest, not until I walked into the lobby of Hotel le Pavillon Hotel and saw you."

His declaration momentarily rendered Georgie speechless, then she sighed and hugged him to her. "You don't know how long I've waited for a man to say something like that to me. Now, I don't know what to say . . ."

"You don't have to say anything," Clay told her and pulled her down to kiss her soundly.

Georgie turned on his lap until she faced him and when his full mouth descended upon hers, she met his kiss with gusto. She felt safe and secure in his arms and his big hands on her back made shivers of delight course through her. If she lived to be a hundred, she would not forget this moment—the instant she fell in love with Clay Knight.

Her mouth felt swollen when they parted. She looked up into his eyes. "You're right, that says it all."

"I can't talk now," the black queen said when she returned Eddie Kovik's call after he'd paged her. "Where are you? I'll come to you."

Eddie took this as a sign she was going to overlook his latest blunder. He gladly gave her his room number at the Parliament Hotel—a seedy circa 1930's dump on the edge of Roxbury.

He lay on the bed after hanging up. The springs in the mattress poked him in the side. He was tired. He hadn't slept well in two days, just snippets of sleep. He was too keyed-up to relax.

After he finished the job, he would be on the next plane to Mexico. He could rest there, on a beach in Acapulco.

Extremely restless, he couldn't concentrate on the sitcom on the black-and-white television set. It was one of his favorites, too—the episode of I Love Lucy in which Lucy and Ethel get jobs in a candy factory. Even the sight of Lucy with her mouth crammed full of chocolates couldn't lighten his mood.

He felt his shirt pocket. Maybe another cigarette . . . No, he was out. He removed the empty package from his pocket and angrily threw it to the floor, crushing it under his boot. Life just wasn't worth living.

He wished he could get just one thing right in his pathetic life. Ever since he'd gotten mixed up with Tonya in Florida, it had been one disaster after another. She'd lied and said he'd beaten her, but, in reality, he'd just been defending himself. Tonya could pummel him in a fist fight any day.

The phone rang, snapping him out of his thoughts. Just as he was about to reach over and answer it, someone knocked on the door. Indecision wracked his brain. The phone won.

"Yeah?" he said rudely. "Make it fast, somebody's at my door."

"Eddie," the frantic male voice said. "Don't open the door, man. She'll kill you."

That's all Eddie needed to hear. He dropped the receiver and headed for the window, hoping it wasn't nailed shut. Dives like this had problems with customers skipping out on the bill. They didn't care about fire codes.

On the other side of the door, the black queen had heard the phone ring. Then silence. Kovik must have answered it. She listened intently for a couple of seconds, then she got out her tools and made short work of the lock. It had been easier than the service door entrance.

She flung the door open and stepped into the room with her gun drawn. After her eyes adjusted to the darkness, all she could make out was the back end of Eddie as he scampered out of the window onto the rain-spattered fire escape.

"You slippery snake!" she shouted, running toward him. "Stop!"

Eddie peered behind him and that small movement made him lose his balance. He tipped, head-first, farther out the window, his derriere perched precariously up in the air. The black queen took aim and fired, hitting him in the right cheek.

Eddie howled in pain, pulling himself onto his hands and knees. Crawling onto the steel surface of the fire escape, he found the first rung of the ladder and started descending.

The black queen was at the window, squinting down at his ashen-with-fear face. "You have ruined me, you toad," she said venomously. "They've identified you. It won't be long before they catch you, and you'll be spilling your guts. I can't have that."

"Lady, please," Eddie cried pitifully. "I'll disappear. You'll never see me again."

"That's the plan, Mr. Kovik," the black queen said with finality.

She fired, point-blank, at his chest.

The impact sent Eddie flailing backward off the slippery ladder. His last thought, as he fell two stories to the pavement, was of his sister, Kate. She deserved a better brother than him. His parents could rot for all he cared. They'd used him up, and when he could no longer play chess, they'd abandoned him. But Katie had always tried to steer him clear of trouble. She'd loved him. And this was how he repaid her devotion—by dying in the alley of a seedy hotel.

Nine

The paramedics took Mrs. Hughes, who protested all the way, to the V.A. Medical Center, the closest available hospital. However, Charles' personal physician, Dr. Lawrence Hamlin, made a house call to treat his old friend and patient. Charles thought it best to keep the shooting quiet as long as possible. He knew, from experience, that hungry newshounds staked-out area hospitals looking for stories. He hadn't had a moment's peace when his wife and son were killed nearly five years ago.

Dr. Hamlin knocked on Charles' bedroom door before entering. Charles lay propped-up in bed. Toni sat on a chair next to the bed. For the last few minutes, they'd been talking about their Berkeley days. Toni found she could talk about the past without acrimony. Charles was grateful for any time he could spend with her.

"What is this I hear about your getting shot, Charles?" Larry Hamlin said, his kind deep-brown eyes resting on Toni with curiosity.

Toni, thinking she was in the way, started to rise from her chair but Charles reached out and grasped her by the hand.

"Don't go," he said, his expression tender.

Toni looked into his face as she sat back down. It was the face she'd known thirty years ago except, in the intervening days, hours and minutes, subtle changes had been wrought. She could not help feeling cheated. She should have been with him, day-to-day, watching the boy mature into a man.

"Feel free to stay," Larry Hamlin said amiably. He was in his sixties. A black gentleman with laughing eyes and an easy-going manner. "That is if you don't mind seeing him buck naked."

Charles sat up against the pillows, eyeing his friend with a sardonic grin. "Larry," he said, "would you cut the malarky? I want you to meet Antoinette Shaw."

Larry went around the bed to shake Toni's hand. His sharp eyes rested on her face. "How are you, Miss Shaw? I recognized you the moment I saw you, although, I know you best as Serena Kincaid. I've read all your books. They are wonderful. My wife, Geri, introduced me to them. If I'd known you were going to be here, I would've brought them so you could've signed them."

"Finally," Toni said, looking into the friendly physician's eyes. "A man of taste and refinement."

Larry, remembering the reason he'd been called to Greenbriar, began his examination. The wound wasn't bleeding any longer. "Small caliber bullet," he explained to Toni and Charles. "It seared the flesh, that's why you didn't get much bleeding. That and the fact that you were fortunate an artery wasn't severed." He looked up at Charles. "How'd it happen?"

"An intruder," Charles said simply. "The authorities have been notified."

"One night, over dinner, you'll tell me the whole story," Larry said as he cleaned the wound. His eyes raked over Toni appreciatively. "I'll bring Geri and Toni/Serena can join us."

"Will you stop flirting with Toni long enough to bandage my shoulder?" Charles cried. "I'm in pain here."

Larry pressed down as he applied the bandage.

"Nonsense. There shouldn't be much pain. Don't be a baby."

"Oww . . ." Charles protested to the contrary.

"He's just looking for sympathy," Larry told Toni.

Toni sat smiling at their easy repartee. She figured they'd been friends a long time. Charles wouldn't allow just anyone to get away with quips like those.

"There," Larry said, finishing up. "Try to keep the shoulder still for the next twenty-four hours. I'll drop back in tomorrow afternoon after I leave the office. I'll recheck the wound for infection, but I don't think you have anything to worry about."

Reaching into this black bag, he produced a small bottle of pills. "You can have one of these every six hours if that 'pain' gives you problems."

He winked at Toni. "It's been a pleasure, Toni."

"Thanks for coming, Larry," Charles said.

Toni walked the doctor to the door.

"He's really all right?" she asked, concerned.

"He'll be fine," Larry assured her. His brown eyes met hers. "I'm really pleased to see you here, Toni. Charles has told me your story. How he foolishly allowed you to slip through his fingers. He's regretted that for a very long time."

Surprised by the doctor's candidness, Toni smiled. "He said that?"

"Yes, he did," Larry replied.

He went to kiss her on the cheek. "May I?"

"Of course."

He kissed her cheek.

"I saw that," Charles said from his bed. "Get out of here, Larry, or I'll tell Geri what you do on your house calls."

Laughing, Larry left.

Toni went back to sit beside Charles. "He was very nice," she said.

Charles was watching her face. He loved every spectacular angle of it.

"Toni," he said. "Why is youth wasted on the young?"

Toni regarded him with a quizzical expression. "Speak English, Chuck."

"I was so stupid when I was young," he explained. He reached for her hand and she gave it to him. "Why couldn't I have the wisdom I possess now back then? I could have saved myself a lot of heartache. I would have told my parents I didn't want their money. And you and I would've gone to New Orleans and gotten married in your family's church."

Toni went to sit on the bed, close to him. "What are you trying to say, Chuck?"

"I won't say it, Toni, because you deserve much more than I could ever give you. I see you with our girls and I marvel at the way you brought them up. You did it all by yourself. I see what a wonderful woman you are and I kick myself for not doing the right thing by you and our daughters." He paused, looking down at their clasped hands. "I wish there were something I could do to make it up to you and the girls."

"Two days ago, I would have told you there was nothing you could do to make up for your behavior, Chuck," Toni told him. "But this morning, when you were shot trying to protect your daughter, I knew that was no longer true. That you would risk your life for your child tells me more about the man you've become than all the words in the English language."

"I can't take credit for that," Charles told her, raising his eyes to hers. "I didn't think, I just reacted."

"Exactly," Toni said. "Just as you did thirty years ago when you turned your back on me. You reacted then, too. If you had known all the facts, especially that I was carrying your child, maybe you would've made a better decision."

"Don't be kind, Toni," Charles said. "It'll only get my hopes up."

"Tell me what you want, Chuck," Toni said softly, her hand gently touching his cheek.

"I want our lives back, Toni," Charles said vehemently. "I want the chance to be your husband and to be a father to our children."

Toni's heart was racing. She'd waited a long time to hear him say those words. Now she had her revenge. She could reject him. Stomp on his pitiful dreams of a reconciliation. She could make him suffer as badly as she had when he'd chosen wealth over their love.

The appropriate biting words were on the tip of her tongue when she saw them—tears. Rolling down Charles' face. She was so shocked by the sight of them that she was unable to utter a word. She didn't know what to do, so she just sat there with her arms around him.

* * *

Later that night, at dinner, an affair that was catered due to
Cook's absence, everyone expressed concern over Charles' condition. Toni sat next to him at the dinner table, Bree on the other
side. Georgie and Clay sat opposite them, along with Benjamin
and Cassie, who actually took the night off from her work at the
laboratory. The last member of the party was Anne, who had
stayed late finishing up some work for Charles and had been
invited to stay for dinner by her guilt-ridden employer. He'd made
her slave all day and wasn't about to send her home to her cold
apartment where she'd probably open a can of soup. At forty-four,
Anne had never been married and her family was in Springfield.
Charles imagined Anne didn't have much of a social life because,
although she was quite attractive, she was painfully shy. So they
dined on a variety of Italian dishes delivered to them by Charles'
favorite restaurant, Antonio's.

Bree couldn't help noticing the solicitous manner in which
her mother was treating her father. Placing a cloth napkin in his
collar. Even, at one point, wiping the corner of his mouth clean
of some spaghetti sauce.

Bree sent meaningful glances in her sister's direction, silently
advising her to observe the rapport between their parents. Georgie got her sister's signals and was, frankly, disturbed by what
she saw. Had her parents kissed and made up? Hardly. Something
was definitely wrong with this picture. She hoped her mother
wasn't planning her own unique form of punishment for her father. Make him fall in love with her all over again and *then* rip
his heart out. That was too cruel to imagine. She'd have to have
a chat with her mother later. In the meanwhile, there was a certain
detective who was on her mind. At the moment, they were playing
footsies underneath the table.

"I'd like to talk to you in your father's study after dinner," Clay
said in her ear.

"Everyone's going to begin to wonder why we spend so much
time alone in there," Georgie said, smiling at him.

"I think they already know the answer to that," Clay replied.
He took her hand and held onto it for the rest of their companions

to see. "Besides, the way your parents are looking at one another, I'd say they have other things to think about."

"What do you think is going on between those two?" Georgie asked.

"I've been meaning to tell you," Clay said in a low voice. "I had a hunch, from the beginning, that your father had unresolved business with Toni. I think he's still in love with her."

Georgie sat back on her chair, her gaze on her parents. If what Clay said was on the money, that talk she was going to have with her mother was more urgent than she'd assumed.

"I'm flying to Poughkeepsie in the morning," Ben said. Seeing Georgie's raised eyebrows, he explained, "One of our plants is under attack by an environmental group claiming the plant's run-off is polluting the ground water and causing various illnesses in the area's residents."

"Maybe you ought to take Cassie with you," Georgie suggested. "You'll need a good scientist to test the water."

"The plant has already had the water tested by qualified chemists," Ben said. "There is no trace of the chemicals they claim are polluting the ground water." He smiled at Cassie. "But I'd love for you to come."

"I'll see what I can do," Cassie replied, clearly flattered.

Cassie was twenty-nine and a native Bostonian. Her parents could trace their families all the way back to the first black residents and were what historians referred to as the Brahmin class—that class of wealthy, intellectuals who were said to be the backbone of their race. Cassie was embarrassed whenever her grandmother, who tended to hang on to the old ways, brought up the term.

She'd met Ben when he'd come to one of her parents' dinner parties. The stars must have been on her side that night because she'd had no intention of attending but her supervisor, Dr. Penhall, had come to the lab and ordered her home. He felt she'd been working too hard and reminded her of the mishaps that could occur when a scientist was fatigued.

Her mother had been aghast when she'd shown up in a cocktail dress that was two years old. Teresa Morelle religiously followed fashion trends. "Good Lord, Cassie," Teresa had said. "You really must get out of that laboratory more. Do a little shopping every now and then."

That was when Ben had walked up and rescued her from her mother's demeaning appraisal.

"I think she looks lovely," he'd said, offering Cassie his hand. "I'm Ben Waters. You must be Cassandra."

Teresa Morelle didn't have anything to say after that. Her daughter had caught the eye of the most eligible bachelor in Boston.

She and Ben made an attractive couple. She was five-six to his six feet. Where he was golden-brown complexioned, her skin was a dark, rich brown with red undertones. Her black hair was long and thick and she wore it swept back from her high-cheekboned face. Tonight, however, she'd worn it down and it fell to her shoulders in soft curls. Ben was happy he'd taken Georgie's suggestion and invited her over to dine with them.

"Anne, would you give me the number of a reputable cab company?" Bree asked her father's personal assistant.

Anne had been lost in her own thoughts. Absently pushing her food around on her plate all night, she didn't appear to have much of an appetite.

She raised her brown eyes to meet Bree's. "What?"

"A cab company," Bree said. "I need a number of a good company."

"Carrington will take you anywhere you want to go," Anne told her. "Just give him a call. He lives above the garage."

"Sometimes I'd just like to get away on my own," Bree said. "I'm beginning to feel like a prisoner in this big house. I don't want the chauffeur to squire me around town. I want to just go, you understand?"

Anne smiled. "Of course. There is a list of reliable companies on the bulletin board in the kitchen. Occasionally, the staff has need of them."

"Thank you, Anne," Bree said, hoping she hadn't piqued Anne's curiosity with her request. She was planning to blow this joint on Thursday night if the case wasn't wrapped-up by then.

And she didn't want her mother or her sister to get wind of her plans until it was too late to stop her. She was going to make that audition.

Ari had sent her the script via FedEx, and it was everything she'd ever wanted in a role. The role she would be auditioning for, that of the princess, Romalia, would require her to explore every facet of her emotions. Romalia was a futuristic monarch who had seen her home planet invaded by other-worldly marauders. It was up to her to save her people and it would take all her mental, physical and spiritual powers to do it.

The role would be a challenge for Bree. She needed the change of scenery because she was still reeling from her break-up with Pierre. Working on a big project like *Dark Universe* would be just the diversion to get her back in the swing of things. Working with Peter Hogan and Dominic Solomon couldn't hurt either. They were two of Hollywood's most eligible bachelors.

"What does a single girl do in Boston on a Saturday night?" Bree asked Anne brightly.

"Oh, there's so much to do in Boston," Anne said, smiling. "We have the opera. The theater. The ballet. Great restaurants. What are your interests, dear? I'm sure we can come up with something."

Bree sighed. Could you come up with a decent male for me? she thought doubtfully. "Have you ever been to a club, Anne?" she asked her shy companion.

"Oh Lord, no," Anne said looking wistful. "I wouldn't know what to do in a club."

"But I bet you'd like to find out, wouldn't you?" Bree said, a mischievous gleam in her light-brown eyes. "If my foot wasn't injured, we'd go boogie until the cows came home, Anne."

Anne laughed. "With my luck with men, that's just what I'd bring home afterward, something that looked like a cow."

"Get off it," Bree said. "You're an attractive woman."

"I'm too reserved," Anne said. "Most men give up before they get through all my layers. They go on to someone easier to get to know."

"Then they don't deserve you," Bree told her. "You've got to tell yourself you're the most beautiful, most desirable woman on earth, and anyone who can't see that needs glasses."

Anne giggled delightedly.

"Is that how you maintain your alluring image?"

"That and the magic of a Hollywood make-up artist," Bree confided with a grin.

The phone rang and Maggie answered it. She brought the cordless phone to the table and handed it to Clay.

"It's a Detective Bendini," she said.

Everyone at the table fell silent as Clay spoke into the phone. "Yeah, John?"

"I think we may have a break in your case, buddy," John told him. "The V.A. Medical Center. Get down here, pronto."

"Will do," Clay replied.

He hung up and looked into Georgie's questioning eyes. "John thinks he has something. I've got to go."

"I'm going with you," Georgie said at once.

"All right," Clay said. To Charles and Toni, he said, "We'll fill you in when we return."

He and Georgie left the table.

"I should be going, too," Cassie announced soon afterward. "I have to get a few things done before our flight tomorrow. What time?"

"Ten," Ben told her, rising to walk her to the door. "I'll pick you up."

Maggie was there to hand Cassie her wool coat.

"Thank you, Maggie," Cassie said, smiling at the young maid.

"Ma'am," Maggie said. She went back to the kitchen where she and the other maid, Kate, were engaged in a fierce game of bid whist, awaiting the time when the diners would be finished with their meals and she and Kate could clean up and then retire for the night.

Ben kissed Cassie good night after he'd seen her to her car, then he went back inside to talk to his uncle. They needed to plan their strategy for tomorrow's meeting in Poughkeepsie. They had already gone over it, but they liked to go over last minute details together before a major meeting. Ben smiled to himself. Imagine, his uncle and Toni Shaw falling in love all over again. The signs were unmistakable. He was happy for Uncle. He'd had enough tragedy in his lifetime. Now it was time again for a little happiness.

By the time he returned from seeing Cassie off, his uncle and Toni had retired to the library. He was told this by Bree who said she was going upstairs to get Pierre to take him for his nightly walk. Anne had already said her good nights and departed.

Ben stood looking after Bree as she ascended the staircase. There was something about her eyes that reminded him of . . . No, Bree had told him her father was an actor who lived and worked around San Francisco. He had to stop allowing his imagination to run wild.

Pierre leapt into Bree's arms the moment she opened her room door.

"Hello, precious. Miss me?" Bree said. "Ready for your nightly stroll? We can both walk off a few pounds. I ate like there was no tomorrow. *Two* servings of spaghetti." She shook her head disdainfully. "José is going to have a field day with me. And knowing that tyrant, he's going to enjoy every minute of it."

Putting Pierre back on the floor, she opened the door and the minuscule pooch ran outside. He knew the way now. But he liked the scenic route. First, he had to visit every room whose door sat open. It was a big house and his curiosity knew no bounds. Finally, after Pierre had explored each room on the first floor, Bree picked him up. "Listen, monsieur le dog, I don't have all night. I have lines to memorize."

Once outside, she set him back down.

Pierre ran in the direction of his favorite clump of trees where he marked his territory.

Bree was standing, looking up at the night sky, which was sprinkled with stars, when she heard raised voices.

Initially, she thought they were coming from the house, but then, after a few seconds of listening, she realized the shouting was coming from the direction of the garage. Recalling that Anne told her Carrington lived over the garage, Bree figured he'd gotten into an argument with a late visitor.

Peering in the direction of the voices, she thought she recognized the rear end of Anne's late model Volvo. Curious, she began walking toward the car. Maybe Anne wasn't as innocent as she let on. Not if she and Carrington were yelling at each other like that. It sounded like they were really getting into it. You didn't argue with a casual acquaintance with such ferocity.

It *was* Anne's champagne-colored Volvo.

Enjoying the adventure, Bree tiptoed closer, until she was directly underneath the picture window, which had been left ajar, of the garage apartment Carrington was said to inhabit. Standing in the shadows, she eavesdropped.

"I told you not to come here anymore," a male voice, probably Carrington's, said. "You've said there's nothing between us, so why come here?"

"I need your help!" a female voice, presumably Anne's, screeched. "If not for you, I . . ."

"If you had listened to me, we'd be far away from here now," Carrington interrupted her. His voice got lower, more intimate. "We could still go away together."

There was silence and then Anne said, "You're refusing to help me?"

"I love you, but I won't be used by you any longer," Carrington said, sounding defeated. "I'll be out of here by morning."

"You'd leave me alone?" Anne said incredulously.

"The decision was always yours," Carrington said sadly.

The next sound Bree heard was that of a door slamming and footsteps descending the garage-apartment's outside steps.

Bree hung back in the shadows until she heard Anne get into her car and speed off. Then, she swiftly ran back to where she'd left Pierre. She couldn't wait to tell Georgie about Anne's conversation with Carrington. Anne had apparently had an affair with the big, good-looking driver. But now he was fed up with being just a source of pleasure. He wanted more and Anne didn't. At least that's what she made of the conversation.

She found Pierre chasing his tail on the front lawn. Silly dog, she thought. You'll never catch it. But, perhaps, that was the point. It was a game Pierre enjoyed season-in-and-season-out.

He never tired of it. Who was she to knock his fun? Looking down to make sure Pierre hadn't left any surprises on the lawn, she sat and watched the stars.

The V.A. Medical Center was in Roxbury. It took Clay half an hour to drive there and throughout the drive, he was fielding questions from Georgie.

"Why do you think he wants to see you?" she asked as soon as they turned off of Greenbriar's drive onto the highway.

"It must be something important," he told her. "John wouldn't have me come all the way across town if it wasn't."

That wasn't enough to satisfy her curiosity.

"Do you think they caught up with Kovik and he decided to shoot his way out?"

"You've been watching too many Jimmy Cagney movies," Clay said lightly, smiling at her naivete. "Kovik is the type who'd run like a scared rabbit if he found himself cornered. Believe me, he isn't a tough guy."

"And how did you come to that conclusion?" Georgie wanted to know. She moved closer to him on the seat in the Explorer.

"His rap sheet speaks for itself," Clay explained. "He has a history of beating up women. Burglary. Car theft. Experience tells me he isn't the 'you'll-never-take-me-alive' type. Kovik is a scab on the butt of society. A scab who'd like to live to see another day."

"Why the hospital?" Georgie inquired. "They must have wounded him. Or maybe he's dead, and you have to identify the body. I've never been to a morgue before."

"You haven't missed anything," Clay assured her. He frowned. He hoped he wasn't going to have to identify Kovik's body.

At the information desk of the V.A. Medical Center, Clay asked for Detective Bendini and was instructed to go to the critical care unit down the hall.

"Press the buzzer on the outside of the double doors," the middle-aged black nurse told him. "Detective Bendini will come outside."

"Critical care," Georgie said. "That's a step up from intensive care, isn't it? Maybe Kovik is going to survive after all."

"Stop making assumptions, Georgette," Clay ordered her briskly as they followed the arrows to the critical care unit. He pressed the button outside the double doors and a couple of minutes later, John appeared.

He looked pretty jolly considering where he was. He pumped Clay's hand. "Clay." His brown eyes rested on Georgie. Clay hastily introduced them.

"Miss Shaw, Clay's description of you pales in comparison to your actual presence," John said gallantly.

"Don't leave me in suspense, John," Clay said, frustrated. "Why have you brought us down here?"

John smiled slowly, obviously enjoying the mystery he was creating with his silence. He let it drag out a few seconds longer, until Clay's face had reached the thunderous phase, then he spoke: "We've got Kovik. He was shot by the woman he agreed to do the hit for . . ."

"Woman?" Clay said impatiently.

"She shot him, point-blank, in the chest," John informed them.

"And he survived that?" Georgie said in disbelief.

John removed a heavy gold chain from his pocket. He held it up for them to inspect. It was a St. Christopher medal with a dent in it the size of a small caliber bullet. "He kept rambling on about how his sister, Katie, gave him this years ago and told him to always wear it close to his heart, and it would always lead him back to her." John laughed. "I guess she was right. It saved the weasel's life."

"Can we talk to him, John? Did he give you a description of the woman?" Clay asked.

"It's a no-go on seeing him. He's out like a light. The painkillers they gave him knocked him slam out. But I'll tell you everything he said about the black queen. That's what he calls her."

"Yeah?" Clay prompted him.

"She's a black woman, around five-six. He never saw her face clearly. She always wore a scarf and dark glasses."

"Age?" Clay asked.

"He couldn't tell."

"An accent?" Georgie put in, hopefully.

"No noticeable accent. Educated, good elocution. A classy dame, he said. That is until she started shooting at him."

"Then I suppose we've got two choices," Georgie deduced.

Clay nodded in agreement. "Yeah, from that description and taking into account that it's someone close to your father, it's either Anne or Lillie."

Clay thanked John for his help and he and Georgie turned to leave.

"Hey, Georgie," John said. "How long are you going to be in our fair city?"

"That depends," Georgie said, looking at Clay.

"In that case," John called, "make him bring you by to meet Margarite and the kids. We'll throw some steaks on the grill."

"What did I tell you about matchmaking?" Clay said, irritated. He smiled at Georgie. "You don't have to answer that joker."

"It's a date," Georgie told John.

"All right!" John exclaimed and went back to the critical care unit.

"Listen to me, Clayton Knight," Georgie said as they walked toward the exit. "What I feel for you isn't a crisis crush. And, unless you want me to, I'm not going to vanish from your life once this case is solved."

They stood on the sidewalk in front of the hospital. It was around thirty degrees out and there was a brisk wind besides. Clay pulled Georgie into his arms, his big duster enveloping the both of them.

She lay her head on his chest. "She shot him," she said. "Imagine how desperate she would have to be in order to do that."

"It was survival, Frisco," Clay told her. He gently rubbed her back. "Come on let's get out of this weather."

"We could go to your place," Georgie said sultrily, her dark eyes looking deeply into his with unspoken desire.

"You're safer at the mansion," Clay told her, ever the vigilant bodyguard.

"A hotel?"

"I'm not taking you to a hotel, no matter how elegant," Clay told her as if it was the most ridiculous notion. "Hotels are for trysts. I respect you too much for that."

"Kiss me then," Georgie said. "Kiss me good and kiss me long."

Clay bent his head and kissed her as she'd asked him to. Their arms wrapped around one another and they succumbed to the magic that was new love. The rest of the world ceased to exist for them and though the weather was cold outside, they generated enough heat between them to keep them warm.

"Get a room!" someone yelled from a passing car.

Georgie and Clay parted, looked at each other and burst out laughing. Then they clasped hands and sprinted to the waiting Explorer to begin the drive back to Greenbriar.

Bree was in the library with her parents running her lines with Benjamin, who was really getting into his role as Khan, Romalia's nemesis and the role Peter Hogan was slated to play.

"I'll never bow to you!" Bree shouted in her most proud tones. Romalia was royalty, after all.

"If you want to save your world, you will not only bow to me," Benjamin spoke for the nefarious Khan, "but you will be my consort."

"I'll see you dead first," the Romalia character responded. "And then," Bree told her rapt audience, "there is a sword fight."

Everyone, save Charles whose right shoulder was bandaged, applauded.

Bree bowed as though she'd just turned in a superlative performance as Ophelia in Hamlet. "Thank you, thank you," she cried, hamming it up.

She walked over to Georgie and Clay who'd sat down on the love seat closest to the fireplace.

"I've got something to tell you guys," she said anxiously.

"What is it?" Clay said.

Bree went on to recount the argument she'd overheard between Anne and Carrington. With dramatic license, of course.

When she was finished, Georgie looked at Clay and said, "What do you suppose she needed his help with?"

Her delicate eyebrows arched questioningly as she continued to watch Clay.

"Carrington saying he'd be gone by morning could mean that things are getting too hot for him around here and he wants to split before we're on to him. *Or,* as Bree believes, it could be an argument between ex-lovers and Carrington's just getting out so he doesn't have to face Anne every day," Clay said.

"There's one way to find out," Georgie suggested, looking as if she was the cat who'd swallowed the canary.

Ten

William Carrington didn't even make it out of his apartment at 12:40 a.m. Sunday morning. Clay and Georgie had had the garage-apartment under surveillance ever since Bree told them about Carrington's conversation with Anne. If necessary, Alec O'Hara would have taken over at three.

"Going somewhere, Carrington?" Clay inquired, appearing in the doorway.

Carrington looked as if he'd seen a ghost. He stumbled backward, his big, square body tense.

The huge suitcase he was carrying dropped to the wooden floor with a loud thud. Breathing hard, he stuttered, "W . . . what are you doing here, Mr. Knight? Can I help you with something?"

Georgie walked into the apartment, flipping on the light switch next to the door as she did so.

"Shall we sit down?" she asked politely.

Carrington sat down hard on the couch, his eyes on first Clay, then Georgie. He squirmed nervously. Georgie sat on the chair opposite him while Clay remained standing, blocking the exit should Carrington decide to bolt.

"Calm down, Mr. Carrington," Georgie said quietly. She hoped that she and Clay could question the chauffeur without resorting to threats. He'd shown his hand by trying to abscond in the middle of the night. Still, the only evidence they had was hearsay and Georgie knew that wouldn't hold up in a court of law. They needed concrete proof that Anne was the person behind the three attempts on her life and Carrington could be their best hope of acquiring that proof.

"We'd just like to ask you a few easy questions," Georgie told him. "Nothing you probably wouldn't be glad to get off your chest."

Carrington was six-feet-six, four inches taller than Clay. He had a beefy block head on a body made strong by hard work. He looked tough, but Georgie, who'd interviewed many criminals in her line of work, would put him in the category of the petty criminal, not the hardened variety.

A talk with John revealed he'd spent two years in Joliet Prison in Illinois for burglary. That was twelve years ago. Since then, he'd kept his record clean. Coincidentally, his hometown was Springfield Massachusetts; that was his connection to Anne. Georgie would be willing to wager that they'd been romantically involved in Springfield before coming to Boston and Greenbriar.

Carrington looked up at her at last. "Ask," he said with a belligerent tone. "But I ain't promising I'll answer."

"Why were you leaving like a thief in the night?" Clay asked, just as bellicosely. He didn't like Carrington's attitude.

"It's a free country, ain't it?" Carrington replied tersely. His dark eyes sent daggers at Clay.

"How long have you known Anne Ballentine?" Georgie asked coldly. She figured Carrington had set the tone for their conversation. If he wanted aggression, she could most definitely give it to him. She was itching for a good fight, anyway. She missed the courtroom.

"Listen . . ." Carrington began ominously. He started to rise and Georgie shot up in an instant and shoved him back down.

"No, *you* listen," she said, up in his face. "You could spend five years in the Massachusetts State prison system for aiding and abetting Anne in the commitment of a crime. Your friend, Eddie Kovik, is *dead*. Shot down by Anne because he bungled my murder three times. She had to get rid of him before he got caught and identified her—and you. You're the one who introduced Anne to Kovik, aren't you? We have witnesses who can place you at Clancy's on several different occasions. Maybe you

didn't know what Anne had in mind when you turned her on to
Kovik. Still, you're an accessory."

Georgie could tell by the horrified expression on William Carrington's face that she'd hit the nail on the head. She had him
sweating now.

"The trouble was: Kovik was a liar and a braggart. He made
up a resumé he didn't possess. He duped you both about his
proficiency as a killer, but by that time, it was too late. Anne was
stuck with the Jerry Lewis of assassins. Kovik couldn't hit the
side of a barn with a tank. Am I close, Carrington?"

She paused to stare into his eyes. Her dark, almost black, eyes
boring into his with the intensity of a cobra about to strike. That
look had made the most fearsome opponent relieved to escape
her presence after she'd trounced him in court.

"She didn't know what she was doing," Carrington said in a
low voice. He shifted in his chair. "She's obsessed with her son.
She's been wanting to confess she's his mother for years. It's all
she lives for. I guess she thought that with you out of the way,
all her plans of living happily ever after as a Waters would fall
into place. I tried to talk her out of it, but nothing I said made
any difference whatsoever."

Clay and Georgie's eyes met across the room as the meaning
of Carrington's words dawned on them.

"Anne is Benjamin's mother!" she exclaimed.

Carrington nodded. "She had him when she was fourteen. Her
parents made her give him up for adoption. She never forgot him.
And she never stopped searching for him until she found him
ten years ago."

"When she came to work for Charles," Clay put in.

Carrington looked down at his big hands, a sad expression in
his dark brown eyes. "I knew all about Anne's past because we
grew up together in Springfield. When I came to Boston back
in eighty-seven, we met by chance, in the supermarket of all
places. We started talking. She knew I'd served time and how
hard it is for an ex-con to find a job. She offered to try to get me
on here. She'd just started, but Mr. and Mrs. Waters liked her.

They took her word for it when she told them I was a reputable character."

He paused, looking at Georgie. "Actually, she told them the truth because I'd sworn never to commit another crime. All I wanted was the chance to redeem myself. A decent job, a decent place to live. Anyway, after I got on here, Anne and I started seeing one another secretly. She had an image to maintain. She didn't want it to be known she was the chauffeur's woman. I loved her. I still love her."

"Yet you sent her to Kovik," Georgie said.

"She was like a woman possessed. She'd fallen in love with Mr. Waters. In her mind, she had it all figured out. She would foil your father's plans of ever having another heir. He would turn to her for comfort and then she would reveal that she was Benjamin's birth mother and they'd all live here at Greenbriar. I tried to tell her her plan was doomed to failure, but she wouldn't listen." He wrung his hands nervously. "She was going to have the perfect family or die trying."

"Do you know who Benjamin's father is?" Clay asked.

"She would never say," Carrington replied. "But when she conceived, the rumor in Springfield was that it was the son of the family her mother, who was a maid, worked for—the Covingtons. Brant was his name."

This time it was Clay who was privy to information Georgie was in the dark about.

"Brant Covington heads the biggest textiles-manufacturing firm in Massachusetts. The last thing I heard about him, he was thinking of running for the senate."

Georgie sat back down on the chair. She'd heard enough for one night. She'd heard enough secrets the last few days to hold her for the rest of her natural life. She blew air between her lips and settled back on the chair. Looking at Carrington, she said, "You know Anne better than anyone else here. What do you think she'll do next? Has she gone over the edge or do you think we could make her see reason and turn herself in?"

Carrington shook his head regrettably. "The way she carried on last night, I don't know. She's already killed once . . ."

"We were just bluffing about Kovik," Clay told him. "Anne didn't kill him, she only wounded him. He'll be all right."

Carrington breathed a sigh of relief. "Thank God. I—I've got to go to her. Maybe if she knows he isn't dead, she'll turn herself in."

Georgie and Clay exchanged glances. Georgie nodded in the affirmative.

"Okay," Clay said. "We'll go together."

"But if she sees you two, she'll think I've given her away," Carrington said, trying to reason with them.

"We'll stay out of sight," Clay told him. "And if she turns violent, we'll be there to diffuse the situation."

"Okay," Carrington agreed. He didn't see that he had any choice in the matter. He'd already confessed to being Anne's confidante. But, if they hurried, perhaps they could save Anne from doing anymore harm, either to someone else or to herself. In her present state of mind, if she should find out that Eddie Kovik was still alive, she might do something drastic like turning the gun on herself and pulling the trigger.

Anne couldn't sleep. She lay in bed flipping from channel to channel on the television, her mind in fast-forward. How did she think she'd get away with it, anyway? All she had been thinking of was Benjamin. How would his life be affected if Charles brought in Georgette? And yesterday, after hacking into Charles' private files by guessing that his code word was "Chuck" for his son, she learned that Briane was also his daughter. She and Georgette were twins. Charles had been so elated to find his children, he couldn't resist expressing his joy in his private journal. Anne would have known Bree was his without that piece of evidence, though. Bree had his eyes. She also had his spirit.

Suddenly, as she paused on a local station, the anchorperson, a too cheery woman called Wendy Hitemann, began talking about a man who'd fallen two stories from the historic Parliament Hotel in Roxbury. Anne sat up in bed, swinging her legs onto the floor and rising. She stood in front of the set, her attention riveted to Wendy Hitemann's expertly made-up face.

"The unidentified man," Wendy reported, "is said to have sustained a gunshot wound in his right buttock. He also received cuts and bruises from his fall. He is listed in stable condition and is expected to make a full recovery. Back to you, Jim."

Anne switched off the set. That little snake was alive. Alive. Why hadn't she gone downstairs and checked for a pulse after she'd shot him? And how could he have survived a shot to the chest at such close range?

None of that mattered now. He was alive. He'd seen her face. The police could be on the way to her home right this minute. She had to get out. She ran to her closet and hastily pulled a few items of clothing off hangers and tossed them into a carry-on bag. She didn't have time to pack properly. This done, she hurried into a slack suit and a pair of flats. Looking down at the shoes, she realized they didn't match her suit. For the first time in her life, she didn't give a damn.

As she tore out of her mid-town condominium with only her purse and the carry-on bag, she knew where she would go. But first, she had a few things to take care of before leaving town.

She purposefully side-swiped another car as she sped out of the parking lot. She needed witnesses who would testify to the fact that she'd been driving like a maniac. Out on the highway, she drove too fast, passing every car in front of her. She had other drivers blaring their horns at her and giving her the finger.

She only slowed down a little as she got in the vicinity of the bay. She could smell the sea air and it reminded her of the time, when she was fourteen, that her mother had taken her to live with her great aunt, Della, in the coastal town of Gloucester. It was there that she gave birth to Benjamin. She had begged her mother to let her keep him. But her mother had said a young girl like her had her whole life ahead of her. If she gave this baby up for adoption, she had a better chance of one day getting married and having all the children she desired.

Anne had proven her mother wrong, though. She'd never married. Her life had been consumed with her search for her baby.

It was ironic. If her mother had let her keep her child, none of this would have happened. Anne would have been content with her life. Benjamin would have had a loving mother, instead of that fashion-conscious bird brain, Victoria Waters. Victoria couldn't be inconvenienced by a pregnancy. She couldn't have that reed-thin body stretched out of shape for nine months. Therefore, she'd had Benjamin, Sr. buy her a son—a son with pale golden-brown skin to match her own. And Benjamin, who'd been the product of a black mother and a white father, suited her needs.

Anne slowed the Volvo at the wharf. Looking around her, she was pleased to see only a few boats anchored in the bay. She got out of the car, leaving it in neutral. Throwing her purse and bag off to the side, she gave the car a shove and gravity did the rest. The car coasted into the bay. She ran to scoop up her belongings and hid in the shadows of a public restroom nearby. She expected the noise the car made as it hit the water would awaken the residents of the yachts anchored in the bay. Sure enough, she saw lights appear in two of the luxury boats. On one of them, a man and a woman came on deck wearing pajamas. She thought she heard the man say, "Oh my God, a car just went off the ramp into the water."

Anne smiled with satisfaction. It would take them days to drag the bay for her body. By the time they concluded that she hadn't been in the car when it went off the ramp, she'd be long gone.

Georgie and Clay observed from the Explorer as Carrington knocked repeatedly on the door of Anne's condominium. No answer. They weren't surprised when Carrington reached into his pocket and retrieved his keys. He unlocked Anne's door and walked inside.

"You don't suppose she'd kill herself?" Georgie wondered aloud.

"I don't know. She's definitely unbalanced," Clay said.

Their curiosity was satisfied when, after a few minutes inside,

Carrington came back to the car. "She took off," he told them. "Looks like she threw a few things in a bag and left in a hurry."

"Get in," Clay said brusquely.

Carrington got in and Clay pulled away from the curb.

"Where do you think she'd go?" Georgie asked Carrington.

Carrington hunched his great shoulders. "I don't know. She wouldn't go to her mother. That's the first place the authorities would look. She has no close friends. I don't know, I just don't know."

"Well think!" Clay suggested strongly. "We've got to find her before she harms anyone else."

"Would she go to the hospital to finish Kovik off?" Georgie proposed. Turning around to look Carrington in the face, she added, "You said she might try something rash if she found out he was still alive. Conceivably, the local television stations could have run a late news story about the shooting."

"True," Clay said. "But what would she gain by going to the hospital to finish the job? She could end up getting caught." He reached down for the cellular phone and handed it to Georgie. "Here. Call John. Tell him what you suspect. He probably already has a man at the hospital. He can be on the lookout for her." He gave her the number and Georgie dialed.

John's voice was groggy with sleep when he answered. Georgie quickly ran down the events of the evening for him.

"Your father's personal assistant?" John said incredulously. "It's always someone close. Okay, we'll cover the hospital. I'll also get someone on the airport and bus stations, just in case."

Georgie hung up. "The hospital's covered."

"Then we go back to the mansion," Clay said. Meeting Carrington's eyes in the rearview mirror, he said, "That is, if we can trust you not to skip town."

"I'm not going anywhere," Carrington said, resignedly. "I just want to find Anne and get her some help."

They rode in silence the rest of the way to Greenbriar.

* * *

Anne had a two mile hike back into town where she hailed a cab and had the driver take her to the Greyhound bus station. A police car sat idling in front of the station, so Anne had the driver take her to the hotel a few blocks down from the terminal. She walked back to the bus station and walked right past the young officer as he was talking into his radio.

"Good evening officer," she greeted him brightly.

The baby-faced officer nodded curtly in her direction. "Ma'am."

Anne strolled into the station and purchased a seat on the next bus heading to a large city.

"That would be the two-ten to Worcester," the clerk told her.

Anne paid in cash and then went to the cash machine in the station and withdrew the maximum amount. She wasn't prepared to flee in the middle of the night. If she made it to Worcester, she'd use her American Express card to buy an airline ticket. From that point, she didn't care if the authorities were able to trace her movements or not. All her dreams were shattered and careful scheming had brought her to this: being a fugitive. It didn't matter. If she couldn't be a mother to Benjamin, she had no reason to live.

She sat down on one of the bright orange hard plastic chairs which were bolted to the floor. Every bus station she'd ever been in, and she'd been in plenty, boasted this garish decor. Loud plastic chairs, harsh lighting, the stench of urine. Crying babies. Transients roaming the terminal looking for a handout or the chance to steal something. She placed her purse between her side and the chair's side and her carry-on bag served as a pillow beneath her head. If anyone tried to grab it, even if she drifted off, she'd awaken instantly. She had no intention of drifting off, but she was so tired that there was the possibility she might.

She wasn't sitting there fifteen minutes before an elderly man in a ragged coat and holes in his shoes shuffled over to her. "Can you spare a little loose change for a cup of coffee, lady?"

Anne reached into her purse and gave him a dollar. "Don't bother me again," she warned him. "I'd like to get some rest."

The man grinned, revealing discolored teeth. "You bet," he said happily. "Thank you, lady. God bless you."

God bless you. Anne sighed and closed her eyes. If God wanted to bless her, He should have done it thirty years ago. It was too late for that now.

Charles, Toni and Bree were all anxiously awaiting Georgie and Clay's return. They sat in the library as Clay recounted the events of the last couple of hours, beginning with Carrington's confession. They'd left Carrington at his apartment. Otherwise, Charles might have tried to strangle him, as he was so furious when he learned of Carrington's involvement.

"So, Anne is on the run," Charles said, shaking his head gravely. "I would never have thought she could be guilty of such perfidy."

He paced the floor, looking quite worn-out. Toni had tried to convince him to go to bed, but he'd insisted on waiting up with her.

"You haven't heard the most shocking news yet," Georgie told her father. She went to him and caught him by the shoulders, looking him in the eyes. "Anne was motivated to do away with me to insure that her son inherited the bulk of your estate upon your death."

Charles frowned. "You mean Anne is Benjamin's mother?"

"It appears so," Georgie said. "According to Carrington, she has been trying to work up the nerve to confess to Benjamin that she's his mother."

Charles gratefully sank onto the nearest chair. "I can't believe I trusted Anne with every detail of my life. No wonder the culprit was always one step ahead of us. The woman had access to everything. I've been such a fool!"

Georgie placed her arm about his shoulders in sympathy.

"It's totally bonkers," Bree said from her seat next to her mother. "Anne seemed like such a levelheaded person."

"That's what's so frightening about all of this," Toni said. "Anne appears as rational as any of us."

The phone rang.

"Will this night ever end?" Toni cried.

Clay looked up at Charles. "May I?"

"Please do," Charles assented.

"Hello?"

"Clay. John here. Sorry to bother you so late, but I know you'll want to hear this. We got several phone calls about a crazed driver over near Dorchester Heights. When a couple of our guys got over there, a man flagged them down and told them he saw a car go into the bay. Anyway, one of the earlier phone calls was from a guy who lives in the same complex where Anne Ballentine has her condominium. He says she ran into his car, caused quite a bit of damage and kept going. He knows it was her because he's been her neighbor for the last three years. He says he'd know her Volvo anywhere."

"You think she panicked and went into the bay in an escape attempt?" Clay asked. John was a good detective, but sometimes he loved the sound of his own voice. Clay wanted to get to the point.

"Wait a minute," John told him. "Another caller wrote down the tag number of the vehicle that nearly caused an accident because of reckless driving. The number belongs to Anne Ballentine."

"So you do think she went into the bay," Clay said, glad his pal had finally gotten to the point.

"That's the way it looks. We can't get anyone down there until morning. And it'll probably be days before her body floats to the surface."

"John, do you have to be so graphic?" Clay protested.

"You've gotten soft since leaving the force, buddy," John laughed. "Anyway, it looks as though your case is solved. If those salvage guys are on the ball, we may have some physical evidence for you in a couple of days. Until then, we don't know a thing."

"All right," Clay said, sighing. "Thanks for your help, John."

All eyes in the room were on him.

"John thinks Anne drove her car into the bay."

"Suicide?" Toni said in disbelief. She felt sick to her stomach. "That poor woman."

"Yes," Bree said. She turned to her mother and warmly placed her arms around her. "In a way, I feel sorry for her. She was so young when she had her son wrenched from her arms. Then she spent the better part of her life looking for him and never got the chance to claim him."

"Let's not lose sight of the fact that she tried to have your sister killed," Clay said, refusing to allow sympathy to overshadow reality. "Anne was a wounded soul, for sure, but she was also a very dangerous woman. I'm just glad she's not still out there plotting her revenge."

They all agreed with his reasoning.

Soon afterward, Toni said good night, pleading a headache which she knew to be caused by fatigue. Charles insisted on walking her upstairs.

Bree also turned in, leaving Clay and Georgie alone in the library.

"Well," Georgie said, turning into his arms. "It's over and we all survived. I'd say you've done a great job, Boston."

Clay pulled her into his arms. "I have a feeling of incompleteness about this, Frisco."

They hugged tightly.

"You don't think she could have survived?" Georgie asked, looking up into his hazel eyes.

Clay reached up to smooth a few errant braids behind her ear. "I know that if I wanted to buy myself time, I'd fake my death. No one would be looking for me, and I could make a clean getaway."

"Yes, but given her state of mind," Georgie proposed, "would she have thought of such an elaborate plan?"

"We'll have to wait until they drag the bay to find out," Clay told her. "And that, my dear, is the beauty of the plan. She could be half way around the world by the time that's done."

Georgie tiptoed and kissed his mouth. "Clay, I'm so tired of this case. Can we just assume, for the night, that it's over?"

Clay smiled down into her lovely face. "You're tired. I'll walk you to your room."

They left the library arm-in-arm, with Georgie leaning on his strong shoulder. She was tired, but she was also eager to put the case behind them. She wanted to spend time with Clay without his constant vigil as her bodyguard. She wanted them to experience each other as just a man and a woman.

At her bedroom door, she put her arms around his neck and said, "See you in the morning, Boston."

Clay smiled. "I doubt if I'll be able to sleep after listening to John's mouth tonight."

"I could rock you to sleep," Georgie said sultrily.

"Not under your father's roof, you won't," Clay told her. But the offer was enticing.

"You and your rules," Georgie said, pouting. "Not in a hotel. Not under my father's roof. Are there any more places you won't . . ."

She didn't get the opportunity to finish her sentence because Clay's mouth was covering hers in a deep, soul-stirring kiss.

"Your place or mine, Frisco," he said when he raised his head. "That way, we can talk all night without any interruptions. I can give you a back rub, and we can sip good wine, and I can watch the sunrise reflected in your eyes."

The way she felt at the moment, Georgie knew she would agree to anything he said. No man had ever kissed her with such abandon, such whole-hearted sensuality. If he could make her feel like she was floating with just a kiss, his love-making would be her undoing.

"All right," she murmured dazedly. "Your place or mine." She sighed as she reached behind her and turned the doorknob. "Good night."

"Good night," Clay said. He waited until she'd gone inside and closed the door behind her before going next door to his room.

Georgie languidly removed her clothes, folding them and placing them on the chair next to the bed. Reaching under her pillow, she got her nightgown and slipped the silken material over her head. At least her last memory of the night was a pleasant one. She'd dream about making love to Clay instead of drowning in Dorchester Bay as poor Anne had done.

On Monday morning, Charles awoke with his mind set on tying up loose ends. The first order of business was to deal with Carrington. Since Anne had met such an ignoble end, he'd decided to show mercy to his chauffeur who had apparently acted out of misplaced devotion to Anne.

Carrington strode into Charles' office with his head lowered, afraid to meet his employer's gaze. He stood stiffly.

"Mr. Waters, sir, I'm very sorry for playing a part in all of this. I tried to talk her out of it. I should have gotten her some help. She might be alive today if I'd . . ." His voice broke.

"We haven't notified the police of your involvement, Carrington," Charles said bluntly as he stood. "This may prove to be bad judgment on my part, but I'm not going to press charges against you. Anne's gone and is beyond judgment. I hope that you will be able to one day come to terms with what you've done, Carrington. Over the years, I've come to think of you as an honorable man. A decent fellow. I was sorry to learn of your part in this."

Carrington met Charles' gaze. "You can't begin to imagine how awful I feel sir. I've spoiled ten years of exemplary behavior with my silence. If I'd come to you when Anne hatched her plan, all of this could have been avoided. I deserve whatever punishment that's coming to me."

"I'm letting you go, Carrington," Charles said. There was regret in his deep set eyes. "Aside from this incident, you've been a remarkable employee, but I could never trust you again. It was my *daughter* that Anne wanted to dispose of and, by God man, you stood by and did nothing to prevent it. In a court of law, you're also liable." Muscles worked in Charles' jaw as he continued. "But, in return for your confession and cooperation last night, I'm not going to inform the police. Go now, before I change my mind."

Carrington left the room without uttering another word. He had expected to be sent to jail for his collusion. At least now, he had the chance at a life. He'd saved practically his entire salary for the last ten years. He could move to another state and maybe open that garage he'd been dreaming of all these years. His nest egg should be a pretty good down payment on a nice piece of property. His mind was on Anne as he walked down the hallway to the front door. He wondered why he wasn't good enough for her. They could have had a happy life together if she could've given up her obsession with being recognized as Benjamin's mother. Now she was gone forever. He was sad to his very core.

Charles' next task took a bit more finesse.

"I saw it coming, Charles," Lillie said, her eyes meeting his. She stood next to his desk in his office, looking elegantly turned out in a dark aquamarine silk pantsuit. Her light-brown eyes were demur. "I realize you and I had an understanding. We both went into our relationship with our eyes open. You had need of a discreet companion and I, well, you know of my financial worries."

"Yes," Charles said sympathetically. "Why didn't you tell me about your son, Lillie? I could've helped you."

"You did help, Charles," Lillie said, a smile tugging at the corners of her generous mouth. She walked around the chair she'd been leaning on and sat down on it. "Jaime is autistic," she explained. "He's never spoken." Her voice broke. "He's never looked at me, Charles. At first, I tried to handle it on my own. My ex-husband had abandoned us. I would spend hours just talking to him, trying to break through his wall of silence, to no avail. Then, I heard about a special home in San Jose that did astounding work with autistic children. It's been a long, arduous process, but Jaime's made some progress. At least now, he'll allow me to touch him, and occasionally, he will even take a quick glance at me."

"I'm sure that makes you very happy," Charles said.

"You have no idea how happy," Lillie confirmed. She looked at him and sighed. "No, I suppose you do. It must be wonderful to get to know your daughter after so many years apart, Charles."

Charles laughed softly. "I feel positively reborn."

He opened the top drawer of his desk, removed his checkbook and began writing out a check for Lillie. "Lillie, I want to help ease your mind where Jaime's concerned. The company has a program that offers aid to families with chronically-ill children. I'll have my people call you about that, and we'll get you signed up. But this," he said, indicating the check, "is to help you move back to San Jose where you can be near Jaime."

"But I can't accept that, Charles," Lillie protested. "You're more than generous offering to help with the medical bills."

"The program I mentioned will pay all of Jaime's medical bills, not just a portion of them," Charles informed her with a gentle smile. "Or, if you have medical insurance, it will take care of all the costs not covered by your insurance."

Lillie looked heavenward, fighting back tears. "Thank you, Charles. On Jaime's behalf, thank you."

Charles finished writing the check, ripped it out of the checkbook and handed it to Lillie.

Lillie met his eyes. "It isn't for services rendered, is it Charles?"

"It's nothing of the sort," Charles vehemently denied. He stood and placed the check in the palm of her hand. "We both knew our relationship had certain restraints on it," he told her. "But I want you to know I grew quite fond of you, Lillie, and I never thought of you in those terms. You're a class act and you deserve the opportunity to meet someone special—someone you can have a future with."

"You're a kind man, Charles," Lillie complimented him. Now tears coursed down her cheeks. She wiped them away with a tissue from the dispenser on his desk. She smiled at him. "Did you ever notice that when you'd give me a gift, whether it was a diamond bracelet or some other expensive trinket, I'd wear it a few times and then you wouldn't see it again?"

"Yes, I did notice that peculiar habit," Charles admitted, returning her smile.

"That was because I'd wear it to prove I appreciated your thoughtfulness. A few weeks later, however, I'd sell it and send the proceeds to Jaime's care facility. Can you ever forgive me for that, Charles?"

Charles laughed delightedly. "I thought you'd stop wearing the old things to make room for something new."

Lillie laughed along with him. "And you'd always buy something new. So, you see, you've been helping to pay Jaime's medical bills all along."

Her hand finally closed around the check. She looked serious. "I hope you find what you're looking for, Charles. I really mean that."

It was only after she'd left Charles' office that she glanced down at the amount written on the check. He'd given her enough to start a new life in San Jose. She'd never be tempted to compromise herself again. She'd always be grateful to him for that.

After Lillie departed, Charles felt he should also take the bull by the horns concerning his situation with Bree and Georgie. Now that they were out of danger, it was time he sat them down and had a long talk with them. Especially now that he and Toni had decided to try to work things out amicably. She had not expressly given him a modicum of hope that they would some day be a couple again—yet. She *had* warmed to him considerably since their meeting on that rain-spattered tarmac a few days ago though.

He almost felt he owed a debt of gratitude to Eddie Kovik for putting a bullet in him. The incident had been the catalyst that started swaying Toni's opinion of him for the good. He left his office and went in search of his daughters. *His daughters*. The thought of them made him grin like a Cheshire cat.

Eleven

"Here's your chance to tell the old man off," Charles told his daughters lightly after they were seated in his study. He'd invited Toni to sit in, but she'd declined, saying what happened should not have any bearing on the fact that she was present at the time. Her girls might feel less inclined to speak their minds if their mother was in the room.

Charles had wanted her there for moral support. She knew them—he didn't. If she saw him about to put his foot in his mouth, she could give him one of those looks she was famous for and perhaps he could pull himself out of the hole he would have dug. However, since she wasn't there, he felt like he was flying blind.

He forged ahead in spite of his handicaps, though.

"I can see by your expressions that you already know why I asked you here," Charles said self-consciously. "Georgie?"

"I've had a lot of practice reading people, sir. The talent comes in handy in my line of work. Maybe I can make this easier on all of us." She paused. "I can't fully accept you until I know Mom has forgiven you for what you did. Now, I realize that what happened between you two should be your business, and it shouldn't affect our relationship but, in my heart, my allegiance belongs to Mom. She was there. She was not only there, but she was one hell of a parent. I think Bree will back me up on that."

Bree nodded vigorously. "I do," she said. "One hundred per-cent." She smiled at her father. "Please try to understand. I was overwhelmed to learn I have a living father. Not knowing my father has been the greatest disappointment of my life. Both Georgie and I suffered from father-hunger. We used to dream about how better our lives would've been with you in it."

Charles' eyes were sad. "What if your mother never forgives me?"

Georgie and Bree exchanged glances.

"We don't think that's very likely," Georgie spoke for the both of them.

Their father's thick eyebrows shot up in surprise.

"Do you know something I don't?"

"Let's go back to the argument that you and Mom had years ago that broke you up," Georgie suggested. "Do you suppose Mom doesn't have regrets about the way she reacted to your parents when you brought her here to meet them?"

"She told you about that?"

"Yes," Bree said. "She told us if she had it to do all over again, she'd be careful not to allow them to insult her. She thought she was overly sensitive because she knew she was carrying your child. And here were your parents: two color-conscious people who couldn't see past her dark skin."

A faraway look came into Charles' eyes and the girls knew they were in for a glimpse into their parents' past. "I was so in love with her. I didn't think for one minute that they would not love her as well."

Charles could envision that day as clearly as if it were yesterday. It was in November. November again. He'd phoned his parents and told them he was bringing a friend home to spend Thanksgiving with them. Before he'd gotten off the phone, his mother had wangled the fact that the friend he was bringing home was the girl he was in love with.

Charles was twenty-two and his parents were ecstatic that he'd finally found the woman whom he fancied himself in love with.

So, it was with much anticipation that his parents met him and Toni at the door that cold November morning and found them standing on the front portico looking like rejects from *Hair*—the broadway musical popular at the time. Toni's afro was huge, and Charles had let his hair grow as well. To compound the effect, he was sporting a goatee and a pair of pink-lensed granny glasses. When they removed their coats, his parents were almost blinded by their matching psychedelic dashikis.

Drunk with the hubris of youth, Charles thought their outlandish apparel was happening. Besides, the folks were part of the establishment. They could do with a bit of shaking-up. He was strangely pleased by the look of horror on his parents' faces. For all his life, they'd dictated his every move. Now they'd learn who was the true captain of his fate.

Toni, a southern girl, was raised to respect her elders. She was very polite. But unbeknownst to her, there was nothing she could do to win his parents' favor. She had been instantly condemned because she didn't look like a boarding-school, cotillion, tea-swilling, charm school, Ivy League college kind of girl. They didn't know she'd earned a full academic scholarship, was at the top of her class, and had recently been published by a literary press.

They were rude to her and made snide remarks about what kind of parents she must have to allow her to carry herself the way she did. Toni took offense. Who wouldn't have? Charles defended her.

"If you can't accept Toni," he told them. "Then we'll both leave."

They took his threat seriously for all of one day. The final straw came the following day when his mother insisted on taking Toni to her beauty salon in order to have her hair dresser "put some reins on that unruly mop *she* calls hair."

They were having a party that night in honor of Charles' homecoming and would cancel it before they allowed their friends to meet Toni. And to Toni's horror, Charles had succumbed to his father's ribbing and had had his hair cut and his much-loved goatee shaved off.

Toni flatly refused to have her hair straightened. She was in one of the guest rooms, shoving her few belongings into a knapsack when Charles burst in to try to talk her out of leaving.

"Toni, please don't go. I told you they were strict disciplinarians. You promised you'd stick it out, no matter what. For my sake."

"That woman," Toni shouted, referring to his mother, "wants me to have my hair fried. The way God made it isn't good enough for her bourgeois tastes."

Charles had gone to her and taken her into his arms. He gently stroked her natural, jet-black hair. "I adore your hair, Toni. I love everything about you."

They kissed.

"Then you'll understand the reason why I'm leaving," Toni said after he released her. Her eyes assessed him and found him lacking. "Oh Chuck, your spiritual growth has been stunted by your parents. Instead of allowing you the freedom to be yourself, they set out to mold you into a replica of themselves. You've got to put your foot down, Chuck—or you'll never know who you really are."

Charles had reacted just the way most men do when confronted with the truth about themselves—he became incensed. "You call showing respect for my parents allowing myself to be stifled?"

"You've buried your individuality, Chuck. Look at you. Twenty-four hours back here and you're a preppie again. Except for your darker coloring, I can't tell you from the white boy down the street. Where did your parents find you anyway? On their doorstep? Surely they could have come up with a lighter-skinned specimen? Or perhaps you've been in the California sun too long? A few months in these Northern climes and you'll revert, is that it?"

"Don't say something you can't retract, Toni," Charles had warned her.

"I'm going to say this and then I'm leaving, Chuck. You told me you love me. I love you, too. But I could never live under this tyranny."

"Tyranny? Toni, you've been attending too many peace rallies," Chuck commented in an attempt to lighten the mood.

"Tyranny, Chuck!" Toni had shouted. "I know we've talked about getting married. But I won't marry a boy. Especially not a boy who won't stand up to Mom and Dad. And I definitely won't have a child of mine grow up in this prejudiced environment. It's one thing to be hated by another race, but to be hated by someone of your own race simply because of the color of your skin is intolerable."

Charles knew he was lost then. No one could get a word in edgewise when Toni stepped up on her soapbox.

The enlightenment he'd gained from his memories gave Charles a new lease on life. He went to Georgie and hugged her, then he hugged Bree with just as much enthusiasm.

"Thank you," he said, beaming. "You two have helped me recall a very salient event in Toni's and my past."

"What?" Georgie said. "Tell us."

His eyes were somber when he met her gaze.

"I used your mother. I brought her here for the express purpose of shocking my parents. I was never brave enough to tell them they were stifling me and that I resented them for it. So I put the point across by throwing your mother in their faces. It was my fault. I set them all up and I just remembered something else. Toni tried to tell me she was expecting just before our final blow-up. And I was too stupid to realize it."

"Don't you think you ought to apologize to her for that?" Bree said. "I believe a sincere apology would put you over the top."

"You think so?" their father asked hopefully.

Toni was enjoying the beauty of Charles' rose garden. She'd never seen so many varieties in one spot before: Hybrid Teas, such as the Charlotte Armstrong, which was a faint red; the Crimson Glory, a rich red; and the Peace, her favorite, yellow. There were also climbers, hybrid perpetuals, Floribundas and Grandifloras. She knew the names because she'd once done research on the rose family for a book she'd written about a widowed florist who fell in love with a man who came into her shop every Friday and ordered a single rose. The florist found out the gentleman was buying the rose to place on his late wife's grave. Once they started communicating, their relationship blossomed into a beautiful love story.

Toni bent her head to breathe in the heady fragrance of the Peace rose.

"Why don't you cut a dozen or so and take them up to your room, you can enjoy them all day long," Charles suggested.

Toni started. "I didn't hear you come in."

"I wanted to talk to you."

She faced him. "I'm listening."

He told her, without mincing words, how he'd been a fool thirty years ago. And he apologized with feeling.

Toni threw her head back and laughed.

"Get real, Chuck. I don't give a damn about that after nearly thirty years. I knew you were rebelling against your parents. Who wasn't back then? What I'm angry with you about is: when I told you we had a child together, you didn't do anything about it. You thought I wanted something from you. Maybe you figured I was trying to break up your marriage. But I would never have done that. You had your life. I had mine. But your daughters were innocent children. They didn't ask to be born. The moment they were conceived, however, they became our responsibility. I only phoned you that day because I felt you had the right to know you had a child. Not because I was pining away for you in the hope that one day you'd come back to me. I knew it was over."

"So, what do we do now?" Charles asked plaintively. "Where do we go from here, Toni?"

"You get to know your daughters, and I will return to New Orleans," Toni told him.

"They've said they cannot accept me until you forgive me," Charles told her.

"Then I forgive you, Chuck," Toni said simply.

"Is it that easy for you?"

"My girls want to be a part of your life. I will not deny them that. If I have to pretend you are back in my good graces, I'll pretend," Toni said, smiling at him. "That's what parents do, Chuck—make sacrifices for their children."

"We've got one more problem, Toni," Charles said quietly.

"What's that?"

"I'm falling in love with you all over again," he said tenderly. He reached out and trailed a finger down her arm. "Be honest with me. Don't you find me a little attractive?"

Toni looked up into his eyes. Her dark eyes were faintly amused. "We'd better get out of this enclosure. I think you could use some air."

"Don't be coy, Toni," Charles pleaded with her. "I've been honest with you. Can't you let go of the past long enough to embrace the future?"

"Oh, that's rich!" Toni cried, turning to walk away. "Coming from a man who ran from his past for thirty years."

"That's good," Charles encouraged her. "Let it out. Come on, Toni. Tell me how you really feel."

He caught up with her at the entrance to the greenhouse and grasped her by the arm. "I'm forty-eight years old. I don't need this sort of nonsense in my life, Charles Waters. Let go of me."

Charles stood in front of her. "I need you, Toni. I need this kind of nonsense in *my* life. What are you afraid of? Are you afraid I'll hurt you again?"

Toni's eyes were steely when she turned her gaze on him. "You'll never get the opportunity to hurt me again, Chuck. So stop dreaming."

"Kiss me, Toni."

"What?"

"I can't very well grab you and force myself on you with my arm in a sling," Charles joked. "Look, if you can kiss me and then tell me there's nothing left between us, I'll let it drop. Otherwise, I'm going to court you whether you like it or not. I'll show up on your doorstep in New Orleans every single day until you go out with me. And you know I'll do it. I'll pester you so badly, your parents will toss you out the door into my arms to get rid of me."

"You wouldn't."

"You know I would," Charles stated emphatically.

Their eyes met and held. Toni frowned. "One kiss?"

Charles nodded in the affirmative.

Toni paused, her eyes narrowing as though she were weighing the pros and cons. Then she stepped forward and gently kissed Charles on the lips.

His good arm wrapped around her waist and he tipped her backward. He was not as helpless as he'd let on. His mouth firmly covered hers, and momentarily, Toni thought she was eighteen again. He hadn't lost his touch.

They parted and both were a little shaky. "Well?" Charles asked, hoping for a reprieve.

"That only proves we're fully-functioning human beings, Chuck."

She left then, opening the door and walking into the cold garden outside. Charles was right behind her. He sighed. "Whatever you say. So, when are you returning to New Orleans? Will you stay for Thanksgiving? It's only three more days. You can put up with me for that long, can't you?"

"I don't know," Toni tossed over her shoulder. "If you keep this up, I might get the next plane back home."

Charles raised his hand in defeat.

"Fine," he said calmly. "You don't have to get testy."

Toni turned and glared at him. "Don't make me get down and dirty with you, Chuck."

In his best Ivy League tone, Charles sighed and said, "I think I'd rather enjoy that."

Toni couldn't help herself. She laughed.

Georgie and Bree were in their father's study watching their parents' actions.

"Oh my God," Bree said happily when her mother kissed her father. "She kissed him." She looked at Georgie. "Whatever possessed her to do that?"

"Our father is quite the charmer," Georgie said, smiling. "No one has broken through Mom's cool reserve in some time now." Her eyes stretched in panic. "They're coming back inside. We'd better make ourselves scarce, we don't want them to know we were spying on them."

"I don't mind," Bree hesitated.

Georgie grabbed her younger sister by the arm and yanked her toward the door. Bree limped along.

"How is your foot doing?"

They were able to close the door of the study behind them before their parents entered the room from the garden door.

Bree leaned against the wall in the hallway. "It's better."

"Are you going to be able to make that audition in San Francisco on Friday?" her sister inquired, watching Bree's face which always told the truth whether her mouth was lying or not.

Bree winced and her sister knew she was still in considerable pain.

"Bree, are you sure you're all right?"

"Georgie, I don't care if I have to do that audition from a wheelchair, I'm going to be in San Francisco the day after Thanksgiving."

"I'll go with you," Georgie offered.

"And miss spending time with Mr. Knight? You have to be back in San Francisco yourself on Monday. If I were you, I'd make sure I took back a few delicious memories of your detective to tide you over until you can see each other again. You get my meaning, Sis?"

"In living color," Georgie told her with a grin.

She placed her arm around her sister's waist and allowed her to lean on her the rest of the way down the hall.

"I just hope I haven't forgotten how to . . . make delicious memories. It's been a while."

"I've got a feeling you won't need an instruction manual with Clay," Bree said. She looked wistful as she continued. "Sometimes I wish I *was* having as good a time as some of those rag magazines say I am."

Georgie giggled. "You remember when they had you linked with Dominic Solomon? And you've never even met the man."

"Oh, no," Bree cried. "I hope he doesn't read the tabloids. I'll just die of embarrassment if he remembers that story."

"Don't worry about it," Georgie said confidently. "Even if he did read it, it happened six months ago. He's probably forgotten it by now."

The next day, Clay dropped by the Back Bay police station to have a word with John about the progress of the dredging crew presently trying to raise Anne Ballentine's Volvo.

John was on the phone when Clay stuck his head in the door.

"Hey," John greeted him, his hand over the mouthpiece. "Have a seat, I'll be off in a minute or so."

Clay sat on the straight-backed chair across from John's desk. He looked around the standard-issue furnished office. A metal desk with file cabinets along the wall. A small table with a coffee-maker on top. For six years, this place had been his home away from home.

John replaced the receiver and looked up at Clay.

"That was Jarvis. He's the guy who owns the salvage company that's raising the Ballentine vehicle. They got the car. No sign of a body though. He said the car was shifted into neutral. He doesn't think the impact did that. The make of the car negates it."

"That lends credence to my suspicion that she might have staged her death," Clay said, shaking his curly-maned head.

"She could still be out there," John agreed. He reached over to take a sip of his coffee.

"My gut tells me she is," Clay said. He rose. "Thanks, John. I've got to go give Georgette the latest news. She isn't going to be pleased."

"You're in love with her, aren't you?" John asked. He waited expectantly.

"Yeah," Clay said with a smirk. John wouldn't be pleased until he knew. "I'm in love with her. Happy?"

"Ecstatic," John confirmed with a grin.

Clay turned to leave. "Get our names right in the precinct's newsletter."

"That's Knight with a K, right?" John joked, enjoying a laugh at his friend's expense. "I can't wait to tell Margarite. The mighty Knight has fallen."

Shaking his head, Clay said, "I'm glad I could make your day." He left.

It was after five in the afternoon by the time Clay arrived at Greenbriar. Carson let him in.

"Good afternoon, Mr. Knight," the elderly butler greeted him.

"Hello, Carson. Is Mr. Waters available? I need to talk to him."

"He's in his study. I'll announce you."

"That isn't necessary," Clay began, then seeing the severe expression on Carson's face, he deferred to the butler's better judgment. "Of course. I'll wait here."

By the time Carson walked to the study and back, five minutes had passed. I really need to control my impatience, Clay thought.

"Mr. Waters will see you now," Carson informed him in his sedate manner.

"Thanks, Carson," Clay said, in a rush in spite of his good intentions. "I know the way."

"Come on in, Clay," Charles responded to his knock.

He looked up from papers he'd been going over and smiled.

"Hello, how are you? Happy to have this case under your belt?"

"That's what I wanted to talk to you about," Clay began.

"Sit," Charles said, gesturing to the chair across from his desk.

"We have reason to believe Anne might have survived her plunge into the bay," Clay remarked after sitting and stretching his long legs out before him.

"Yes?" Charles replied, leaning forward. A frown creased his brows.

"There is no sign of her and the car was purposely shifted into the neutral gear. Sir, I believe she put the car in the bay, then made her escape."

"If that's true," Charles proposed, "then where do you suppose she is now?"

Clay sighed. "She could be anywhere."

"It's just a theory though, isn't it?" Charles insisted. "The car was in neutral instead of drive. Couldn't that have happened when the car hit the water?"

"It's a possibility," Clay allowed. He knew why Charles was reluctant to believe Anne was still out there somewhere. He wanted to put all this behind him and get on with his life. His daughters and, probably, Toni, were the most important things on his mind now.

"What do you want to do about it?" Charles inquired. He was a man who needed to know the bottom line if he were to effectively deal with a situation.

"Until a body turns up," Clay suggested, "we should not let down our guards. If Anne *is* alive, she has nothing left to lose. She's probably embittered and blames you for all her problems. All her plans hinged on you. You didn't return her love. In her unbalanced mind, you deserve to be punished and how better to make you suffer than through your children?"

Charles held his head in his hands in despair.

"I so hoped this was over with, Clay. But, if you think we should maintain our vigilance until we have proof that Anne is out of the picture then I will bow to your judgment. Do whatever is required to keep my daughters safe."

"What about my audition?" Bree cried in disappointment after Clay finished telling her, Georgie and their mother of his theory concerning Anne.

They had been in the kitchen welcoming Mrs. Hughes back when Clay went in search of them. Mrs. Hughes suffered no after-effects from being, as she termed it, electrocuted. She had Toni and the girls cracking up at her description of her harried ride to the hospital in the ambulance.

The attendants had insisted she lie down on the gurney and

then they had difficulty lifting her into the back of the ambulance. She had gotten up, walked into the ambulance then laid back down on the gurney. Looking into their faces, she had then said, "If you have any problems driving this contraption, I can do that for you, too."

Mrs. Hughes, after shamelessly eavesdropping on their conversation in the kitchen (it *was* her domain after all), said to Bree: "Pardon me, Miss, if I put my two cents in. But if Mr. Clay says you all should be careful, then you should listen to him."

Bree was warmed by the cook's concern. She smiled at Mrs. Hughes. "I know Clay is looking out for our best interests. But if I don't make that audition in three days, I'm going to kill myself anyway."

"Don't be melodramatic, dear," Toni chided her, laughing.

"Maybe you can phone Ari and reschedule," Georgie suggested.

"I'll try," Bree said. Looking at Clay as though he were a traitor to her cause, she turned to leave. "Excuse me."

Clay sighed. "I've just made an enemy."

"Nonsense," Toni told him. "Bree was just being petulant. If she doesn't experience a crisis every few days, she creates one."

She placed her arm through his and smiled up at him. "We know you're only trying to keep the girls safe, and we appreciate it."

Before his arrival, the women had been having cups of Mrs. Hughes' rich coffee and even richer coffee cake. Mrs. Hughes poured Clay a cup and cut him a slice of the cake.

"Sit down," she ordered him. "Have some of my cake."

Clay looked up at Cook and winked at her. "You do know how to cheer a guy up."

"What's going on in Boston, Bree?" Ari demanded to know after Bree got through to her. "Spill, girlfriend, I'm beginning to get worried about you."

Bree saw no reason not to tell Ari everything now. Anne was

out of the house. Everyone knew that she had been behind the attempts on Georgie's life, hence there was no lingering need for secrecy.

"I'll try to contact Dominic and reschedule," Ari promised after hearing the full story. She sighed. "But if I can't swing it, don't get down. There will be other films."

Bree took Ari's pessimism as a sign of her impending doom. "Oh no. You can forget that, Ari. I'm making that audition."

"But what about that crazed woman?" Ari cautioned her.

"If Anne comes between me and that interview, she'll have *me* to fear," Bree said with conviction. "The audition is scheduled for two at the Fairmont Hotel? Can you meet me there and take Pierre off my hands while I read for Dominic?"

"Sure," Ari said at once. "But I don't think it wise for you to come, Bree. What if she tries to harm you? I'd rather have you doing those Jody Freeman movies for the next decade than not have you around at all. You wouldn't be the first actress stalked by a lunatic, you know."

"You're not going to talk me out of it," Bree said stubbornly. "Just be at the Fairmont. I'll show up."

"Please, don't," Ari pleaded with her.

"You promised you'd be there," Bree reminded her friend. "Bye, love."

"Bye." Bree could hear the disappointment in Ari's Spanish-accented voice.

Bree replaced the receiver and sat back on her bed. Pierre hopped up onto the bed, wagging his tail happily. She picked him up and hugged him. "You don't think I've taken leave of my senses, do you?" she asked, looking into his brown eyes. Pierre licked her face. "I knew you'd agree with me."

Now there was only the matter of making airline reservations. She could do that over the phone using her Visa Gold card. The modern world offered so many ways to get into trouble with just a push of a button.

She'd go straight to the audition from the airport and afterward, she and Pierre would spend the night at Georgie's place. Years ago, when they both started living on their own, the sisters made it a practice of exchanging keys. They visited one another so frequently that it was convenient for them to do so.

"Anne is probably dead, poor thing," she said as she laid back on the pillow. "Clay is good at his job, but you can't depend on gut feelings all the time. My instincts didn't serve me well with St. Martin, that rat. Clay could be wrong."

Someone knocked on her door.

"Come in," Bree called.

Her father walked into the room.

Bree sat on the edge of the bed.

"Your mother told me how you reacted to Clay's news," he said sympathetically. "I hope you were able to set up another time for your appointment."

He sat down beside her. Bree leaned on his uninjured shoulder.

"No problem." She lied. She didn't allow him to see her eyes.

"Are you certain?" Charles inquired softly. "Maybe I could phone this Solomon Dominic fellow."

Bree laughed. "It's Dominic Solomon."

Her father laughed, too. "At any rate, I'd be happy to fly him and whomever else out here to you."

"That's kind of you, Dad," Bree told him. "But it isn't necessary."

Charles hugged her. He was pleased by the upgrade in titles.

He stood, lovingly gazing down at her. "You look like a forlorn little girl. Come back downstairs. Ben is back home. I'm sure he'll be delighted to learn that he has a second cousin."

Bree rose, a look of surprise on her face. "Ben," she said. "Are you going to tell him about Anne?"

"I don't see how I can avoid it," her father said listlessly. He wasn't looking forward to the task. How do you tell someone you care so much for that you've located his birth mother, she is a mad woman who has either drowned in Dorchester Bay or is still a fugitive bent on revenge, in one breath?

Twelve

At 11:00 p.m. on Tuesday night, Jonathan J. Crenshaw, a retired University of California—Berkeley English professor, following his normal routine, went into the kitchen to put the kettle on to boil. As he waited for the sound of the whistling to begin, he went to the pantry adjacent to the back door and retrieved the tin of Sleepy Time herbal tea. He enjoyed the soothing flavor and he was partial to the picture of the brown teddy bear attired in an old-fashioned red-and-white striped nightshirt and cap. It reminded him of his childhood.

Jonathan was seventy-six years old. He was a tall, spare man with kind green eyes and a head full of wavy white hair. He lived in the same Victorian home in Pacific Heights that his parents had raised five children in, three boys and two girls. Prior to his parents' possession of the home, it had belonged to his father's parents, Jonathan and Beatrice. They'd reared a brood of twelve in the Pacific Heights home.

Jonathan and his wife, Penelope, hadn't been blessed with children. And when Penny passed away seven years ago, Jonathan, already retired, thought he would go stir-crazy alone in the big house. So he'd had the top floor converted into an apartment and rented it out.

He hadn't been lucky with the first few tenants. One guy was an artist and kept Jonathan up all night with the sound of his hammering as he molded copper into decorative wall hangings. Another threw wild parties that lasted until the wee hours. Two years ago, Jonathan had lucked-out when a caterer, Alana Calloway, moved in. She was wonderful and he grew quite fond of her. However, several months ago, she'd gotten married. Luckily for Jonathan, Alana's pal, Georgette Shaw, moved in shortly afterward. He liked Georgie right away. She was a friendly girl who made him homemade bread and when she brought it downstairs to him, they always enjoyed a slice together with real butter and various flavors of jam along with strong cups of Colombian coffee.

The only complaint he had about Georgie was that she rarely made enough noise for him to know when she was at home. So, when he heard footsteps upstairs a few minutes after he'd taken his cup of tea to bed with him, his curiosity was immediately engaged. For one thing, Georgie had told him she wouldn't be returning from New Orleans until Sunday night. She usually returned from a trip the day before she had to go in to work. He hoped nothing had gone wrong at home. He knew her mother, Toni Shaw. Toni had been one of his best students when he was a young instructor at Berkeley. He'd followed her career since he learned she was a writer. He liked to think he'd had some influence on her style.

As he lay in bed, he decided to give Georgie a call. She was already up, so he wouldn't be waking her. He dialed the familiar number. The phone rang six times. Georgie didn't have an answering machine. He didn't know why she didn't have one. Everyone else in the civilized world did. He replaced the receiver. Maybe she was in the shower.

The next morning, he had to go shopping for a birthday gift for his baby sister, Ginger. Ginger was turning seventy, the whippersnapper. Every last one of the brothers and sisters would be gathering at Ginger's to celebrate the occasion. Now, all five of the Crenshaws would be in his seventh decade. They'd hired a male stripper. Ginger would get a kick out of that.

Before he left on his shopping excursion, he'd leave a note on Georgie's door welcoming her back and inviting her down for coffee. He intended to find out why she'd cut her trip short. He didn't hear another sound from upstairs. Picking up the mystery novel he'd been reading the last few days, he settled into the story. He was certain the culprit was the sexy widow of the curmudgeon who'd been bludgeoned to death in the first chapter.

"Uncle," Benjamin said, getting to his feet, "Cassie and I have an announcement to make."

Charles and Bree had just entered the living room. Charles paused in his tracks. "Yes, Ben?"

Benjamin had an attentive audience as he cleared his throat and placed his arms about a smiling Cassie's slim shoulders. His uncle, his two cousins, Toni and Clay awaited his next words.

Benjamin's face broke into a grin. "We're getting married," he said quickly.

Good news for a change, Georgie thought. She was sitting next to Clay, her hand in his. They were past the stage of being embarrassed by public displays of affection. Everyone in her family knew she was attracted to Clay by now.

Stepping forward to shake Ben's hand, Charles smiled broadly. "That's wonderful news, Ben. Cassie," he said.

Cassie's light-brown eyes were tearing up. She batted her lashes, attempting to hold back the tears.

"Thank you," she said. "We didn't mean to spring it on you so suddenly, but we were so happy, we wanted to share it with you."

Pulling her into his arms, Charles hugged her affectionately.

"You may bring me news like this any time, my dear," he told her. "Welcome to the family."

Everyone else in the room came up, in turn, to congratulate the happy couple.

Georgie pulled her cousin aside to tell him, "You see what a little closeness can do?"

Their eyes met and they smiled at one another. "You've been my good luck charm," Benjamin told her. "Ever since I started taking your advice, Cassie and I have been on the same wave-length." He looked serious. "We read about Anne in this morning's paper. It's so sad. I've known her for years. It's difficult to believe what they wrote about her is the truth. She was always so kind to me. I was very fond of her."

Georgie's heart went out to him. She felt it wasn't her place to offer her opinion on Anne. He would know all the details soon enough. She wished there was some way to lessen the blow for him when it did come.

"Yes, it is sad," was all she would say.

"Ben," Charles said, coming to stand next to Georgie. "Could I have a word with you in private?"

"Of course," Ben said, looking up.

At that moment, Toni grasped Charles by the arm. "Chuck, before you speak with Ben, there's something I'd like to say to you."

Her dark eyes made it a command. Charles went quietly. "Excuse us," he said to Georgie and Benjamin.

In the privacy of his study, Toni closed the door behind them and turned to face him.

"Must you ruin this night for him? He just announced his engagement. Let him have this night, at least, to feel truly wonderful. Surely you can recall the feeling of elation at realizing you loved a woman to such an extent you'd gladly spend the rest of your life with her."

Charles was watching how the irises in her dark eyes seemed to expand when she was angry. He stood smiling foolishly at her.

Toni's anger dissipated at the sight of the expression on Charles' face. She suddenly grasped his lapels with both hands and shook him until his head snapped back. He only smiled. "Stop it, Chuck. It isn't going to happen, so give it up." She meant his conquest of her.

She let go of his lapels. Turning on her heels, she headed for the door. She looked back at him. "What are you going to do?"

"I'll wait," he said simply.

Charles remained in his study a couple of minutes after Toni left the room. What a woman. He had been a total jerk to have treated her so badly.

When Toni returned to the living room, Georgie sidled up to her and said, "You didn't hit him, did you?"

Toni looked up at her eldest daughter and laughed.

"I should have, but I didn't. He was going to tell Ben about Anne tonight. I talked him out of it, that's all."

Georgie looked up and saw her father entering the room. "He looks quite happy. Did you kiss him to sway him to your way of thinking?"

Her mother laughed even harder. "Kiss him? I'd rather kiss the south end of a skunk."

"You seemed to enjoy that passionate clinch in the greenhouse," Georgie said lightly.

"You were spying on us?"

"Yes. Bree and I were concerned. You two alone in the same room? There could have been fireworks. Oh, wait a minute. There *were* fireworks."

"It was a harmless kiss with no passion whatsoever," her mother disavowed. "He dared me. I did it to prove there is no spark left to rekindle."

"And the outcome?" Georgie inquired, watching her mother's face.

"I don't care if he's changed," her mother said, avoiding answering the question directly. "I'm still not going to get involved with that man."

Georgie's mouth was agape. She clamped it shut. "He's serious?"

"He wants to date me," her mother guffawed.

"Clay was right," Georgie said, her voice filled with wonder.

"About what?" Toni asked, her grin disappearing.

"He said he thought our father was still in love with you, and that's why he came looking for us."

"He should have sent flowers instead," Toni quipped.

Benjamin wanted to know why Charles had wanted to see him in private earlier. Charles, thinking quickly on his feet, said, "I wanted to tell you of the true identity of Miss Shaw here." He pulled Bree into the crook of his arm. Bree smiled radiantly. "Benjamin, meet your other cousin."

Benjamin, his hand clasped in Cassie's, laughed softly. "I *knew* it," he cried.

"You knew it?" Charles repeated, looking puzzled.

"I found myself staring at Bree and wondering how she could have your eyes and not be your daughter as well," Benjamin explained. He reached for Bree's hand and he stood between her and Cassie holding both their hands. "A bride and a cousin, all in one night. I'm a lucky man, indeed."

Georgie and Clay left the room, venturing into the library where they could talk alone.

"I hate this waiting," Clay said, sighing heavily. "I know she's out there. I just can't figure out where."

"I don't think she would have stuck around here," Georgie said of Anne. "Why would she risk getting caught when she could escape to Mexico or some other country?"

"Try to think like she does," Clay suggested. "A long time ago, her mother made her give up her child. Now, in a sense, your father has done the same. She was found out before she could realize her dream of a perfect family with your father and Benjamin. She'll undoubtedly blame your father for spoiling that dream."

Georgie placed her head in her hand and squeezed her forehead. She felt a headache coming on. "My head is spinning." She met Clay's eyes. "I wish I could get away from here, just for a few hours."

They closed the space between them and Clay pulled her into his embrace. Looking down into her upturned face, he said, "We could go to my place."

"You said it wasn't safe enough," Georgie reminded him with a smile.

"It isn't as safe as Greenbriar, but I don't plan on letting you out of my sight for a moment."

"That sounds inviting," Georgie said, her head tilted back and her braids cascading down her back. "When do we leave?"

Clay caught her hand in his and brought it to his mouth, kissing her palm.

"How about in an hour? I can have someone over here by then. They'll stay with Bree while you and I . . ."

"Make delicious memories?" Georgie offered mischievously.

"What?"

"I'll explain it to you later."

William Carrington was staying with his sister, Yvonne, in Springfield when he awoke with a start Wednesday night. He'd been having a nightmare in which Anne's reanimated dead body walked out of Dorchester Bay, covered with murky brine. She raised a bloated arm, pointed at him and said, "It's just like the last time. If you had helped me when I asked you to, I wouldn't be dead. I wouldn't be dead . . ." She kept repeating those words until Carrington awoke, clutching at the covers and sweating profusely.

As he lay there, his heart hammering in his broad chest, he hoped he hadn't cried out in his sleep. Yvonne was a light sleeper, and she'd come running to ensure everything was all right. Will didn't want to be a burden on his younger sister. She had gone through a painful divorce and was raising two daughters on her own. He'd felt badly when he'd told her the reason he was there.

She'd looked at him and said, "You used bad judgement, getting involved with Anne Ballentine. She hasn't been wrapped too tight since she lost her baby years ago. But then you were always sweet on her."

Yvonne was thirty-seven, tall and smart. Where Carrington's features were blunt and square, hers were delicate, well-sculpted. Life hadn't been easy for her and the trials she'd gone through had helped to shape her character. She faced challenges head-on, and when her husband had walked out on her, she'd gone back to college and earned a nursing degree. She was a head nurse now.

Sure enough, Yvonne appeared in his doorway pulling her bathrobe on. She knocked on the door frame. "May I come in?"

The door was sitting wide open. She was already in. "Come on in," Carrington said sheeplishly.

Yvonne sat on the edge of the bed.

"I heard you shouting her name." She reached up and wiped his brow with a tissue from the box on the nightstand. Her gesture fleetingly reminded him of their mother.

"There's something you're not telling me, isn't there?" Yvonne surmised. Her intelligent brown eyes looked into his. "Will, if you're ever going to exorcise Anne's ghost, you're going to have to talk about it. You know that whatever you tell me is going to stay right here between these walls. Out of all of Mama's children, you and I have always been the closest." She grasped his clammy hand, squeezing it gently. "I want to help you, big brother. Let me."

Carrington told her about the dream in all its vivid detail. Yvonne was shaking her head and grimacing when he concluded the narrative.

"God, that was awful," she said.

Carrington was sitting on the side of the bed next to his sister now. She had gone to the kitchen, made them cups of cocoa and returned with them. He took a sip of his and raised his eyes to hers. "Sis, what I'm about to say will be more awful than that dream, because it's real. It happened."

Yvonne steeled herself. "Go ahead, I'm listening."

Carrington nervously rocked back and forth as he began. "One day about five years ago, Anne came into the garage while I was working on one of the cars. We'd been lovers for some time by then. I was always delighted to see her. While I was bent over the car, repairing a loose hose that was connected to the car's brakes, she casually began asking me questions about what I was doing. Flattered that she was paying attention to me and seemed genuinely interested in my work, I readily answered all her questions." Carrington sighed. He held his head in his hands, his eyes downcast. A look of shame clouded his dark face. "About a week later, Mrs. Waters and her son, Charles the third, were killed in a car accident. The police said the brakes gave out while Mrs. Waters was driving."

"Oh my Lord," Yvonne cried, horrified. "And you believe Anne tampered with the brakes?"

"I'm certain of it," Carrington said. "It all makes sense now. She wanted Mrs. Waters and Charles the third out of the way, just like she wanted Georgette Shaw out of the way."

"Then it's good she's dead," Yvonne said stoically. She placed her arm around her brother's shoulders. "She was sick, Will. Now, she won't be able to harm anyone else."

Alec O'Hara arrived at Greenbriar in under forty minutes. He was pleased Clay had phoned him. There was something about the case that didn't sit well with him. Like Clay, he didn't believe the Ballentine woman would commit suicide by driving her car into Dorchester Bay.

Bree, who had become fond of Alec on his first visit to the mansion, greeted him at the door.

"Don't tell Carson I did his job," she joked lightly, ushering him inside. "Hi, Alec. Have you come to guard my body?"

Alec laughed. "It appears so," he said, his blue eyes twinkling in his tanned face.

Bree took his arm, walking with him to the living room where everyone else waited. "You know," she said, "I'm getting tired of being cooped-up in this house. Could I bribe you to help spring me?"

"I'm afraid not," Alec answered shyly. He was always a little tongue-tied around beautiful women. He didn't know how he'd managed to win the fair Dian.

"You detective types are no fun at all," Bree returned, pouting.

Alec only laughed.

"It's snowing," Georgie said, going to the window and peering out onto the lawn. Bree joined her.

"Will you two stay away from the window?" Clay spoke up. He walked over and took Georgie by the hand. "Do I have to remind you that the former rules still apply? No standing near windows . . ."

"All right," Georgie said, slightly irritated. She met his eyes. "I'm sorry." For a moment there, she had forgotten she was still under protective custody. She'd never seen a heavy snowfall before, except in photographs. They didn't get much snow in San Francisco or New Orleans, the two cities she'd spent most of her life in.

"It's okay," Clay said dismissively. He thought it was quite sweet the way her eyes had lit up at the sight of the snowflakes coming down outside. "Shall we go?"

"I'll get my coat," Georgie said, her smile restored.

They walked out to the car as Clay had had her practice—with him between her and the open space of the outer estate. That way, if anyone was out there with a high-powered rifle, Georgie would be out of the line of fire.

Once in the Explorer, Clay said, "Okay, you know the routine."

Georgie sighed and slouched in her seat. "I don't think Anne is still in Boston, Boston."

"Just stay there," Clay sharply ordered as he put the car in gear and they drove away from the house.

"Where are we going?" Georgie asked from the floorboard. "Are we actually going by to see John, as you told my parents?"

"Yes, we are. John is supposed to be trying to trace Anne's movements via her credit card company. He may have something."

"But wouldn't he phone you if he did?"

"Look," Clay said, "if we don't go to the Back Bay police station, I will have lied to your parents just to get their daughter alone. Do you want to make me out a liar?"

Georgie laughed. "I can see chivalry isn't dead after all."

At the station, John told them he hadn't come up with any new information. However, with Georgie present, he had the opportunity to tell her a few tales from the period in time he and Clay had been partners.

Georgie enjoyed listening to John. She sat atop his desk with her long legs swinging down. She was wearing button-fly jeans and a bulky red sweater that brought out the red undertones in her dark skin.

"The first time I saw Clay, he looked like a statue. In the Marine Corps, he'd been taught to stand at attention, and his back was so rigid, I thought he walked like he had a pole stuck up . . ."

"John," Clay interrupted, "remember we have a lady present."

"I get the picture," Georgie assured John with a giggle. Her eyes met Clay's. "He was the model Marine. And I bet he was a 'by-the-book' cop as well. Tell me something I don't already know."

"She'll do," John told Clay, impressed with Georgie's chutz-pah.

Clay rose and reached for her hand. Georgie took his hand and hopped down off the desk.

"We'd better go, John," Clay said. "We don't want Chief Kowalski to come in here and catch you gossiping. He might want a bite out of your . . ."

"Go," John said hurriedly, his brown eyes filled with laughter and his dark face crinkled at the eyes and mouth. "Stay safe, children."

"He's a real character," Georgie said when they were halfway down the hall.

Clay held her close to him as they made their way through the partitioned office. "He's happy to see me happy."

Georgie stopped to stare up at him. "You mean that? You're really happy with me?"

"I'll be even happier when Anne is caught."

They continued walking. Georgie let it drop. What they felt for one another was physical attraction. A couple of days ago, in an unguarded moment, she'd thought she was in love with him. But what did she know about Clay Knight other than he was loyal, trustworthy and damned fine? Nothing, really. She had to think rationally, as she'd been trained to do in law school. Deal with the facts and the facts alone.

She was afraid for her life. Clayton Knight had saved her life in that alley in New Orleans. She was grateful to him. But was she so grateful that she was willing to risk her dignity on a one-night stand? What if, after all of this was over, they never saw one another again?

Clay's place was a loft in Jamaica Plain. The neighborhood was upscale, peopled by mostly young, upwardly-mobile African-American families. There were also a smattering of Hispanics, Irish and Italians.

"This is nice," Georgie complimented Clay on his taste as she stepped onto the polished hardwood floor. Her footsteps reverberated throughout the cavernous space. She was immediately taken by the masculine decor: black leather furnishings and bold, colorful African-inspired paintings on the walls.

Clay paused to lock the door behind them then re-engaged the alarm and shucked off his duster. He was wearing jeans as well, with a heavy wool shirt and a T-shirt underneath. He went to Georgie and took her coat. He hung both of them on the hall tree near the door.

"Who's your favorite artist?" Clay asked, walking over to the entertainment center housed in a walnut cabinet buffed to a warm patina.

Georgie ruminated briefly. "Lately, I've been listening to the Fugees, but my old standby is that fellow formerly known as Prince." She laughed at her description of the popular artist. "Oh, and anything Motown. I like the Temptations, Smokey Robinson and the Miracles, Marvin Gaye and Diana Ross and the Supremes."

"Well let's see if you know this guy," Clay said as he put a compact disc onto the player.

"Oh, she may be weary . . ." the distinctive, soulful voice crooned. It was a song about how best to nurture a woman. When all else failed, try a little warmth, sensitivity, and love, it advised.

Clay moved forward and reached for Georgie's hand. She gave it to him, her brown eyes seeking his. They began to sway to the rhythm and when the tempo picked up, their steps did as well.

Georgie found her inhibitions vanishing as their bodies got in sync with their separate movements. By the second song, she was having a good time imitating Clay as he did a dance he called "the Pony."

"I think I saw James Brown do that once," Georgie told him, laughing.

The object of the dance was to slide to the left, wiggle the left leg and repeat the motion, going to the right.

"When I was kid," Clay told her, a happy expression on his handsome face, "my mother showed me all the dances they would do in her day. She was a great dancer."

"That's probably where you get your talent from," Georgie complimented him.

Clay smiled down at her. "Do you know how beautiful you are?"

"How am I supposed to answer that without appearing either conceited or self-deprecating?"

"It isn't a question you need to answer. It's a fact," Clay said.

"Beauty fades, a good heart lasts forever," Georgie stated emphatically. "That's what Gran always taught us."

A slow song came on and Clay pulled her close.

"Have you figured out who's singing?" he asked.

"I knew it was Otis Redding with the very first lick," Georgie informed him confidently. "I have that CD at home."

"I've been loving you a little too long . . ." Otis Redding's mournful voice filled the air.

Clay's hand at the base of her spine sent currents of electricity shooting throughout her body. She breathed in the heady scent of his aftershave. It was a mild musk whose fragrance when combined with his male scent appealed to the female in her.

She didn't think they'd even make it back to the bedroom if he kept this up. Something in her was attuned to his every gesture. Thankfully, the CD concluded and Clay released her to go put on another one. Georgie took the opportunity to pull back from the moment and gain control of her runaway libido.

She walked over to the black leather sofa near one of the ceiling-to-floor windows, and sat down. A large square coffee table made of pine sat in front of the sofa and on top of it were various photography books and magazines.

"You're a photographer?" she casually asked as Clay walked toward her.

"I dabble," he said modestly.

"What kind?"

"I like photographing people, mostly—old houses, too, when the mood strikes me," he answered. He sat next to her and took her hand into his.

"You don't have to be nervous, Georgette. Nothing has to happen here tonight if you don't want it to."

She looked up into his square-chinned face. His hazel eyes were tender. She inhaled and slowly exhaled. "You could sense my reticence, huh?"

Clay sat back on the couch, still holding her hand. "I know how you feel. We don't know each other well. Under different circumstances, I would ask you out. We'd feel each other out."

"In our case," Georgie said, picking up where he left off, "we know we're attracted to one another. But we just haven't had the time to talk."

"So let's talk tonight," Clay suggested. "You start."

"Okay," Georgie said softly. "Any question?"

"Anything," Clay said.

"Do you blame yourself for your wife's death?"

Clay hesitated. He released her hand and his expression darkened. For a moment, Georgie thought he might react with anger to her impudence. She'd been too bold asking that question so soon in their relationship. She cursed her habit of always desiring to get down to the nitty-gritty.

"I'm sorry. I shouldn't have asked that," she said regretfully.

Clay laughed shortly, looking at her. "It's all right."

"It's none of my business," Georgie went on. She was thoroughly embarrassed. "I'm truly sorry."

"Frisco," Clay began, looking into her dark eyes and loving her more than he did a second ago. "That's one of the things I like about you. You ask the tough questions." He actually grinned at her. "I was so proud of the way you got Carrington to talk. The guy didn't have a snowball's chance in hell of getting away from you."

"That was different," Georgie said. "He was hiding facts that led us to the person behind this whole mess. What I just asked was way too personal."

"Yes," Clay answered suddenly. He wanted her to stop beating up on herself. "Yes, I do blame myself."

"Oh, Clay . . ." Georgie breathed. She got up on her knees on the couch and wrapped her arms around him. Clay laid his head on her bosom.

"I was supposed to meet her at the theater. We were going to see some local playwright's debut. I can't even recall the guy's name now. I was late. Chief Kowalski had John and me staking out the house of a known drug dealer trying to catch certain individuals coming and going. You know, the guys who deal in the neighborhoods. They'd come pick up the drugs from the dealer and distribute it in the neighborhoods. Anyway, to our amazement, while we had him under surveillance, he tried to murder one of his distributors over a dispute about how much money was owed him. We had to prevent the murder and wound up at the police station filling out arrest forms for the next couple of hours. Chief Kowalsi is a stickler for procedure." He blew air between his lips. "By the time I got home, Josie had gone to the play alone. Hours later, she still hadn't returned home. Then I got the phone call. They'd found her body. She'd been shot by a mugger."

Georgie held him against her. "I can see why you blame yourself." She paused to plant a kiss on his forehead. "But you couldn't have done anything differently." She bent her head to kiss his cheek. "I know, if I were in your place, I'd feel the same way. My mother tells me I've always been too serious, always wanting to take on more than I could handle." Tears sat in her ebony eyes. "But this is too much for any one person, Clay."

Clay reached up and wiped her tears away with a finger. His eyes rested on her full lips. Right now, he wanted to take her in his arms and press them against his. He needed to experience her warmth and invite her lovely spirit to reside inside of him, if only for one instant in time.

Georgie didn't wait for him to build up the courage to take what he wanted. She kissed him gently. Their lips touched and parted. Then she took his lower lip between her teeth and lightly pulled on it. Clay moved against her more aggressively, his tongue parting her lips, and they fell back on the couch as the kiss deepened.

His hands were in her braids, caressing her hair. Hers were on his muscular back petitioning more closeness. He could never get close enough for her. I love everything about him, Georgie thought. Is it wrong to want more?

Realizing the depth of his love for his wife had only made her certain of her feelings for him. She cared for this man and she knew that, given time, the caring would turn into love.

However with caring, comes responsibility. All her life's lessons had taught her that, first, you must not harm the one you love in any way. If she made love with Clay tonight and somehow, before all of this was over with, Anne got to her and finished the job she had started, what of Clay? What would her death do to him? For three years now, he'd blamed himself for his wife's death. Georgie didn't want to cause him additional pain.

She broke off the kiss and gazed into his green-brown eyes. Her breathing was labored when she found her voice. "I, um . . . I think we should slow down, Boston."

Sitting up on the couch, Clay regarded her with a quizzical expression. He knew she wanted him, so why the sudden change of heart? He was a gentleman, though, and wouldn't press her to explain. As far as he was concerned, when a relationship moved to the intimate level was always left up to the woman.

He grinned at her. "Whatever you wish, Frisco."

Getting to his feet, he reached down and pulled her up with him. "You missed dinner, didn't you? I bet you're hungry."

"I could use a little something," Georgie agreed, grasping at any reason to change the venue.

They went into the kitchen, a professionally outfitted room with the stove built into the center island and various sized copper-bottomed pots hanging from the ceiling.

Georgie sat on a stool at the breakfast nook while Clay opened the refrigerator to peer inside. He looked back at her. "I've got some roast beef. How about a sandwich?"

"Mustard," Georgie said, smiling slowly. Her emotions were so raw at the moment, tears threatened. What was going through his mind? Did he think she had rejected him because she'd found him lacking in some fundamental way?

She lowered her head and her braids spilled across her face, obscuring it. When she looked up again, Clay was watching her with a smile on his lips.

"Don't sweat it, Georgette."

They stared into one another's eyes for only seconds, but the intensity of emotion communicated in their expressions made it seem like much longer. In an instant, he was standing in front of her, pulling her firmly into his strong arms. She knocked the stool she'd been sitting on over in her rush to meet him halfway.

He bent his head and covered her mouth with his in a rough kiss. Georgie's arms went around his powerful neck as she wholly gave herself to him. Their bodies clung to one another as though they instinctively knew where each curve, every angle fit most perfectly. When he raised his head, he did so only momentarily, and then his mouth was on her throat, her face, her ears.

Georgie's hands were in his short, black hair, her fingers combing the silken curls. Eyes closed, her head thrown back, she felt her body tense in a crescendo of sensual stimulation. As her arousal increased, her resolve diminished. Her desire for him was unprecedented; no other man had made her reach this level of abandon before.

Clay raised his head. Georgie's eyes came open to stare at him curiously.

"I love you, Frisco."

Georgie smiled and parted her lips to speak, but Clay silenced her with a light kiss.

"Don't say anything. I know this is hard for you. You deal in logic and, unfortunately, love is rarely logical. So think about it. Take your time, I'm not in a rush. When we make love, when you confess your feelings, I want it to be a special moment for us. Everything has happened so fast. I can't believe I've only known you four days. It feels like so much longer, like I've always known you." He grinned down at her, revealing straight, white teeth in his dark, copper-colored face. "There, Frisco, you know how this big lug feels. I've said enough."

Too full of emotion to speak, Georgie simply smiled at him. He loved her. A man like Clay didn't take those words lightly. She felt blessed.

Thirteen

On Wednesday afternoon, Jonathan walked straight upstairs to show Georgie the birthday present he'd bought for Ginger: a pair of brown leather Birkenstocks. Georgie would get the private joke. Ginger had been wearing Birkenstocks since she was a hippie hanging out in Haight-Ashbury. She swore by the comfortable sandals, crediting them with the fact that she'd never suffered a bout of arthritis in her life. She power-walked in them, shopped in them, went to church in them. Jonathan was certain her final request would be to go to her grave wearing them.

He frowned when he saw the note he'd left on Georgie's door that morning still taped to her door. Perhaps she hadn't gone out yet, therefore she had not seen the note.

He rang the doorbell. No answer. He knocked. No reply. She had to be in there. It didn't make sense for her to go out without removing the note he'd written to her.

Puzzled, he turned away. Maybe I'm getting dotty in my old age, he thought. He laughed out loud. He'd actually thought he'd heard someone moving about in the apartment last night. Well, he didn't have time to ponder his sanity. He was driving to San Mateo this afternoon for Ginger's party and he was staying over for Thanksgiving tomorrow. Two days with his brothers and sisters. They didn't get many opportunities to be together. He was looking forward to it.

* * *

"We're going to miss spending the day with you too," Georgie told her grandmother over the phone the next morning—Thanksgiving Day. Spending Thanksgiving anywhere other than the house on Poydras Street in New Orleans felt strangely unsettling. She was used to awakening on that special day to the aromas of sweet potato pies baking in the oven and her Gran's delicious savory cornbread dressing. The kind that wasn't stuffed into a bird but baked in its own dish because, quite frankly, it was so good it didn't need a bird to play off of.

Bree was standing next to her, reaching for the phone. However, Marie was not finished talking to Georgie.

"How are things going with you and that darling boy, Clay?"

"What do you mean?" Georgie asked innocently.

"Don't try to deny it," Marie said with laughter in her voice. "Your sister told me how much time you two have been spending alone. I mean there's guarding you and then there's *guarding* you. Which one is it, the former or the latter? Give your grandmother something to dream about. I'm way overdue for a great-grandchild."

"All right," Georgie said, laughing. "I'm somewhat drawn to Mr. Knight."

"Has he kissed you?"

"Yes."

"On the cheek or the lips?"

"Gran . . ."

"Then it was the lips," Marie deduced from her granddaughter's reluctance. "How was it?"

"Gran, you're embarrassing me . . ."

"That means you *really* enjoyed it," Marie said, satisfied. "I'll expect him for Christmas. Okay, let me speak with your sister. Love you, baby."

"I love you, Gran," Georgie returned, fighting back laughter. Her grandmother was always able to make her laugh.

She handed the receiver to Bree, but not before fixing her with an accusatory stare. "I didn't tell her anything. I swear," Bree cried, holding up her right hand as though she were ready to swear to it on a stack of bibles.

"Right," Georgie said, unconvinced.

She left Bree in the library on the phone with their grand-mother and went in search of her mother, whom she'd last seen in the kitchen with Mrs. Hughes. Toni and Mrs. Hughes were sitting at the kitchen table talking companionably when she en-tered the kitchen.

"Georgie," her mother said, looking up at her. "Adelaide, here, has been telling me some interesting things about your father's wife and son and the circumstances surrounding their deaths."

Georgie pulled up a chair at the large, rectangular table and sat down.

"It was a car accident, right?"

"At the time, the police believed that the brakes simply failed to work," her mother explained. She had that excited look on her face that she always wore when she was plotting a story. "So they didn't attempt to connect anyone with the occurrence."

"But," Mrs. Hughes said, adjusting her considerable bulk on her chair, "what your mother and I were wondering is—what if Anne did it?"

"She had a motive," Toni said, looking into Georgie's face to see if she found their reasoning plausible. "In light of everything that's happened recently, we think she was the only one close enough to this family to do something like that. And yet, five years ago, no one suspected her."

A chill came over Georgie.

"If what you say is true," she said in hushed tones, "then that means Anne is even more dangerous than we assumed. She's already killed once. No wonder she didn't hesitate to shoot Kovik. She's killed before and got away with it. She probably figured she'd get away with his death, too."

Maggie came running into the kitchen at that moment, her cheeks red from the exertion. "Adelaide, you'll never guess who had the nerve to show his face at the front door . . ."

"Carrington!" the three women at the table said in unison.

They all rushed from the kitchen to witness what would unfold next in the continuing drama of the Greenbriar household.

* * *

Carson was just returning from showing Carrington to Charles' study when the women cornered him in the hallway. The old gentleman was backed up against the wall by their steady barrage of questions.

"I don't know why he's here," he told them sternly. He took it as a personal affront that they would be so openly curious about the master's affairs. "Pardon my saying so, Miss," he began directing his remark to Toni, "but if Mr. Waters wants you to know why Mr. Carrington is here, he will surely tell you." Pulling himself up to his full five feet, nine inches, he continued. "And I'm surprised at you, Mrs. Hughes. You were trained properly." With that, he turned and left them.

"He's getting more crotchety every day," Mrs. Hughes complained good-naturedly. She sighed. "Well, I guess we'll just have to wait and see."

In the study, Benjamin was preparing to excuse himself, believing his uncle wished to speak with the dismissed chauffeur alone. Charles, however, asked him to stay. "You should hear this, Benjamin," he said.

Wondering why but obeying nonetheless, Benjamin returned to his seat in the leather wing chair near the French doors. His uncle remained behind his desk and Carrington stood.

Charles regarded Carrington with as much patience as he could muster. He had been thinking that he may have behaved too rashly by allowing the chauffeur to walk away unscathed.

"What is it, Carrington?" he said sharply.

"There's something I think you need to know, Mr. Waters," Carrington began. He shifted his weight from leg to leg, trying to get up the nerve to say what had to be said.

"Out with it, man," Charles said impatiently.

Carrington told him the account of how Anne had come to the garage that day, five years ago, full of questions and of his suspicions that she was behind the deaths of Mariel and Charles III.

"I don't have any proof," Carrington concluded. "But everything points to her. I had no way of knowing, at the time, the depth of Anne's feelings for you or the lengths to which she'd go to . . ." He glanced furtively in Benjamin's direction.

"Yes, yes," Charles said hurriedly. "I see what you mean. Is that all, Carrington?"

"Yes, sir. I'm sorry. I truly am sorry," Carrington said, backing from the room.

Charles was gripping the edge of his desk so tightly, his knuckles were nearly white. Mortified, trembling with rage, he rose from his chair. Seeing murderous intent in his former employer's eyes, Carrington made a hasty retreat.

Benjamin, shocked and incensed by what he'd just heard, went to his uncle and caught him by the shoulders. "Could it be true, Uncle? Could Anne Ballentine have been responsible for Aunt Mariel's and Chuck's deaths?"

Water sat in Charles' eyes when he raised them to his nephew's face. He hadn't had time to digest the information himself, but with a strong sense of duty, he pressed on. "Ben, my boy, there's something you should know."

Ben laughed nervously. "Uncle, you're scaring me."

"Believe me, if I could alter the events which have led us to this moment, I would. But, as in all things of this nature, I'm completely powerless," his uncle told him sadly. "Ben, you have known you were adopted for some time now."

"Of course," Ben replied shakily.

Remembering the document that had recently been faxed to him from the courthouse in Gloucester, Charles went to his desk to get it. Coming back around the desk, he handed it to Benjamin. "I believe this will explain things a lot better than I ever could," he said, clarifying his actions.

Benjamin looked down at the document for a few moments, then back up at his uncle. "This is my birth certificate," he said, his voice quivering.

Charles nodded.

"Anne is my mother?"

"Yes, Benjamin. Anne Ballentine is your birth mother," Charles said. He wished he could spare Benjamin the hurt that knowledge was sure to cause. Lately, he'd come to realize that all the wealth he'd worked so hard to accumulate hadn't been able to cushion the blows of life. He hadn't been able to protect his wife and son from a madwoman. Money hadn't made him a better father to his girls. Money had come between him and Toni. And now, wealth and power would not erase the stigma of being the son of a killer for Benjamin.

"We only found out recently," Charles explained further. "It seems she came here so that she would be near you. I don't know why she didn't simply tell you she was your mother and leave it at that. She was mentally ill, son. She thought that if my family were no longer in the picture, I would turn to her, and then she'd reveal her true identity and we'd all be one happy family."

"Anne is my mother," Benjamin repeated as though he were a record stuck in a groove. "Anne is my mother." He looked into his uncle's eyes. "You know what this means, don't you?"

"It doesn't mean anything, Benjamin," Charles told him emphatically, guessing what Benjamin was thinking. His mother was unbalanced—perhaps it was a genetic disorder. "It's simply a happenstance of birth. The fact that Anne is your birth mother has no bearing whatsoever on who you are."

"You can't be serious, Uncle," Benjamin shouted. The veins in his forehead were visible. "My mother was a murderer. She had to be stark raving mad!"

The women, who had been standing outside the study ever since Carrington left in a hurry, shuddered. Toni decided they'd heard enough and turning to Georgie, said, "I think we can all find something better to do."

Even Mrs. Hughes could agree to that. She headed back to the kitchen, feeling quite contrite. Maggie followed. Toni and Georgie went in search of Bree.

"Do you suppose there were no murderers in my gene pool?" Charles asked. "Come now, Ben. We both know that being related to someone who is guilty of atrocities does not make us guilty by reason of association. If that were so, then the parents of past murderers should have been put to death alongside their offspring. It's preposterous. It was Anne's environment, her constant conviction that she'd been wronged by having you snatched from her arms, that drove her insane. She became obsessed and she fed that obsession until she had to somehow make her twisted desires a reality."

Charles paused to place a strong hand on Benjamin's shoulder in reassurance. "Don't start doubting yourself, my boy. There's absolutely nothing wrong with you. You are the most decent young man I've ever had the pleasure of knowing."

Benjamin didn't appear convinced. He was breathing hard and his eyes were wild. "Oh, God," he said, his eyes stretching, "Cassie. I've got to break our engagement. I'd never subject Cassie to the embarrassment sure to follow when this gets out."

He broke free of his uncle's hold and hurried to the door. Looking back, he said, "You can expect my resignation on your desk by this afternoon. And I'll be moving out as soon as possible."

"Ben! Ben!" Charles called after him.

Benjamin, however, didn't look back.

Charles ran after him, to no avail. Benjamin had youth and determination on his side. Then, too, some part of Charles knew that Ben would have to go through this crisis on his own. He was confident that Ben's intelligence and his strong common sense would win over his present panicked state of mind.

Charles stood looking after Ben as he stormed from the house, slamming the door after him. And he, once again, cursed everything that came with wealth and position. He was certain that Ben wouldn't have reacted as strongly to the revelation if he'd been brought up differently. But with the trappings of wealth came the belief that you were better than others. And when Ben had learned of his birth mother, he therefore assumed he was no longer the man he had been all his life. He no longer deserved Cassie. He no longer deserved his position with the company.

Rubbing his shoulder, which had begun to throb, Charles turned and began walking toward the back of the house to the kitchen. He needed a drink and, although Cook didn't know he knew, the good bourbon was kept in the kitchen. For once, he was going to break his rule of never drinking hard liquor before nightfall.

* * *

Anne was enjoying the comfortable coziness of Georgie's apartment. Whenever Jonathan Crenshaw was in, she had to be as quiet as a mouse, but that didn't cramp her style. She was a quiet person anyway.

A few minutes ago, she had watched from the window as the old man had gotten into his Chevrolet Impala, circa 1982, and driven off. She didn't know how long he was going to stay, but she assumed he would be staying overnight because he'd been carrying a duffle bag and a garment bag. He was probably attending a dress-up affair. She hoped he had a good time. He seemed like a nice fellow. The note he'd left on Georgie's door attested to that: "Dear Georgie," he'd written, "Welcome back. Come downstairs the first chance you get. I've got a new Sarah Vaughn CD I want you to hear. She's divine."

Thanksgiving dinner at Greenbriar was a sombre affair. Mrs. Hughes had done a wonderful job on the meal. In keeping with the tradition of the house, she'd roasted a duck instead of a turkey and the side dishes were fresh peas with pearl onions; cornbread dressing, which she'd prepared because she'd overheard Georgie say she was going to miss her grandmother's; glazed sweet potatoes; mustard greens, a bow to her own Southern roots. Mr. Waters usually loved her mustard greens, but today, his plate came back half full.

Toni, sitting next to Charles at the head of the table, looked out over the rest of the diners. Georgie and Clay were in their own world. Bree, uncommonly quiet. When she was a little girl, Toni would always know Bree was up to something when she was in a pensive mood. She wondered what was going on in her mind now. She was supposed to be in San Francisco tomorrow for her big audition. She was undoubtedly still upset about having to miss it.

"Listen," Toni said to the entire assemblage, "I know things aren't the way we'd like them to be. But, by God, I think we can each name at least one thing we're grateful for today." Looking at Charles, she said, "Chuck, you go first."

Charles, his mind wholly on Benjamin at the moment, forced a wan smile.

"I think it's obvious what I'm most grateful for," he said. "I thank God that you all are in my life, at last."

"Bree?" Toni prompted her daughter.

Bree reached across the table and took her father's hand in hers. "I'm grateful for the same thing," she replied, smiling into her father's eyes. "I realize I may never get the opportunity to work for Dominic Solomon, but I have to be philosophical about it. At least I'm alive."

"I knew that if you dug deep enough, you'd come up with something," Toni joked. "Clay?"

Clay looked at Georgie in such a way that everyone at the table knew what he was grateful for. "I'm just grateful to be here," he said simply.

"Me, too," Georgie agreed, looking into his eyes.

"We all know what you two are grateful for this year," Toni said, a smile on her lips. "All right. Here's what I'm grateful for: I'm happy that the truth has been told, no matter what the consequences may be. I lived for nearly thirty years with a lie, and I'm relieved to have it revealed." She reached over and grasped Charles' hands. Her daughters let out audible gasps. "I know you're worried about Benjamin," she said to him. "But if he's as good a man as I think he is, he will survive this. Cassie will help him, I'm sure. She will make him realize what's important and what isn't. So, try not to worry." Her dark-brown eyes now rested on Bree. "And my youngest? You're talented. There will be more opportunities for you. I've no doubt that one day, I'm going to be sitting in the audience at the Oscars watching you receive an award."

A single tear ran down Bree's right cheek.

"You see what I mean?" Toni said, pointing at it. "You're already rehearsing your acceptance speech."

Everyone laughed.

"Now, you two," Toni said to Georgie and Clay, "all I'm going to say is: Bravo, for finding some light in all this apparent darkness. I won't embarrass you further."

Georgie mouthed the words, "Thank you."

Benjamin was supposed to pick Cassie up at her parents' home in Brookline at 6 p.m. By then, Cassie would have spent time with her relatives, close and distant. Then she could have made her apologies and left without having to make too many excuses. Ben was late. He'd stopped at a bar and had two Jack-and-Cokes. Teresa Morelle wiggled her nose distastefully at the odor of the Jack Daniels on his breath. She didn't say anything, however.

"Mrs. Morelle," Benjamin said as he stepped into the foyer, "I need to see Cassie right away."

"Ben." Teresa had never seen him lacking composure. Oh no, she thought, what has that girl done now? I hope Cassie hasn't done anything to ruin the wedding. Teresa had already phoned the best wedding planner in Boston and discussed her ideas. "Come on in," she said to Ben now. "I'll go round-up Cassie for you. I think she's upstairs in her grandmother's bedroom."

"I suppose Benjamin Waters will do," Elizabeth Morelle was saying to Cassie at that moment. Seventy-two years old, Elizabeth was sitting in bed with a frilly pink bed jacket over her gown. She didn't receive visitors in her gown alone. She had taken to her bed because Teresa had invited, Beryl, Elizabeth's sister to Thanksgiving dinner, and she and Beryl were involved in a long-standing feud. Ten years ago, before both their husbands' deaths (some say they occurred to escape the sisters' continual bickering), Beryl had made the unforgivable mistake of revealing Elizabeth's true hair color to her stylist. Soon, all of their friends knew that Elizabeth dyed her hair. Knowing full well that Beryl was the only person who could have revealed the secret since Beryl was the only soul she'd told (as Elizabeth colored her own hair to avoid being found out), Elizabeth had not spoken to her sister in over a decade.

"Of course we may never know his true heritage," Elizabeth continued haughtily. "God knows what kind of people he came from. But he is a Waters now and that counts for something in this world. Cassandra, are you listening to me?"

Cassie smiled politely. Actually, her grandmother had lost her when she'd started expounding upon the importance of the right set of parents. Cassie didn't believe that anymore than she believed the moon was made of green cheese. Look at her. She came from social-climbing parents and a grandmother who lived in the past because she thought it was a more genteel time. A time when poorer blacks bowed to her on the street and looked at her with awe in their eyes. Yet, Cassie believed a person created herself. One made choices, good or bad. Those choices were what decided the kind of life one led.

Looking into her grandmother's pale, rouged face, she sighed. "It's really a shame you didn't get downstairs today. Aunt Beryl looked especially smart. I hear it's because she has a new beau— Chester Montgomery. You know him, don't you? He's one of the *Salem* Montgomerys."

Frowning, Elizabeth quickly swung her legs off the bed and rose. "Why that little minx. She knows I'm interested in Chester." Purposefully walking toward the door, she looked up at Cassie. "Is she still here? I want a word with her."

"Don't you think you ought to get dressed first?" Cassie asked, smiling.

"Oh, yes," Elizabeth said, looking down at her feminine nightgown in surprise.

Cassie turned to leave. "I'm glad you're feeling better, Grandma. I'll go downstairs and make sure Aunt Beryl stays put while you get dressed."

"You do that," Elizabeth called after her.

Smiling, Cassie left the room. Well that put some pep into the old girl, she thought.

She met her mother on the landing as she was going downstairs.

"Cassie," Teresa said, "Ben is here. What's going on between you two? He looks awful. Did you two get into a fight so soon after the engagement?"

Cassie stared at her mother.

"Where is he?" she asked. She had no intention of allowing her mother to play on her insecurities today. Cassie knew of the troubles going on over at Greenbriar, and there may have been serious developments.

"I left him in the foyer," her mother replied. Curiosity was eating her up. "Cassie?"

Cassie continued her descent. "I'll call you, Mother," she said.

Teresa Morelle knew what that meant. Sometimes, when Cassie was working on a project in the laboratory, she wouldn't hear from her for weeks at a time.

"Don't forget to phone, Cassie," she admonished.

Cassie's heart skipped a beat when she saw Ben. He was pacing nervously and his clothes were disheveled. But it was the look in his eyes that disturbed her the most. He had a panicked, caged-animal expression in his light brown eyes.

Pausing at the hall tree next to the front door, she grabbed her coat. Ben woodenly helped her on with it. She took his hand and led him outside.

Outside on the portico, she put her arms around him and held him tightly.

"No matter what it is, Ben, we'll work it out together," she told him, her voice emotion-filled. Her eyes met his. Something in Ben's began to pulse with life again. Cassie saw that glimmer and it calmed her somewhat.

"Now tell me," she said calmly. "Tell me everything. Don't leave out anything."

"Anne Ballentine was my mother," Benjamin commented dryly. "I think that says it all."

"Let's walk," Cassie said. She stepped down off the portico, descending the steps. Ben followed.

Her parents' home sat on two acres and was surrounded by spruce trees. They walked away from the house, past the late model automobiles owned by the friends and relatives inside enjoying Teresa and David Morelle's hospitality.

"This is a shock," Cassie said, looking up at Ben. "You must be reeling. But with all shocks, you've got to distance yourself from it in order to cope with it. Give yourself time for your head to stop spinning."

"I don't need time," Ben told her. "I came here to tell you the wedding's off. I can't marry you knowing my mother was mentally deficient. And now, we've recently learned she may have been a killer. I'm her son. I may be a time bomb waiting to go off. I can't subject you to that, Cassie." He related to her Carrington's theory about Anne's motive for getting rid of Charles' family.

Afterward, Cassie stepped forward and tried to hug him to her. Ben moved away from her, turning his back to her. "I don't want your pity. I've already made up my mind about this. You don't need me hanging around your neck."

Energized by her outrage, Cassie went to him and jerked him around to face her. "Look at me, Ben."

He reluctantly met her gaze.

"You did not inherit Anne's neuroses. Her experiences made her what she was. Take it from a geneticist: you are not a time bomb waiting to explode. We aren't able to pick and choose who our parents are. God knows I would have chosen less materialistic parents. But I'm stuck with them, and you're stuck with Anne. Who knows what happened to her to make her disassociate the way she did? We'll never know the hell she went through. But you can't start obsessing about your becoming like Anne because then you will be feeding your psyche the wrong message. Ben, we all have skeletons in our closets. Take my family, for example. For all my grandmother's boasting about coming from the elite class of Bostonians, her father was a bootblack. But did that make him a bad person? No. I only knew him briefly as a child, but Grandpa Nathan was the sweetest man, next to you, I've ever known. I sometimes detest my grandmother for never talking about him. Since she married a Morelle, she wants everyone to think she just appeared out of thin air, that she has no background."

The cold wind whipped their coats about them, but Cassie was unmindful of the temperature. She had to get through to Ben. Their lives together depended on it, and she was not about to give him up.

Cassie placed Ben's hand over her heart. "I love you, Ben. I guess I've loved you since the moment we met, and you told me how pretty I was in my outdated dress." She smiled, however, tears sat in her eyes. "I don't want to lose you over this. We can move past this. We're strong enough to survive."

Tears rolled down Ben's cheeks. He pulled Cassie into his arms.

"Cassie, Cassie. What cloud did you come down on?"

Cassie didn't answer that. Relief flooded her body. She buried her face in his chest and reveled in the moment. Then, she looked heavenward and silently thanked God for helping her come up with the words she'd spoken. She most definitely hadn't done it on her own.

Bree sat cross-legged on her bed in her room going over her checklist of things she had to remember to do in order to make a clean getaway tonight.

First, she had to disengage the alarm. She'd watched Clay enough to know how to do that efficiently. She'd written down the codes and memorized them. Numbers had never been her forte, but it hadn't been that difficult to do.

Next, she had to avoid Mrs. Hughes on her nightly raid of the refrigerator. Bree was leaving by the back door, and she had to time her escape just right in order to not be detected by the cook. For two nights in a row, she'd observed Mrs. Hughes make her rounds at approximately midnight. She figured she would be able to sneak out the back door at half past midnight. Mrs. Hughes usually took her booty back to her bedroom instead of consuming it in the kitchen. She probably watched the late show while chowing down. It was how she maintained her impressive girth.

Finally, she had to travel light. A few clothes thrown into her overnight bag in one hand. Her purse on her shoulder and Pierre in his travel cage in her other hand.

She patted the bed, getting Pierre's attention. He had been sitting on the window seat looking longingly outside.

"Okay," Bree said, "I think I have everything down pat. All I have to do now is wait."

Pierre pounced up on her, answering her call. She smoothed the hair out of his eyes. "You need a haircut," she said.

"Quabird?" Georgie said skeptically, looking at Clay over the Scrabble board. "That's not a word."

"Of course it's a word," Clay said confidently. "It's a type of heron."

"You don't say."

"I do say," Clay replied, smiling at her. "Look it up if you don't believe me. And while you're looking it up, you may also make a note of the fact that practically every word in the dictionary that begins with a 'q' is followed by the vowel 'u.' Such as: quack, quadrangle, quadrant and so forth."

They were in the library and Georgie walked over to the huge dictionary on its own pedestal sitting next to the globe and looked up the word "quabird."

Going back to her seat across from Clay, she laughed. "You were right. It's a black-crowned night heron. What? Do you sit up nights reading the dictionary?"

"After Josie was killed, I read through the dictionary, and the Bible and the works of William Shakespeare," Clay said. His deep hazel eyes held a melancholy light in them. "I suffered from insomnia that first year."

Georgie reached across the table and placed her hand atop his. She had no response to that.

"Your turn," Clay said, breaking the silence.

The phone rang just as Georgie added letters to the word "row" to form the word "throw."

"Should we get that?" Clay wondered. "It's after eleven, Carson should be retired for the night."

"If Dad doesn't get it in three rings, then we'll get it," Georgie said.

"Dad? Did you just call your father Dad?"

"I like the sound of it. Before I'm done, I may call him Pop or Daddy or Papa. That's what Mom calls Granddad. I sort of like the ring of that. Anyway, I'm getting my feet wet with this father thing. Okay?"

Clay smiled at her. "The phone stopped ringing. Your Dad must have gotten it."

A moment later, the phone buzzed there in the library. Clay got up to answer it.

"Hello?"

Charles' voice said, "Clay, Detective Bendini is on the line. Would you speak with him?"

"Of course. John?"

"Clay," John said without preamble, "She's alive. On Monday morning, she took a flight out of Worcester. Her destination: San Francisco."

"Damn!" Clay uttered harshly.

"Sorry, buddy," John said regrettably. "Looks like you're heading to San Francisco in the morning."

Charles and Toni appeared in the doorway. They looked expectantly at Clay who hadn't yet hung up the phone.

"All right," he said into the mouthpiece. "Thanks, John. I owe you one."

"I didn't do anything," John said modestly.

"You didn't tell me I was nuts when I told you I thought she'd escaped," Clay told him seriously. They rang off.

Clay turned to find three pairs of eyes on him.

"She's in San Francisco," he told them. "She took a flight out of Worcester Monday morning. She has been in San Francisco all week."

"Where's Bree?" Georgie asked her mother. "She ought to hear this."

"She went to bed," Toni replied. "Let her sleep. She'll know soon enough. At least she'll get a good night's rest."

At 12:30 a.m., Bree carefully cracked her door and looked down the dimly-lit hallway. Easing out of the bedroom, she made certain the door didn't slam shut behind her, or that she accidentally scraped Pierre's cage against the door frame. As she passed her sister's room, she noticed a stream of light coming from underneath. Georgie stayed up late reading. She paused, listening. Then, she hurried down the carpeted hallway, mindful that she'd told the dispatcher at the cab company that she'd be downstairs waiting at the back gate promptly at 12:45 a.m.

When she got down to the kitchen, she waited at the entrance until she saw that the coast was clear. Mrs. Hughes had come and gone already. She breathed a sigh of relief. Fearing for her safety, Mrs. Hughes would think it her duty to prevent her from leaving the house in the middle of the night.

At the back door, she quickly punched in the appropriate numbers on the security alarm's panel. She then made sure the door was locked after her. Stepping onto the back porch, she realized it was snowing. She pulled her coat closer around her and hurried down the back steps. She was grateful her father didn't own a pack of Doberman Pinchers. She and Pierre wouldn't have lasted a second against them. But then, she would have devised a different plan, if there had been dogs involved. In one of her Jody Freeman movies, she had placed a mild tranquilizer in a pound of ground beef and fed it to watchdogs at a nuclear plant she'd been breaking into. Maybe that would have worked.

She was out of breath by the time she reached the gate which sat a good two hundred yards from the back door. Drat! The cab hadn't arrived. She disengaged the alarm on the back gate and stepped outside of the property. She hadn't wanted to go outside until she saw the cab approaching, for her own safety. However, since he was late, she'd have to go outside because standing near the gate, anyone could plainly see her illuminated in the security lights pointed at the gate.

The cab arrived five minutes late. She climbed in and berated the driver.

"You're late, what kept you? It couldn't have been the traffic at this time of night."

"I got lost, lady," the Pakistani driver said, hunching his shoulders apologetically. "This isn't my normal route."

Bree settled back on the seat. It didn't matter. She was out of there. She would get the red-eye to San Francisco and, God willing, be walking into the Fairmont by 2 p.m. tomorrow afternoon.

Pierre barked.

"Hey, what've you got back there, lady?" the cabbie asked nervously. "No animals loose in the car."

"All right, all right," Bree said impatiently. "He's in his cage. Don't worry about it. Logan International Airport and step on it."

Bree smiled to herself. She'd always wanted to tell a cab driver to step on it.

"In this weather?" the prudent driver asked incredulously. "Are you crazy, lady?"

Yes! Bree thought triumphantly. And I'm going to make that audition.

Fourteen

Bree was almost tempted to return to her warm, cozy bed at Greenbriar when she heard the shattering news: Logan International Airport was snowed-in until further notice. She sat in the waiting area silently fuming.

A middle-aged brunette with a short, tapered hairstyle and warm, open brown eyes, sat down next to her. "Can you believe this?"

"It can't be snowing that hard," Bree complained. She was a veteran traveller and had taken-off in worse conditions than these. She glanced out the window. It wasn't even snowing any longer.

"If you ask me," the woman said, "their instruments are probably fouling up. They're blaming it on the snow to keep us from panicking once we get on the plane."

Bree looked into the woman's clear, brown eyes and frowned. "You think so?"

"Like you said," the woman replied, "it isn't snowing that hard."

"In that case, I'll gladly wait," Bree said. "I don't want to get on a plane that isn't fit to be in the air."

She bent her head to peer at Pierre in his travel-cage. "Are you okay, sweetie? We're going to be a little delayed, but we'll get to Frisco on time. A little snow isn't going to stop us."

"Are you from San Francisco?" the woman inquired.

"No," Bree told her. "I'm going there for a meeting."

"The day after Thanksgiving? Didn't you get a four-day week-end?"

"It's an important meeting," Bree said.

"It must be," the woman said. She yawned. "The only reason I'm going home is because my son was in a motorcycle accident yesterday. He's doing okay, but I'd rather be with him than with the in-laws, you know?"

"I'm sorry to hear that," Bree said sympathetically. She offered her hand to the woman in greeting. "I'm Briane Shaw."

"Briane . . ." the woman said thoughtfully. "Briane, you look so familiar to me. Have we ever met before?"

Bree smiled. "No, but you'd be surprised by the number of people who ask me that question. I work as an actor. I've done quite a bit of television work. You probably saw me in passing once or twice, and that's why I look familiar to you."

The woman's smile broadened. "That's it! Jody Freeman. I *love* those movies. I've seen all of them. You're very talented. I'm Judy Vincent, by the way."

Bree grinned. "Nice to meet you. Thank you."

"No, I really mean it. I'm not just a lay person. I work in television. I direct Uncle Walter's Workshop. You know, the kiddie show . . ."

"I grew up on Uncle Walter," Bree told her. "I learned how to build a bird house watching him."

"I directed that episode," Judy told her proudly.

"Tell me something," Bree said, delighted to be talking to someone in the business. "Why did they replace Dirk Jergen? I thought he was the perfect Uncle Walter. He had that kind, friendly face, and a wonderful voice."

"Dirk has Alzheimer's," Judy said sadly. "I wanted to close down the show after he retired, but the producers brought in Barry Howser."

"Do you like working with him?" Bree asked.

"He's a fair actor," Judy said. "But we all miss Dirk terribly. He was an institution. And you want to know something else? The kindness he exhibited on television translated to his actual life. He is an exemplary human being."

Bree sighed wistfully. "I'm so happy to hear that. At least one of my childhood illusions hasn't been blown to bits."

Judy laughed softly. She smoothed her short, brown hair away from her face. "What's the important meeting you're going to San Francisco for?"

"A job interview," Bree said easily. She liked Judy's forthrightness.

"You're not making any more of the Jody Freeman films?" Judy asked, alarmed.

"Oh sure," Bree told her. "At least one more. I'm under contract to do a Jody film in Jamaica in February."

"Jamaica? Sounds intriguing. What sort of mess has Jody gotten herself into this time?"

Bree laughed. "This time, Jody is up against modern-day pirates who rob and murder wealthy yachtsmen on the high seas."

"I can't wait to see it," Judy told her. "Will there be a romantic interest in it for Jody this time? Poor girl, she never gets the man."

"The man is usually the culprit," Bree reminded her.

"Yes, but most of them were handsome devils, weren't they?"

"Wait until you see the one we have in the can," Bree said. "Patrick Ashton is my co-star and he is *gawgeous.*" She ended with a fair imitation of Patrick's Georgia accent.

"I've seen his work," Judy said excitedly. "I'll have to tell my friend, Gwyn, to look for it when it comes on. She's smitten with Patrick Ashton."

They talked for two hours straight, and Bree didn't notice the time slipping away. Finally, at 3 a.m., the announcer came over the P.A. system and said, "Flight 242 boarding for San Francisco. Anyone with infirmities and people with small children, please board first."

Georgie awoke at six and hastily showered and dressed. Her father had phoned the company's pilot last night to inform him that he needed to be fueled-up and have his flight-plan filed before seven that morning, weather permitting.

After coming out of the shower, she donned her robe and sat on the bed to dial Bree's number. Bree would be pleased that they were going to San Francisco this morning. With luck, she'd be able to audition for the part of Romalia, the warrior-princess, after all.

The phone rang six times before Georgie decided to walk over to Bree's bedroom and knock on the door. Unlike her, Bree was a heavy sleeper. If she had gone to bed dead-tired, it would be even more difficult to awaken her than usual.

Georgie knocked. She waited two or three seconds then turned the doorknob and walked in. "Coming in . . ."

Bree's bed hadn't been slept in. Instantly suspicious, Georgie quickly searched the large suite. On the bureau, she found an almost illegible note: "Sorry, but this is my chance. I couldn't blow it."

Georgie sat on the bed and dialed Clay's room number.

"Yeah? Clay here," he said crisply.

"Bree took off in the middle of the night," Georgie informed him angrily. "That sneaky little . . ."

"Her agent," Clay said, thinking swiftly on his feet. "Her agent would know where the meeting's going to be held. You know her agent, don't you?"

"It's Arieanna Sanchez. She and Bree were in acting school together."

"Do you know how to contact her?"

"I never had a reason to contact her before. She's Bree's friend, not mine," the panic was more evident in her voice now. Anne was in San Francisco patiently spinning her web into which Bree possibly was about to be caught.

"Maybe your mother knows her number," Clay said hopefully. "Are you dressed?"

"Partially," Georgie answered.

"Then I'll talk to your mother while you finish dressing. Get downstairs as soon as possible. We leave in ten minutes."

Toni didn't know Ari's number. They dialed directory assistance and got her office number. The office was closed for the holiday. The recording did, however, give a number where Ari could be reached in case of an emergency.

Toni dialed the number. She, Charles and Clay were in the living room and she looked up into Charles' stricken face as she listened to a busy signal.

"No answer," she said.

"There's a time difference," Clay said. "What is it, a three hour difference? It's only 4 a.m. there. Maybe she took it off the hook in order to get some rest."

"Then why would she leave that number in case of an emergency if she was not going to answer it?" Toni cried, exasperated.

"We can keep trying her number on the plane," Charles suggested. "We should be going."

Georgie entered the room as if on cue, fully dressed and eager to leave. Directly behind her stood Benjamin, whom none of them expected to see.

"What is this I hear about Bree being missing?"

Looking out the window, Clay spied the limousine pulling up out front.

"We don't have time to explain now, Ben. If you'd like to ride to the airport with us, we can fill you in on the way."

They got in the idling stretch-limousine and the new driver—a man Charles had hired directly from an agency who thoroughly checked the references of their employees—drove away from Greenbriar.

Ben's eyes rested on his uncle's face. "After yesterday," he said, "I think I deserve to be apprised of the goings on around here . . ."

"I've already told you there was the possibility that Anne is still alive," Charles began. "Last night, we found out she had been on a flight to San Francisco on the twenty-fourth, Monday. And, sometime last night, your cousin left. Knowing how much the audition with Dominic Solomon meant to her, we believe she's heading to San Francisco."

"I would say that's an accurate assumption," Ben said, catching on. "And I take it you also assume Anne is lying-in-wait for

Bree, for whom she'd guess the audition would be too big an opportunity to pass up."

"Exactly," Georgie said, taking up where her father had left off. "Now, what we have to do is get there in time to prevent Anne from harming Bree."

"We've already tried to phone her agent, with no luck," Toni put in.

"And I'm on the phone with Logan International Airport right now," Clay told him. He spoke into the receiver. "You can't give out that sort of information?" he said angrily. "But it's a matter of life or death. Miss Shaw could be in danger."

He paused, listening intently. Then he said, "Fine, I'll have the authorities contact you."

He hung up. Sighing, he told the others, "I'll call John. He'll get the flight information and phone me back."

He set about doing it.

When Clay got off the phone with John, Georgie reached for the handset.

"I should phone Jonathan and ask him to be on the look-out for Bree. She has the key to my apartment. If her flight arrives early enough, she'll go to my place and leave Pierre there."

"Good thinking," Clay said, handing her the phone. "And John is getting that information. He should be able to call us back with it soon."

Georgie frowned as she pressed the shut-off button on the cellular phone.

"No one's at home on Lombard Street. If he were there, he would've answered." She thought hard, then she recalled what Jonathan had told her last Friday. Ginger's birthday was coming up.

Smiling, she punched in the numbers to the California directory assistance line. "Jonathan's sister's birthday was yesterday. This year it fell on Thanksgiving. He probably went down to San Mateo to help her celebrate and spent the night."

The operator came on the line. "What city, please?"

"San Mateo," Georgie spoke crisply. "I need the number of a Ginger Crenshaw. She lives on Coconut Grove Avenue."

The operator was silent a few seconds and then a recorded voice said, "the number is: 555-2368."

Georgie hung up and dialed the number. "Oh Lord, it's only four o'clock in the morning there. I'm about to awaken a house full of elderly folks."

The phone rang twice and then a spry feminine voice answered with, "Good morning, what can I do for you?"

"Ginger," Georgie said, "is that you?"

"Of course it is," Ginger said, laughing. "You dialed my number, didn't you?"

Georgie laughed, too. "Ginger, this is Georgie Shaw. You remember me. I accompanied Jonathan down there a few months back . . ."

"Georgie. This is a surprise. Are you in California? Jonathan said you and your sister were going to New Orleans for Thanksgiving. But then, last night, he told us this weird tale about hearing footsteps upstairs in your apartment Wednesday night." Ginger went on excitedly. "You probably want to talk with him, don't you? He's up, we all are. We're getting ready to go clamming. The best time is early in the morning."

"Yes," Georgie told her, finally able to get a word in. "It's important, Ginger."

Jonathan came on the line. "Georgie?"

"Yes, Jonathan . . ."

"I thought Ginger was pulling my leg. How'd you find me?"

"I remembered you said Ginger's birthday was coming up, so I just put two and two together. Listen, Jonathan. I can't explain everything to you right now, but I promise I will as soon as things settle down. When are you returning home?"

"Not until Sunday," Jonathan told her.

Georgie realized then that he would be of no help to them. She'd have to think of some other way to head Bree off. She was curious about what Ginger had been referring to earlier, however.

"Jonathan, do you really think you heard someone in my apartment Wednesday night?"

"At the time, I was certain of it. But now, I'm not so sure. Maybe my hearing's beginning to go."

Georgie didn't think that was likely. What if Anne had somehow found out where she lived and broken into her apartment? Her father had said Anne'd had access to his personal files. Anne's resources were probably drying up. She wouldn't want to use her credit card to check into a hotel, the authorities would be able to trace her. However, who would look for her on Lombard Street?

"You be careful, Georgie," Jonathan said, concern apparent in his voice.

"Jonathan won't be returning to San Francisco until Sunday," Georgie told the others after she hung up.

"Too late to help us," Toni said morosely.

"What was that about someone being in your apartment?" Clay asked Georgie.

"Jonathan thinks he heard footsteps upstairs Wednesday night. That would have given Anne time enough to arrive in San Francisco. With delays, stopovers, or whatever else could have held her up, she could have definitely been in San Francisco by Wednesday."

"True," Clay agreed. "And from the description John gave me of the episode in the Parliament Hotel, she knows how to jimmy a lock. It's a distinct possibility that Anne was in your apartment Wednesday night."

"We've got to call everyone we know in San Francisco and ask them to try to get to Bree before she gets to your apartment, baby," Toni said to Georgie.

The two women immediately opened their purses and removed their voluminous date books. The men looked on in disbelief.

"You carry your entire lives around in your purses," Clay stated, representing his brothers.

"You never know what you're going to need," Toni said lightly. "Now, if we didn't have the addresses and phone numbers of our friends in these books, we would be in even more of a mess than we already are."

Looking up at Georgie to coordinate their next line of defense, she said, "I'll phone Margery and Daniel. You try Sammy."

"Right," Georgie said.

Margery Devlin Lincoln answered on the first ring. Toni could imagine her friend of thirty years rolling over in bed and picking up the phone on her nightstand. Daniel Lincoln, her husband, would be awakening, too, and wondering who was calling them at four-thirty in the morning.

In San Francisco, Margery rubbed her eyes gently and switched on the bedside lamp while holding the phone to her ear. She was in her late forties, petite with golden-brown skin that defied aging and sooty black hair that she wore in a short cut that framed her pretty heart-shaped face.

Margery was a veteran actor who was still popular enough after a twenty-five year career to command excellent roles and exorbitant salaries. Her husband, Daniel, was a highly venerated thespian as well. A tall, very dark-skinned man with uniquely handsome features that made his face recognizable to millions of ardent fans worldwide.

He turned over on his side now and continued snoring.

"Hello?" Margery mumbled sleepily. She had not fully opened her eyes yet.

"Margery," was all Toni had to say.

"Toni, my God. Has anything happened to your parents, the girls?" Margery asked worriedly as she sat up in bed.

Toni gave her a shortened version of what was going on. Then she said, "We need someone to go over to Georgie's apartment right away and wait for Bree. We can't let her go inside. Anne may be in there ready to do God knows what to her."

"I understand," Margery said on her end. "Daniel and I will get over there right away. I'm taking my cellular phone with me. Call me if anything else comes up. I love you, darling."

"I love you," Toni said. She shut off the phone and handed it to Georgie. "Your turn."

"If only we could get Arieanna Sanchez," Georgie mused as she punched in Sammy's phone number. "Then we'd know what time the appointment is for and could judge more accurately whether Bree would go straight to the audition or stop off at my place first."

Sammy answered after four rings. "Mmm . . ." was the only sound Georgie heard.

"Sammy Chan!" she cried. "Sammy, wake up."

"Georgie?" Sammy said groggily. "What's wrong?"

"Sammy, Bree's in trouble and I need your help . . ." She went on to explain the situation to him and when she'd finished, Sammy was wide awake.

"I'll see if I can intercept her at the airport," Sammy said. "Don't worry, Georgie. We'll get to her in time."

Georgie hung the phone up and sat quietly for a moment. Clay reached over and took her hand in his. "We'll get there in time," he told her reassuringly, almost echoing Sammy's remarks.

She looked out the window and saw they had arrived at the airport.

They filed out of the limousine. Benjamin was the last to disembark. He stood next to his uncle, a grim expression on his face. "I think I should go with you, Uncle. I may be able to talk to Anne, convince her to give herself up."

Before his uncle could respond to his suggestion, Georgie stepped forward and threw her arms around Benjamin's neck. "Thank you, cousin," she said. "I was hoping you'd say that."

There were five passengers on the company jet bound for California on that cold, overcast morning.

Bree said goodbye to her new friend, Judy, outside the terminal at San Francisco International Airport. One of the world's busiest airports, she was fortunate to be able to hail a cab.

As she slid onto the seat of the cab, Pierre in her right hand, her bag in her left, she consulted her watch. Thanks to two rather long lay-overs, it was already 12:30 p.m. But she was here now. She'd go straight to the Fairmont. If necessary, she could change in the ladies' room there. Ari had promised to meet her at the hotel to babysit Pierre, so she had everything under control. Nothing could go wrong.

Suddenly, she heard her name being shouted. She turned

around and spotted Sammy Chan, her sister's best friend, running toward the cab.

"The Fairmont," she said to the driver. "Hurry!"

Sammy stopped in the middle of the street. Hadn't Bree recognized him? She had looked right at him. Startled by a car's blaring horn, he hurried out of its path. Taking his cellular phone from his jacket pocket, he dialed the number Georgie had given him.

"I lost her," he said when Georgie answered. "She turned around and looked straight at me, then she took off."

"She doesn't know Anne's in San Francisco," Georgie explained. "She is so intent on making the audition, she's risking her own safety in the process."

"Too bad you don't know where it's going to be held," Sammy said.

"You're telling me," Georgie returned, exasperated. "Thanks for trying, Sammy. I'll talk to you later."

"Sammy saw her at the airport," Georgie informed the rest of the group. "She ran from him, thinking we'd sent him to stop her from going to the audition, no doubt."

"That girl will be the death of me yet," Toni moaned, shaking her head.

"You should phone the Lincolns and tell them she may be on the way to Georgette's apartment," Clay said.

Toni did as he'd suggested.

Georgie turned to her father. "Do you think we'll be delayed much longer?"

"The pilot says we should have clearance in a few more minutes," her father told her.

For the last hour they'd been grounded at the Natrona County International Airport in Casper, Wyoming. There was a problem with the jet's fuel gauge. The pilot had set down in Casper to have it checked out. He didn't want to get somewhere over the Rocky Mountains and find out his fuel was low.

The resident airplane mechanic at the Natrona County International Airport was repairing the gauge post haste.

"Margery and Daniel have been alerted," Toni announced.

* * *

"Is any of that coffee left?" Margery asked as she reached for the thermos sitting on the seat between her and Daniel. Daniel didn't reply at once, his attention was on the bedroom window of Georgie's apartment. They were sitting in front of the house across from Jonathan Crenshaw's Victorian home. From there, they were able to see the bedroom window of Georgie's apartment and the front entrance of the house. Every hour or so, Daniel would move the car to a different spot. He didn't want the neighbors to get suspicious, if they weren't already. He and Margery had been out here for six hours. Bree hadn't put in an appearance yet.

"Did you see that!" he said, his baritone rising with amazement.

Margery almost spilled the little bit of coffee that was left in the thermos. "What?" she asked looking at her husband as though he'd taken leave of his senses.

"The curtain," Daniel said. "I saw the curtain move."

"You're getting punch drunk, Daniel," Margery said cynically. "We've been here all morning and that woman, if she *is* up there, hasn't done a thing to give herself away and you think she's going to come to the window?"

His hand on the door's handle, Daniel said, "I'm going up there."

Margery reached over and grabbed his arm. "No you're not. This isn't a movie, Daniel Lincoln. Toni said Anne Ballentine is dangerous. I'm going to take her word for it. Close the door."

Daniel hesitated.

"Please," Margery implored.

Daniel closed the door and sat back on his seat. He sighed, "What we should do is call Nico. He could go up there."

"The police have to have a search warrant," Margery said. She'd also thought of phoning her son-in-law, who was a detective on the San Francisco police force. The police, however, required a search warrant in order to go into a private citizen's home uninvited. Without proof that Anne was up there with the intent to harm someone, they didn't have a legal leg to stand on.

Upstairs, Anne had found what she'd been perusing the *San Francisco Chronicle* for. She rose from her chair at Georgie's kitchen table, neatly folded the paper and placed it under her arm. Since the dark green Range Rover was still parked across the street, she stealthily abandoned the house through the back entrance. She had first noticed the couple in the Range Rover watching the house four hours ago when she'd awakened and gone to the window to see what the day promised. Another sunny California day. She loved this place. She was a little sad about leaving it once she'd completed her mission later on today.

As she walked down the sidewalk, dressed in basic black—a pair of slacks, a crew-necked shirt and a light jacket thrown on for warmth—she looked like any other resident of Pacific Heights out for a leisurely stroll. At the end of the street, she flagged down a cab. As she slid onto the vinyl seat, she smoothed her short, tousled hair away from her face.

The cab driver, a black gentleman in his forties, looked back at her and smiled. "Good afternoon, pretty lady, where to?"

Anne smiled at him, crinkles appearing around her brown eyes. "The Fairmont. There's a symposium on film being held there today. I hear several celebrities are going to put in an appearance."

"You don't say?" the friendly cabbie replied cheerily. "The Fairmont it is."

The Fairmont Hotel, one of the city's last remaining grand hotels, was located on Nob Hill. Bree liked the Old World quality of the architecture. Whenever she stayed at the Fairmont, she was reminded of her trip to Paris, although the personnel at the hotel she'd stayed in in France were not as accommodating as the staff at the Fairmont. Nor did they possess the prodigious memory.

The clerk at the front desk, a young, blonde male with the chiseled good-looks of a matinee idol smiled broadly when Bree approached the desk.

"Miss Shaw," he said deferentially. "It's a great pleasure to see you again."

His nimble fingers flew over the computer keyboard. He raised his blue eyes to hers. "We don't seem to have a reservation for you . . . but I'm sure we can find something. Bear with me."

Bree gave him the benefit of her prettiest smile. "I don't have a reservation . . ." she looked at his name tag, "Thomas. I'd just like to have you phone Mr. Solomon and tell him I'm here for my interview with him. Would you be a dear and do that for me?"

Thomas's relief was apparent in his expression. "I'd be happy to," he said at once, eager to please.

"Thank you, Thomas," Bree said. She smiled at him again and then turned to walk to the lobby area. Thomas' eyes lingered on her legs a while longer, then he went back to his computer and looked up Dominic Solomon's telephone number.

Bree sat on one of the beautiful ivory-colored couches in the lobby and removed Pierre from his cage. She snapped his leash onto his collar and placed him on the floor. After glancing down at her watch, she realized she had a full hour before the audition. She was sure Pierre was overdue for a walk, so she swung her overnight bag and her purse, both lightweight, over her shoulder and began walking toward the exit. Pierre trotted as quickly as his tiny legs would allow him to, leading the way.

"Briane!"

Bree froze. Not another one of Georgie's friends stalking me, she thought.

She looked up and her heart lurched. It was Peter Hogan the biggest box-office draw in the world. She wished she'd had time to change.

Peter was Dutch and had the coloring of his countrymen: fair-haired and blue-eyed. His skin coloring was darker than she remembered. Bree thought he'd probably just returned from one of those islands he was always being photographed on with scantily-clad supermodels hanging all over him. At thirty-seven, he was five-eleven but magazine writers described him as a six-footer. He was in wonderful physical condition. His body, after all, was his claim to fame and fortune.

He recognized *me,* Bree thought suddenly. Her nervousness disappeared as Peter clasped her right hand in both of his. "You made it," he said enthusiastically. Perfect white teeth gleamed in his lightly tanned face. "Dom and I were about to have a bit of lunch, won't you join us?"

Bree thought fast. She had a dog who needed to "go" on one hand and two powerful men who could make or break her career on the other.

"Hello, Mr. Hogan . . ."

"Peter, please."

"Peter," she said, "let me take my poodle to my room and I'll join you in a few minutes."

"Wonderful," Peter said, his blue eyes resting on her lovely face. "Have the maitre d' show you to our table."

"Will do," Bree said. She stood smiling at him until he turned and began walking back to the hotel's restaurant. He looked back once and smiled at her for good measure. When he was out of sight, Bree rushed toward the exit.

The proprietor of a small newsstand on Sunset Boulevard, a Mexican-American man in his fifties, watched as a white limousine pulled to the curb and stopped. A tall, powerfully built, black man got out and walked up to him.

"I'd like all of your daily papers, please," he requested.

The owner of the newsstand handed the man a huge stack of papers and accepted a twenty dollar bill for his trouble.

"Keep the change," the man said and got back into the limousine.

Clay handed the papers around. "Today's Friday," he said. "There will probably be something mentioned in the entertainment section of the paper. Dominic Solomon's well known. Look carefully."

"In the meanwhile?" Charles asked. He was the only one who wasn't turning pages.

"We go to Georgette's apartment," Clay answered. "And I go in."

"We go in," Georgie corrected him.

"I thought that was you I saw as I was driving up," Ari Sanchez said as she approached Bree.

They were in the park adjacent to the Fairmont. Bree had taken Pierre's leash off and allowed him to romp.

She gave Ari a brief hug. "I'm happy to see you," she told her friend. "I arrived a few minutes ago and whom do you suppose I ran into?"

"Dominic?" Ari asked. She was Bree's height, five-eight, and had dusky skin and very dark, almond-shaped eyes. Her long hair was chestnut-colored and hung in waves down her back. She was dressed casually in a sky blue DKNY jogging suit.

"No, Peter," Bree replied. She wasn't over her encounter with the movie star yet. She had worked in the business for seven years and she was still capable of becoming awestruck.

"Isn't he remarkable-looking?" Ari said, trilling the R. She was attempting to appear light-hearted, but her dark eyes anxiously darted back and forth as though she were afraid she'd been followed.

"Whom are you looking for?" Bree asked, curious.

Ari stared at her friend in disbelief. "I've been as nervous as a cat in a room full of rocking chairs ever since you told me about that crazy woman who tried to kill your sister. What do you mean, whom am I looking for?"

"Oh her," Bree said dismissively. "Poor Anne is probably at the bottom of Dorchester Bay."

She whistled for Pierre, who pricked-up his ears and obediently came running. Bree bent down and hooked his leash to his collar. She handed the leash to Ari. "I'd better go. I promised Peter I'd join him and Dominic for lunch. Thanks Ari."

"Where should I meet you afterward?" Ari called. Pierre was wrapping the leash around her legs.

"I'll meet you in the lobby," Bree shouted. She was halfway across the lawn. "Wish me luck."

"Break a leg," Ari said affectionately.

Clay and Georgie cautiously approached her apartment door. Georgie gave Clay the key and he unlocked the door.

"I'm going in low," he told her. "You stay back until I tell you it's safe to enter. Got me?"

Georgie nodded in the affirmative. Her dark eyes raked over his face. "Be careful."

"Always," Clay said.

He pushed the door open and entered quickly with his gun drawn. Because they'd arrived in San Francisco on a private plane, he'd been able to bring his personal weapon—the Koch P7. With his elbows locked and the safety off, he searched each room of the apartment. Coming back into the living room, he called to Georgie. "All's clear," he said.

"What you need to do," Clay instructed her, "is to go through the place and see if you notice anything that isn't the way you left it."

Georgie's eyes scanned the living room. She'd left the apartment clean and neat. She wasn't a neat freak, but she liked her living space to be orderly. She supposed it reflected her logical train of thought.

At first glance, she didn't see anything out of the ordinary. Her bedroom was a large, airy room simply furnished with pale oak pieces she'd bought at an auction. The big, four-poster bed had a golden-hued comforter atop it and the drapes matched the bed cover. She felt something was different here.

Then, she walked into the bathroom of the master bedroom and noticed that the shower curtains were drawn the full length of the tub. She always left the shower curtain open. Drawing it back, she gasped. Floating in the tub was the teddy bear that had formerly been laying on her bed.

Clay entered the bathroom as she was bent over the tub attempting to wring the water out of Buster.

Placing his hand atop hers, he encouraged her to drop it. "It's Anne's way of letting us know she's aware we're on to her, and she doesn't care anymore. Come on, Frisco, we're losing time."

When they returned to the limousine, Toni held up the *Chronicle*, a triumphant grin on her face. "The Fairmont," she chortled. "That's where we'll find that hard-headed daughter of mine."

Georgie didn't notice the two extra passengers in the car until she sat down opposite them. "Aunt Margery, Uncle Daniel!"

"They came knocking on the limousine's window after they saw you and Clay go upstairs," Toni explained. "Daniel says he saw the curtains move upstairs. Did you find anything?"

"She was there all right," Georgie said, frowning. She saw no need to tell her mother of Anne's bizarre act of soaking Buster.

Anne couldn't believe her good luck. She sat forward on her seat in the cab in order to get a better look. She would recognize that mutt anywhere.

"Stop here," she ordered the cabbie sharply.

The cab driver halted the car a block further down the street. "You'd like to walk, huh?" he said. After consulting the meter, he said, "That'll be four dollars and fifty cents."

Anne handed him a ten dollar bill.

She got out of the cab, firmly closing the door. "Thanks, you've been very kind."

The cabbie made change and offered it to Anne. She smiled at him and said, "I don't need it, you keep it."

She stood on the sidewalk and watched him drive away. There are some nice people in the world, she thought.

She walked back to the spot where she'd seen Bree a few minutes earlier and discovered the girl was no longer there. Chagrined, she turned and holding her purse close to her body, hurried the rest of the way to the Fairmont.

Ari didn't know how the little devil had gotten off his leash, but Pierre was somewhere loose in one of the most luxurious hotels in the city.

She searched the lobby area, walking up to perfect strangers, asking, "Have you seen a cute little black toy poodle?"

Some of the people she asked were polite and answered her with a: "Sorry, no."

Others looked down their noses at her and kept walking.

She nearly collided with a petite woman in black as the woman came through the entrance.

"Excuse me," Ari said, grinning sheepishly. "But did you notice a toy poodle anywhere outside when you were coming in?"

The woman gave her the strangest look. "He belongs to you?" she asked sharply, clearly interested in Ari's response.

"Yes," Ari said. "He's black with a rhinestone collar. Did you see him?"

"No!" the woman replied in a huff and continued walking.

What a witch, Ari thought and went in the direction of the restaurant. It would be just like Pierre to try to return to his mistress. He didn't like being separated from her for any length of time.

"You were right. She's Romalia," Dominic Solomon said to his friend Peter Hogan.

Bree had read for him at their table after they'd finished lunch. He'd been immediately charmed by her. He knew her persona would translate powerfully to the big screen.

Dominic Solomon was a genial man of thirty-six. African-American, he had medium brown skin with healthy red undertones and had a full beard which was neatly trimmed. He wore his natural black hair cut close to his well-shaped head, and there were a few prematurely grey hairs at his temples. His dark brown eyes were kind and intelligent. Bree's heart did a flip-flop when he smiled at her. "So," he said after singing her praises, "how did our affair turn out? Did we get engaged? Is there a wedding in the offing?"

Bree wasn't listening. She was in shock. Walking toward her, with her purse still clutched tightly at her side, was Anne Ballentine.

Bree pushed her chair back and stood. She'd stopped breathing. She inhaled a sudden, painful breath.

"Briane?" Dominic rose also and reached over and touched her arm. "What is it?"

Anne sidled up to Bree and said in a low, menacing voice, "If you come with me, no one else has to get hurt." She patted her purse to denote the presence of a weapon.

"Briane," Peter said, rising, "do you know this woman?"

"Y . . . yes," Bree stammered. Where was her acting ability now? She breathed in deeply and exhaled slowly. If Anne went ballistic in the dining room, a lot of people could get hurt and it would be all her fault. She had to regain her composure.

She smiled. "This is my father's personal assistant, Anne Ballentine," she told them. Looking into Anne's eyes, she added, "Dad's condition hasn't worsened has it, Anne?"

"Yes, I'm afraid so," Anne said, playing along. "He sent me here to bring you home."

"I'm sorry, Dominic, Peter, but I have to go," Bree said. She didn't have to feign regret. She'd never felt so disappointed in her life. The feeling wouldn't last long, however. Anne wasn't here for girl talk. She was going to kill her. She was certain of that.

She slowly backed away from the table, Anne moving in tandem with her "bag" trained on her.

When she and Anne turned around to leave the dining room, they were both surprised to find a small portion of the population of Boston blocking their path: Charles, his eyes narrowed; Toni to his right, frowning; Georgie to his left, an angry expression in her brown depths; and Benjamin with a look of utter shame. He stepped forward.

"Mother?"

It was at that moment that Bree thought, where's Clay? He wouldn't allow Georgie to come to her rescue without him.

Anne removed the snub-nosed .38 from her purse, dropping the bag to the floor. She roughly pulled Bree against her. "Stay back," she warned, "I'll kill her."

"Mother, please," Benjamin beseeched. Stepping a bit closer, he reached out to her. "You can still save yourself, Mother."

"I'm not your mother," Anne said harshly. "I thought I wanted to be, but I was too late." Her eyes rested on Charles. "You're just a clone of him now." She laughed. "But that's all right. You've got my son, and now, I have your daughter. It's only fitting." Her gaze moved to Georgie. "This isn't how it was supposed to be. Everything fell apart when I brought Kovik into it. I should have handled things myself."

"Like you did with Mariel and Chuck?" Charles asked, furious. He started to approach her and Anne cocked the gun, pointing it at Bree's head. Charles froze.

"I didn't enjoy it," Anne said. "I liked Mariel and Chuck."

She was holding Bree by the neck, practically cutting off her breath. Bree twisted her head around, attempting to get into a more comfortable position. That's when she spotted Pierre running toward them.

She growled deep in her throat. Pierre, doing what he'd been trained to do, ran forward and sank his teeth into Anne's exposed ankle. Anne howled and loosened her grip on Bree. Clay, coming from behind them, caught Anne by the arm, pointing it upward. He wrenched the gun out of her grasp and Benjamin grabbed her, holding her tightly.

The rest of the diners applauded.

Bree fell to her knees and hugged Pierre. "My hero," she said, hugging him to her chest.

Her mother, sister and father were at her side: Charles hugging her; Toni berating her; and Georgie saying, "You were always trouble, Baby Sis."

Hotel security led Anne away with Clay and Benjamin following to give their statements when the police arrived.

Georgie was warmed by the solicitous manner in which her father was treating her mother. His good arm was casually draped about her shoulders, and, what's more, her mother allowed it to stay there unmolested. Was there a chance that the two of them could now have the life together that they should have had years ago? She hoped so.

Her mother stifled a yawn and, concerned, Charles looked lovingly into her face. "You're worn out," he said. "Come with me, I'll get rooms for all of us. We can spend the night here, it's probably going to take some time for this whole mess to be resolved."

Dominic Solomon strolled over to Bree and taking her aside, asked, "Are you all right?"

"That was nothing compared to the week I've had," Bree joked, sighing.

"Perhaps you could tell me about it sometime soon," Dominic said, his dark eyes smiling into hers. "You've definitely got the part. Anyone brave enough to do what you just did will make a fierce warrior-princess."

Dominic pulled out a chair from a nearby table. "Maybe you ought to sit down."

Bree didn't have to be asked twice. She sat down, still holding Pierre in her arms. "So," she said, looking up at him, "I guess that means we'll be working closely together."

Dominic knelt in front of her, took her hand in his, looked deeply into her eyes and said, "The closer, the better."

Georgie opened the door in stockinged feet and stepped aside for Clay to enter the hotel suite. She'd removed her jacket, too, and was in a state of semi-undress.

"Everything settled?" She gave him an enigmatic smile.

"Anne is in custody," he confirmed as Georgie shut the door and turned to face him.

He stood stock-still as she circled him, busily removing his duster. Finished, she lay it on the back of an upholstered chair next to the bureau. She returned to him and began unfastening his bulky shoulder holster and once that was accomplished, she placed it, with its weapon, in the top drawer of the bureau. Then, she languidly started to unbutton his denim shirt.

Clay stayed her hand at that point.

"It appears as if you're undressing me."

"Apparently," she readily agreed and continued to do so.

Offering no further resistance, Clay allowed his arms to fall to his sides.

"Let's get one thing clear, Frisco." His hazel eyes narrowed as he looked into her upturned face. "Sex without love is just sex."

Georgie opened his shirt and gently caressed his smooth, muscular chest with both palms. She smiled when she felt an uncontrollable ripple of pleasure course through his body.

"Then I'm about to make *love* to you, Boston."

About The Author

After working as a journalist, a loan officer and an elementary school tutor, Janice Sims decided to dedicate her life to writing poems, short stories and full-length novels. She lives in Central Florida with her husband and daughter.

Look for these upcoming Arabesque titles:

July 1997
LEGACY by Shirley Hailstock
ECSTACY by Gwynne Forster
A TIME FOR US by Cheryl Faye
THE ART OF LOVE by Crystal Wilson-Harris

August 1997
SILKEN BETRAYAL by Francis Ray
WISHING ON A STAR by Raynetta Manees
SLOW BURN by Leslie Esdaile
SWEET LIES by Viveca Carlysle

September 1997
SECOND TIME AROUND by Anna Larence
SILKEN LOVE by Carmen Green
BLUSH by Courtni Wright
SUMMER WIND by Gail McFarland

TIMELESS LOVE

Look for these historical romances in the Arabesque line:

BLACK PEARL by Francine Craft (0236-0, $4.99)

CLARA'S PROMISE by Shirley Hailstock (0147-X, $4.99)

MIDNIGHT MOON by Mildred Riley (0200-X; $4.99)

SUNSHINE AND SHADOWS by Roberta Gayle (0136-4, $4.99)